MURDER AT CUYAMACA BEACH

A Bella Kowalski Mystery
Set on California's Central Coast

Sue McGinty

To Joyce & her friede from the Mystery Book Club. Enjoy.

Sue McGinty

—2014—

Book 2

ISBN: 1492892440

ISBN 13: 9781492892441

Acknowledgements

Thanks to members of Novel Idea, my fabulous San Luis Obispo CA NightWriter critique group, especially our wise and patient leader, Barbara Wolcott. Thanks also to early readers Diane Broyles and Myrt Cordon. You convinced me to try a new beginning.

Kudos to Detective Mike Wasley of the San Luis Obispo Sheriff's Office, who suggested a way that Mike, a non-sworn officer, could work cold cases.

Kudos also to Lynda Roeller for the cover photo, and to Patrick and Diane McGinty for posing.

Special thanks to Bev McGinty and Jerry Douglas Smith for reading all those drafts. Any errors that remain in this work of fiction are mine alone.

To Jerry Douglas Smith, 2013-2014 Poet Laureate of San Luis Obispo County. This one's for you.

Cast of Characters

Angelina Sereno Minetti—Dominic, Magda and Loreli's aunt

Bea—Bella's murdered sister, Chris's mother

Bella Kowalski—former nun, now obituary editor of the *Central Coast Chronicle*

Ben Adams—reporter for the *Central Coast Chronicle*

Chris—Bella's nephew

Darrell Vader—Tolosa County Sheriff's detective

Dave Farris—his murder becomes one of Mike's cold cases

Dominic Sereno —head of Sereno Cellars winery

Ed—Chris's father

Father Todd Burton—pastor at Saint Patrick's church, Sereno family friend

Janet—Chris's stepmother

Jeremy Beamer—Marcus's foster son

Kathe Tanner—Los Lobos Librarian, Martin's mother

Loreli Sereno—Magda and Dominic's sister

Magda Sereno—Dominic and Loreli's sister

Marcus Daniels—rancher who takes in the homeless on an as needed basis

Martin Tanner—Tolosa County Sheriff's deputy

Mike Kowalski—Bella's husband, retired detective

Ryan Scully—Tolosa County Sheriff's detective

Sam—Mike and Bella's Golden Lab

Vito—Dominic's former partner

Walter—another of Marcus's foster sons. Walter has Down syndrome.

1

The hour before dawn, a time when night terrors fade and solutions begin. Aware of encroaching winter daylight behind him and the need to hurry, the man forges into the shallows below Bush Lupine Point, nostrils tingling from the acrid smell of brackish water. His neoprene wetsuit and hood protect him from hypothermia and provide anonymity.

Holding the mask strapped to his neck, he spits onto the glass and rubs the saliva around. Its acidity will keep the lens from fogging. Mask in place, he fits the snorkel's mouthpiece between his teeth, blows into the tube to clear obstructions, and pulls on gloves to cover the too-short sleeves that leave his wrists exposed. He's added bulk in the years since he last wore the suit.

Preparations complete, he waits for The Woman—the only way he can think of her now that she knows too much. He could live with the liability she's become, but not the threat. If only she hadn't gotten nosey after Dave Farris disappeared. Still he hesitates to kill her too, knowing it will hurt people close to him.

He's familiar with her routine: kayaking from the marina that lies in the shadow of Mariposa Rock to the sandspit where she welcomes the day with Tai Chi, her new-found passion. By now she'll experience the euphoria Valium produces, but also feel calm and in control. Will she assume a natural high, or sus-pect drugs? She and drugs are old friends.

He waits until the kayak emerges from the cocoon of shad-ows, the paddle in her strong arms windmilling in and out of the water. He watches her, mesmerized by the figure-eight pattern the paddles makes against the dim light. She won't see him, of course. Contact lenses and saltwater sports make bad compan-ions. Time and surprise are on his side.

As she approaches, he again adjusts the mask and seal-like, slips into the water, closing the expanse between them. Kicking easily with oversized flippers, he maintains a distance of twenty feet or so, raising his head occasionally to check their progress from the middle of the bay to the southwest side of the uninhab-ited sandspit that divides the bay from the open ocean. Anyone watching from the opposite shore will see only a woman in a kayak.

They near the sandspit several minutes later. When she stops paddling and drifts into the shallows, he discards his gloves and closes the distance between them. Knowing speed and concen-tration are essential, he steels himself, then rises like Lazarus from the dead behind the craft, reaches forward and grabs her head around the chin with his strong hands.

Senses dulled by Valium, she struggles, but not enough. He closes his eyes, because killing is easier that way, and twists her head sharply to the side as he had been taught.

Now to swamp the kayak and his work will be complete. He opens his eyes and something enters his field of vision. A projec-tile of fur and teeth flies at him, grabbing his exposed wrist. He howls with pain and rage. The dog! She brought the dog.

2

Five years later, Wednesday, December 31ˢᵗ, 2008, 12:15 PM
I stood on the widow's walk that circles our windmill home, binoculars trained on Bush Lupine Point, a mug of steaming Earl
Grey beside me on the railing. The lenses brought into focus the
layered vista of Mariposa Bay and beyond it the ocean, separated
by the dunes of the sandspit. Each New Year's Eve I stand here
and take stock, something I've done since my husband Mike and
I moved to Los Lobos almost nine years ago. This ritual is in
part an homage to Emily Divina, our resident ghost, who leapt to
her death from this exact spot on December 31ˢᵗ, 1893, after her
lover drowned at sea.

That had been the ultimate bad year for Emily, but this one
had been tough for us: problems in our marriage, two murders
in our usually-sleepy hamlet, Mike's heart attack. For me, it had
been the worst time since my sister Bea's senseless, unsolved
murder years ago in Detroit.

I took a gulp of tea and refocused the binoculars, studying
gunmetal clouds massing overhead. Approaching rain heightened the pungent odor of the bay; thunder rolled in the distance. The bay resembled a sheet of tin, so different from the
vibrant hues of warmer weather when it blossoms with sailboats

and kayaks. For just a moment I thought of Loreli Sereno, a real estate broker, who, with her sister, found us this amazing house. She broke her neck in a kayaking accident nearly five years ago.

I shivered, and I wasn't the only one. Beside me, Sam, our Golden Lab, shook himself, rattling the links of his collar. I reached down and stroked his silky head. "What's the matter, boy? Too cold for your old bones?" Sam, then a teenager of two or three, had chosen us the second we walked into the shelter eight years ago. He was, and always would be, a big baby, a teddy bear, a clown in a dog suit. That's why we loved him.

"Okay, Okay." I opened the slider to my study and he barged ahead of me. "Well, excuse you," I said to his departing tail. My cell rang. Mike, from the kitchen in the main part of the house.

"Mayday, Mayday!" he shouted.

* * * * *

"What's the problem?" I said, stepping into the chaos our kitchen had become. Crates of liquor and wine stood by the back door, with cases of beer stacked in one corner by the table where brown grocery bags belched trash. Counters overflowed with pots, skillets and bowls, *kielbasa* lying on butcher paper, *pierogis* in freezer wrap, cans of sauerkraut, plastic glasses, plastic silverware and paper plates. In short, trappings for Saint Pat's fundraiser for our homeless program which began in—I glanced at my trusty Timex—exactly six and a half hours.

Mike exploded. "What's the problem? I need help that's what. Where have you been?"

"We've been in this kitchen since before five and I took a tea break to get my head together before leaving for work. What's the big deal?"

His gray eyes darkened with the cop-like anger that frightens me a little. "What the hell have you gotten us into?" he said, his voice lapsing into the slightly nasal tone of native Midwesterners.

"Wait a minute. That's unfair. You were the one who offered to cater a Polish feast for tonight."

"And if you weren't up to your eyeballs running the whole damn program, I'd have kept my pie hole shut."

"I—" The snappish reply died on my tongue. He had a point, I did over-commit. It's an ex-nun thing. I was going to be fifty soon; old enough to say no.

I took a deep breath, aware now of the soothing aromas of garlic and spice rising from a skillet of sizzling *kielbasa*. "Look, arguing is getting us nowhere. I have to be at the paper in exactly twenty-nine minutes. I can work for a few of those. What's the most helpful thing I can do?"

He pointed to two kettles that filled the kitchen with steam, offering me the crooked grin I fell in love with. "Cook the *pierogis? Please?*"

* * * * *

The promised rain arrived, hurling itself against the south-facing windows of Tolosa's *Central Coast Chronicle*. Thunder reverberated through the tin-roofed building. Outside, windswept branches flailed about like strung-up ghosts. The old year giving us the finger on its way out of town.

I sat at my desk up to my smudged spectacles in obituaries to edit and send to press. Before me sat at least four hours work to complete in two. I'd sworn a blood-oath that I'd be home by four.

From the next cubicle came the sound of foot-tapping and gum popping, investigative reporter Ben Adams fidgeting as usual. "Ben, cool it."

Save your breath, Bella.

The desk phone rang, shrill and insistent. "Mike, what now?" I barked into the receiver.

"Bella?" The husky voice sounded familiar—and troubled. "It's Magda."

It took me a second. "Magda *Sereno*? How are you? Funny you called. I was just thinking about Loreli, God rest her. How are things in Denver?"

Ben, our self-described future Pulitzer winner, became unnaturally quiet. The Serenos were always newsworthy meat.

"Lousy. Home sales are way down there, too. I'm back at the winery in Dos Pasos with my brother Dominic. Um,"—a short pause—"I just got an anonymous call about Loreli's death. Do you have a moment?" She sounded desperate and my heart contracted with concern for her.

"Of course," I lied. "Tell me about it."

"I can't on the phone. How about coffee? I'm downtown."

Oh dear. "I'm on deadline—"

"He claims Loreli was murdered and he knows who did it."

3

Wednesday, December 31st, 2 PM

"What's all this about?" I asked when we were settled at a tiny table at Java World, half a block from the paper.

Magda sat clasping and unclasping her hands, tiny lines around her eyes revealing every one of her forty-plus years. Her chin-length blonde hair lay plastered like wet cotton against her face. My own short "do" had fared somewhat better, but my Birkenstocks took a direct hit in a puddle. I sat there, wet, cold, and time-stressed, the perfect setup for catching a cold.

I took a sip of hot Irish Breakfast to ward off the chill and invited Magda to reconsider her choice of bottled water. She shook her head, wiping tears from alabaster cheeks a model would kill for.

"Okay," I began. "So an anonymous caller wants to give you information about Loreli's death?"

"Not give. Sell."

"Sell? What a bastard."

"True, but he confirmed what my brother Dominic and I have always known. Loreli was murdered." She leaned across the table as though someone might hear. "I think it was Marcus who called."

"Marcus Daniels?" I almost upset my tea. "Why would he want to sell you information? He was engaged to Loreli."

Magda tugged at her black turtleneck as though to cool a raging fever. "Dominic and I broke with Marcus after he gave that statement to the press urging us to accept the coroner's verdict of accidental death. Now he needs money to fix up the Blue Stetson and maybe the Sereno fortune looks pretty good."

"Good point." Daniels was a maverick rancher who drove regulators berserk by offering drop-in lodging to the homeless in facilities that were rundown at best and unsafe at worst. His legendary battles with the county were the third favorite topic of conversation among locals, right after last summer's murders and our Los Lobos wastewater debacle.

She pressed her lips together, hazel eyes filling, knuckles white around the water bottle. "Dominic has bone cancer, stage four. Inoperable. That's the main reason I'm back. Loreli's murderer must be found before he dies. He thinks of little else." She squeezed the bottle so tight I was afraid it would burst. "If Dominic can't get justice, he'll settle for retribution." A tight smile. "Our Grandmother had Sicilian roots and the retribution gene is in our DNA."

I reached across the table, pried her cold hand from the bottle and wrapped it in my equally-cold ones. "Oh Magda, I'm so sorry he's in such torment." Wealth and prestige certainly didn't protect people from tragedy. "Did Dominic get a call too?"

"Marcus would never call him, not after the words they exchanged over the coroner's verdict."

He might. The caller could contact all interested parties to play one against the other and collect from everyone.

Before I could express the thought, Ben Adams walked in. He'd obviously overheard us deciding to meet at Java World. He paused inside the door, set his open umbrella in a corner, slicked back the longish hair he'd adopted recently and passed us with a brief nod. Magda seemed unaware of him. He carried a folded *Wall Street Journal* and a stainless sippy cup, no doubt filled from the office pot.

Cheapskate.

After seating himself behind Magda, he snapped open the paper with great fanfare and leaned back, the better to eavesdrop. I bent toward her. "Assuming the caller was Marcus, did he give you any hint of what he knows?"

A frown disturbed her smooth forehead. "Why are we whispering?"

I tilted my chin beyond her, at the back of Ben's head. "Our investigative reporter is behind you."

"Oh, no." She turned just as a couple vacated a nearby table.

"Come on," I said. "Let's move."

Once we'd resettled, I repeated, "What does Marcus know?"

She covered her mouth with a French-manicured hand as though Ben read lips. He might for all I knew. "Marcus repeated something only the family and law enforcement know—Loreli had Sadie, her Jack Russell, with her in the kayak."

"But she and Marcus were engaged. Wouldn't he know that?"

Magda gulped water, her Adam's apple rippling the turtleneck. "Because Sadie died of a broken neck as well, the authorities thought at first Loreli was murdered. They withheld information about the dog and asked us to do the same."

"If they didn't tell Marcus about the dog, they must have suspected him. Why the ruling of accidental death?" Mike and I were on vacation at the time, so I was hazy on details.

She heaved a deep sigh, struggling for control. "Toxicology reports showed a huge dose of Valium in her system. They decided she broke her neck after falling from the kayak in the shallows near the sandspit."

"And the dog broke his neck, too? Sounds farfetched," I said, and she agreed. "How did Valium get into Loreli's system?"

"Someone slipped it to her. She was in rehab anonymously."

"Really?" I knew Loreli liked to party, but I had no idea she had serious problems. "Wait a minute. She had her *dog* with her in rehab?"

"Yes, they allowed clients to keep pets in a kennel at the back of the property. Good for morale and all that."

"I suppose. But why hide the fact that she was in rehab in the first place?"

"She didn't want Dominic to know. She was his golden girl." She dabbed her eyes with a napkin. It was too late to save her mascara.

"But Marcus knew?"

Magda nodded. "Of course. She wanted to get clean and sober and she was doing so well. She would've never taken Valium on her own after entering rehab."

She paused for breath, her finger drawing tight circles on the table. "We should have challenged the coroner's report, but Dominic wasn't well even then, and I ran away to Denver and shouldn't have, and our Aunt Angelina walked around in her usual state of denial."

"Does your aunt live with Dominic?" I asked.

"Oh God, no. She's very religious and would never sleep under the same roof with Dominic and Vito. She lives in Los Lobos, on Fifteenth Street, so she can be near her confessor, Father Burton."

"Really," I said, apropos of nothing. "Is Dominic still with Vito?" She'd spoken of her brother and his partner often during the escrow process.

"No, he cleared out when Dominic was diagnosed. I presume he went back to his old life of crime."

"Crime?" I asked.

"Yeah, as a Mafia knee breaker. My brother is better off without him."

"So the caller most likely wasn't Vito?" She shook her head.

"How much does Marcus want?"

"A hundred thousand."

"Dollars?" She nodded and I remembered she was broke. "Where can you get that kind of money?"

She glanced at me like that should be obvious. "From Dominic, but I want to talk to Mike first." She grimaced. "Would you, uh, tell him there's no hard feelings before I do?"

"Sure, I understand." Mike and Magda had a tiff over some detail at the end of escrow, important then, but inconsequential now. "Mike's gruff as an old Billy goat, but he doesn't hold grudges. Let's see, today is bad, bad. He's going berserk with the Polish food for tonight, and tomorrow, God help me, we're doing the Polar Bear Dip at Cuyamaca Beach."

"I'll be there," she said, brightening a bit. "A friend and I are surfing before the dip."

"So you still surf?"

"Absolutely. It keeps me sane." She smiled for the first time. "Colorado is too far from the ocean."

"It sure is. I'm really glad you're back. Why don't you wait by the pier until after the dip? I don't think it lasts long." At least I hoped not. I'm terrified of water, but I didn't want Mike in the ocean alone after his heart attack. "If we can't get together for some reason, you can catch him early Friday morning at the shop. Later, he'll be busy pumping."

A slight smile. "You guys bought that septic service after all?"

"We did, though I sometimes wonder why. He pumps, I clean the john and do the books before my shift at the paper. A retired cop's salary doesn't go far these days."

"This damned economy's affecting everyone," she said. "Dominic's lost a bundle in the market." She thumped the table with her palm as though to get the conversation back on track. "I'd better talk to Mike ASAP. I'm supposed to wire money to a special account first thing Friday morning. Marcus, or whomever, promised to snail-mail the information as soon as he verifies the deposit."

Before I had a chance to remark the plan seemed hare-brained at best, and illegal at worst, my cell chirped. Father Burton, Saint Pat's pastor, didn't mince words. "Our volunteer bartender just called. He has the flu. I'm canceling the bar."

Father was an old-fashioned priest, more concerned with saving souls than solving social issues. He wasn't crazy about our homeless program or tonight's benefit, but he'd inherited both from our former pastor. "We'll make a lot more money if we serve drinks, Father. Besides, Mike already bought the liquor and I'm not sure Bev-For-Less takes returns. I'll find us a new bartender. See you at five." I pressed the end button before he finished sputtering.

A glance at my watch reminded me I had a job, in fact several jobs, to do. I polished off my tea, buttoned my raincoat and caught Magda's eye. "How'd you like to tend bar at Saint Pat's tonight?"

* * * * *

I got home around 4:30 after dispatching the obits, chasing my tail all over town doing errands and, at the same time, dealing with several benefit-related crises by phone. I still had to endure the agony of choosing something to wear from my less-than-copious wardrobe. In order to put off the decision as long as possible, I checked the mail first.

Big mistake.

The letter looked like a pitch for an enhanced credit card program, but it contained a time bomb. Like many people with modest incomes, we used our single credit card as a slush fund for emergencies and once-in-a-blue-moon splurges. Long story short: our current balance had crept higher than we intended. We meant to pay it off, but couldn't quite stay ahead of it, and at less than six-percent interest, it didn't seem important.

The letter in my shaking hand stated the credit card company had tripled our interest rate and lowered our available credit by two-thirds. Our balance was now dangerously close to this new limit, meaning new charges would be denied.

After agonizing for several precious minutes, I decided not to think about it, much less tell Mike, until after the fund-raiser. I'd pull a Scarlett O'Hara and think about it tomorrow. Or Monday, the first work day of the New Year.

4

Wednesday, December 31ˢᵗ, 7:30 PM

Billy Ray Cyrus's achy-breaky-heart lament almost melted the sound system, but didn't drown out the New Year's Eve party at the Los Lobos Community Center. Saint Patrick's first annual "Help the Homeless" benefit had cleared the launch pad.

Standing by the stage with clipboard in hand, I surveyed the crowd, allowing myself to relax a bit. We had a good turnout so far. Los Lobos, an unincorporated area, is not affluent even in the best of times, and I'd worried about the forty-dollar ticket price in a bad economy. To make a profit tonight, we needed a sell-out crowd or a miracle from Saint Jude, the patron saint of hopeless causes. February, Saint Pat's month to house the homeless, was exactly thirty-two days away. That meant money we didn't have, for extra utilities, plus coffee and breakfast for our guests. Our homeless program, like everything these days, needed a bailout. This fund-raiser was a make-it or break-it event.

Someone nearby tooted a horn, celebrating early. The jarring noise reminded me I had a more immediate problem. Magda, our bartender, had not arrived. Five more minutes and I'd need to recruit a volunteer. They were in short supply due to the flu bug, and the ones present were swamped.

Jim Sykes, one of our finest, approached, a troubled look on his weathered face. We were short of chairs and the storeroom was locked. "Jim," I shouted over Billy Ray and another blast of the horn, "there's a key on top of the refrigerator. And find someone to help set up those chairs."

"Thanks, Mrs. K." He touched two fingers to his temple in a small salute and limped off, leaning on his three-pronged cane. I gave silent thanks to Saint Vincent DePaul, the patron of volunteers.

I again surveyed the makeshift bar set up between Father Burton taking tickets at the door and Mike at the buffet table. Still no Magda. A current of alarm tingled my spine. Was she okay? I checked my cell, found no messages and heaved a sigh of exasperation. So much of this evening was beyond my control.

Stationed behind a covered trestle table, Mike at least had the buffet under control. He wielded a serving spoon in each hand, doing a soft-shoe dance as he served a few early diners. Walking to their tables, they bent their heads to sniff the sweet and savory scents rising from their plates. The aromas drifted across the room, reminding me I'd had nothing since that cup of tea with Magda. Where was she? Did she have an accident, receive another frightening call?

Mike waved a serving spoon overhead and I did the same with my clipboard. A couples thing acknowledging we'd share a glass or two of red wine later to celebrate the end of this horrible year. The last six months had been hell, starting with Connie Mercado's murder, and then unbelievably, the killing of a local official. The resulting fear and mistrust, plus our ongoing sewer debacle, ripped the fabric of this community in two. I had two goals for tonight: raise money to help the homeless and bring people together.

Enough wool gathering. I hardly know a Martini from a Margarita, but the time had come for me to take command of the bar. I set my clipboard on the stage behind me and when I turned around—Voila! Magda had appeared, and in an outfit best described as just this side of "out there." A red sequined blouse showing the legal limit of cleavage set off her platinum hair, now styled sleekly so two points fell just below those amazing cheek bones. Tight designer Levis and crimson leather boots completed the ensemble.

A volunteer followed, pushing a dolly loaded with two cases of wine. He set both boxes on the floor, then disappeared. She waved to me and stepped behind the bar like she owned the place. I almost swooned with relief.

For the next few minutes I relaxed, watching dancers stepping (and miss-stepping) through a series of line dances, crowds at the door, a line at the buffet and an even longer one at the bar. Maybe, just maybe, this all might come together. Most people wanted a drink first thing, and if Mike was busy, Magda was overwhelmed. Time to trade my clipboard for a bar apron. "How can I help?" I asked.

She smiled and handed me a corkscrew. "Open three red and four white." Then, "Make it four red and six white," when a man ordered two full bottles of white, handed me a fistful of tickets and stuffed several singles in the tip jar.

Magda had donated two cases each of Sereno Vineyard's special Cabernet and *Pinot Grigio*, their signature wines. They'd go quickly and we'd have to fall back on the cheap stuff. By then most people wouldn't know or care.

I grabbed two bottles of Cabernet and stuffed them under the bar. "For Mike and me, one for tonight and one for tomorrow," I explained.

She gave me an enthusiastic thumbs-up. "You earned it." Magda held a bottle of Jack Daniels in one hand and one of Dewar's White Label in the other. From metal spouts she poured shots over ice in two squat glasses with amazing precision. She's had practice, I thought, relieved I had asked her to take over the demanding job.

"Bella, the wine?"

"Sorry. You're doing a great job."

"I know," she said, and I could tell she was pleased. She bent to retrieve a bar towel that had fallen to the floor and a red bandanna waved from her rear pocket like a little flag. That should help the tip jar.

I surreptitiously hitched up the black leggings puddled around my ankles—an unfortunate Goodwill purchase—and straightened the Snoopy-printed scarf I'd tossed over my one decent black sweater. The outfit, which looked so smart in the full-length mirror at home, now made me feel like Eliza Doolittle.

The next half hour passed in a blur. I took drink tickets, mopped spills from the bar and opened bottles of wine and beer. The DJ switched from country to soft rock and couples gyrated around the floor. The first rush for drinks abated, and I was preparing to slip away and help Mike, when something drew my eye to two late arrivals by the door.

Marcus Daniels and a younger man.

After taking their tickets, Father Burton grabbed the younger man's arm and whispered something in his ear. Perhaps the man's fly was open. If so, I didn't want to know and turned toward Magda. "Marcus sighting at three o'clock. Don't look."

Of course she did, and her face went as pale as her hair. "Oh dear God, he's got Jeremy with him."

"Jeremy?" I asked, scrutinizing Marcus's companion, a sensitive-looking man in his early forties.

"His foster son."

"Looks a bit old to be a foster anything."

"True, but Jeremy's been with Marcus forever. I haven't seen him in years"

"You've been away," I reminded her.

"Not long enough," she said, untying her apron. "I can't talk to them."

I moved behind her and clamped my hands on her shoulders. "Magda, if you rush off now, Marcus will know you suspect him. That could put you at risk. Besides, he may not want a drink."

She turned to me and rolled her eyes. "Oh, he'll want a drink all right."

Sure enough, here they came. "Be cool," I whispered as the two men approached.

"Easy for you to say." She mopped the bar top over and over, eyes fixed on the emergency exit.

Marcus halted when he saw Magda and exchanged glances with Jeremy. The younger man's face had gone slack with shock. But he recovered quickly and the two advanced, with the older man in the lead. Marcus nodded at me, but gave his full attention to Magda. "It's been a long time," he said in the sandpaper voice of a lifetime smoker.

"Still drink Sam Adams?" she asked without batting an eye.

"You bet." Marcus pulled tickets from the watch pocket of his Wranglers. The ranch owner was probably fifty-five, but exuded a restless, almost sexual, energy. I could see the attraction he would have for a woman twenty years younger like Magda's late sister.

"Make it two beers," he said after a brief exchange with Jeremy. Deep lines ran down his cheeks and tufts of fading ginger hair showed beneath his Stetson. Granny glasses too small for his full face did not dull the effect of sharp brown eyes that missed nothing. Still, their expression lacked the feral look of someone pedaling information.

Perhaps Magda was wrong about Marcus being the anonymous caller. It could easily have been someone else. Vito, Dominic's money-hungry former partner, again came to mind.

She plunked the beers on the counter. Marcus grabbed his, took a swig and headed for a nearby group of ranchers. Jeremy lagged behind, stuffing singles into the tip jar. Ignoring Magda, he caught my eye, his glance lingering a second too long. Then he joined his uncle, leaving me to wonder what that look meant.

As for Magda, she looked like she'd been whacked with a two-by-four. "We need to talk," she said.

"So let's." I indicated the empty space in front of the bar. "No one's in line right now."

"Not here." She yanked her apron off and threw it on the bar. "Outside."

"Magda, it's thirty degrees out there. How about the bathroom? I'll get someone to take over here."

"Fine. Don't be long." She headed across the room and down a short hall opposite the kitchen where the bathrooms were located.

I inventoried my prospects for a bartender. Mike busy serving, Jim Sykes on kitchen duty, Jack Olson barely keeping abreast of trash patrol. My eye fell on Father Burton chatting up diners at a nearby table. I slipped off my apron, draped it on the bar next to Magda's and approached him. "Father, do I have a job for you."

* * * * *

I pushed open the door, hoping we'd have privacy in the tiny bathroom. "Magda?" No answer. I glanced under one stall and spied a pair of red boots. "Are you okay?"

A sniffle. "Of course I'm not okay. Give me a minute."

"That's fine, but we may not be alone for long." I slipped into the other stall and sank down on the seat, dismayed at how weary I felt. No wonder. I'd been up for almost fifteen hours and the evening was just beginning.

Another sniffle, ending in a sob. "Are you okay?" I repeated, my nun instincts kicking in.

"It wasn't Marcus who called me."

"Are you sure?"

She hesitated. "His voice sounds different now, huskier. And older. The person who called had a young voice."

"Wait, wait," I said, "let's finish this discussion by the sink."

A hand appeared under the divider. "Got paper?"

When I emerged from the stall, Magda stood gripping the edge of the sink, which was so close to the door I worried about us being hit if someone barged in. I touched the small of her back to nudge her away from the hazard and she gasped like she'd forgotten my presence.

"Sorry, didn't mean to startle you." She sniffed, grabbed a piece of tissue and blew, finally regaining some degree of control.

"Okay," I said, "if it wasn't Marcus, who then? Maybe the foster kid, what's his name, Jeremy? He sure looked surprised when he saw you."

"Unlikely. I hardly know him." Her shoulders hunched like it was too much to think about. "I have no idea who called me."

"What about Vito?"

"No, he has an old voice too, sounds pissed all the time, and this guy was young."

"A crank? Someone who found the old death notice or a newspaper article online? There are a lot of sickos out there and they all have computers."

The hazel eyes registered a flick of uncertainty, but she said, "No, whoever called knew the dog was with Loreli in the kayak."

The door opened and we jumped to one side so as not to be hit. A woman seeing us in the midst of a serious girl-to-girl said, "Excuse me, I'll use the men's." Only after she backed out and the door shushed behind her did I realized the intruder was Kathy Tanner, our head librarian.

I gripped Magda's bare arm in the spot where red silk ended and her goose bumps began. "You know, it really doesn't matter who called. I think if the guy's withholding evidence from law enforcement, he could be an accessory after the fact. You might be implicated if you give him money."

Her eyes widened. "I hadn't thought of that."

"Of course not, but you should leave. Use the side entrance. Go home and don't answer the phone. On second thought, don't go home. Do you have a friend you can stay with?"

"Yes, the one I'm going surfing with tomorrow. He has an apartment near here."

"Good. Stay with your friend and go surfing in the morning as planned. You and Mike can talk after the dip."

"What about the bar?"

What about it? I thought of Father Burton mixing drinks, opening beer and pouring wine. "Don't worry about that, it's in God's hands."

She looked puzzled, but said nothing.

"Let me walk you to your car. No one will bother you with me along. Got a coat?"

She didn't and, as we gathered our things, someone or something thudded against the door. We stared hard at one another until I reached over and grabbed the handle, yanked the door open and peered across the hall. The entrance to the men's was just closing behind a flash of denim and the heel of a shoe.

The skin on my forearms prickled. Had someone listened to our conversation, fallen against the door and ducked into the men's to avoid detection? "Come on," I said, "let's get out of here."

I glanced over my shoulder to make sure we weren't followed as we made our way to the side exit. In a shroud of cold rain we hugged each other for warmth and support on the short walk to her gold Lexus.

I pulled out my cell. "Give me your number so I can contact you."

"Good idea." She called me and when my phone chirped I added her number to my directory.

Shivering, I remained in the lot until the night swallowed Magda's taillights, then turned and started toward the side door. No, not that way. Eavesdropper lurking.

Wait. Wait a darn minute.

What about Ben Adams, our investigative reporter? He showed no qualms about listening to our conversation at Java World. I hadn't seen him tonight, but that didn't mean he wasn't here. I peered into the dark, rain-spattered windows of the parked cars and hurried toward the front entrance.

5

Wednesday, December 31st, 8:30 PM

I re-entered the Community Center to a blast of heat and noise and the combined smells of beer and too many bodies in damp wool. It felt good, normal, a place where murder happens only in mystery novels.

I headed for the bar where Father Burton assured me he'd be fine until a volunteer took over. Beside him sat a most un-ecclesiastical looking glass of white wine and a full tip jar.

Marcus and Jeremy stood behind the buffet table, serving spoons at the ready. Great. We could use the extra help. Relieved of duty, Mike relaxed at a nearby table. He had food, two plates of it! He patted the empty seat beside him and gave me a thumbs-up. My heart contracted with love and concern.

My husband has a Tommy Lee Jones kind of face, with large, steel-gray "seen it all eyes" and craggy cheeks. His crew cut used to be the exact color of his eyes. But the hair has whitened since last summer and the eyes have darkened with sadness, the result of an ill-considered decision that led to tragedy and a heart attack for him, and dealt an almost-fatal blow to our marriage. There is about him now a new and troubling aura of vulnerability.

I sank down, grabbed one of the two heaping plates and hugged his neck. "Thank you, thank you."

The grin widened. "Can I have more of that later?"

"Plan on it." After another neck-hug and a wifely pat on the shoulder, I inspected the plate and inhaled: sauerkraut with sautéed onions and caraway seeds, spicy *kielbasa*, *golumpki*, (stuffed cabbage), cheese and potato-filled *pierogis*, (dumplings), more caraway seeds in rye bread slathered with sweet butter. All the Polish food groups.

"Was that Magda Sereno behind the bar?" he asked. "It's been awhile since we've seen her."

With a mouthful of bread, I could only nod. I hadn't had a chance to tell him about our meeting at Java World. "She wants to talk to you tomorrow after the Polar Bear Dip."

Annoyance flashed in his gray eyes, reminding me of Mike's darker side, the one we worked on in therapy. "What about? Can't it wait until Friday? I want to go home, fall on the couch, watch football and eat junk food all day."

"Mike, you know you're supposed to be on a low-fat diet."

"Stop!" He squeezed my leg and gave me a goofy leer, the darkness receding. "And maybe grab a quickie at half-time?"

"We can do all that, Mike, but a little later. She really needs help. You'll never believe what's happened."

"Try me."

While he cut *pierogis* into precise pieces with a plastic knife too small for his wide hand, I explained about the phone call offering to sell her information about Loreli's death, how she thought the caller was Marcus and how, when she heard his voice after five years, she'd changed her mind.

He took a bite, chewed thoughtfully, and swallowed. "You're right. I do need to talk to her, and tonight would be better than tomorrow." He glanced around. "Where'd she take herself off to?"

"She left after Marcus and Jeremy arrived. I thought it best."

He nodded. "You're probably right. I'll catch her tomorrow right after the dip, and make sure she talks to Ryan," he said, referring to Ryan Scully, Tolosa County sheriff's detective and Mike's racquetball buddy.

I stroked his hand. "It's the right thing to do."

I looked up to see Ben Adams in designer Levis and a maroon silk shirt headed toward the bar. So, he *was* here after all. Seeing him got me thinking. "Mike," I said, pulling on his sleeve, "while Magda and I were in the bathroom deciding what she should do, someone fell against the door."

Mike stopped chewing, swallowed. "And your point is?"

"Someone tried to eavesdrop on our conversation, and now that I see Ben's here, I wonder if it was him."

"What makes you think that?" Mike raised a skeptical eyebrow and lowered his voice a notch. "Did he actually open the door?"

"No, I did, and saw only a denim leg running into the men's."

Mike peered around and smiled. "Ninety percent of the men in this room are wearing some variation of Levi's. What about shoes or boots, color of hair, or lack of hair?"

"I saw the heel of a shoe, but think about it, Ben's the most likely candidate for eavesdropper. He came into Java World while Magda and I were talking this afternoon and sat right behind us. He's trying to get something on her for a story. What a sleaze-bag."

"I think you're blowing this out of proportion. Even if you find out the eavesdropper was Ben, so what?"

"I'll go to Amy, that's what."

"He's an investigative reporter. Isn't that what he's supposed to do? I think you're making too much of this."

We'd had this conversation before. Fuming inwardly and too angry to meet Mike's gaze, I turned and found myself staring into the dark eyes of Jeremy Beamer who stood behind the buffet table. Not knowing where to look, I dropped my own eyes to the plate and speared a hunk of *kielbasa*.

"Bella?" Mike said softly.

"What?" I snapped, cutting the sausage into smaller and smaller pieces.

"I'm sorry. It's New Year's Eve and we're both worn out. Let's not fight." He reached for my hand.

I grabbed his large paw in my two small ones and held on tight. "Okay."

"May I join you?" Father Burton stood behind us, sipping a full glass of white wine.

Great timing. Did he notice our tiff? I indicated a place opposite. "Please do. Looks like the fund-raiser's a success."

"I suppose." Our pastor wore a black shirt and Roman collar over Lee slim jeans. Interesting. Did this choice express disapproval of tonight's function? Full "civvies" were usually his choice for social functions. I found Father a conundrum, and the combination of jeans and clerical garb expressed it perfectly. On one hand, he preached hell-fire-and-brimstone. On the other, there was something a bit too worldly about him, especially in those sharp blue eyes. I waited for his acknowledgement of our part in tonight's success.

Nothing, nada, zip.

Oh, for the warm and comforting presence of Father Rodriguez, our former pastor, who took indefinite leave after Connie Mercado's murder last summer. The parish hot line sizzled with rumors that grief over her death drove him back to the Philippines.

Mike half rose from his chair. "Father, let me get you some food. If you've never had Polish before, you're in for a treat."

Father gave him a dyspeptic smile and held his skinny midsection as though stifling a burp. "No, no, thank you." He was not a newcomer to Saint Pat's, having been a fixture here for years before Mike and I moved to Los Lobos. The two of us hadn't seen eye-to-eye then over his old-school ways. Still didn't.

Before he left, Father Rodriguez begged me to take over Connie Mercado's job as volunteer homeless coordinator. The request came at a good time. Being an advocate for a sane wastewater policy had become an exercise in futility. In Los Lobos, it was impossible to mention "wastewater" and "sane" in the same sentence. I could make a real difference helping the homeless.

The benefit was my first big project. I glanced around and attempted to leaven both my thoughts and Father's somber mood with one-sided small talk, which sounded strained and ridiculous. The priest might not make idle chit-chat, but those eyes missed nothing. Even Mike, who's oblivious to such social niceties, seemed uncomfortable.

"Tonight's take should cover all our expenses and leave some for emergencies," I added.

Our pastor tapped his ring on the table. "Any surplus will be used to purchase new vestments."

My jaw suddenly lost all muscle tone. "But... but with the economy in a tailspin, and all the foreclosures, there are a lot more homeless. To get through February, we'll need all of tonight's money, maybe more."

Father sniffed like something smelled bad and my foot jerked with a sudden urge to kick him. "We'll take thirty people each night, and no more. Let the Blue Stetson ranch take the rest," he said, reminding me of Marie Antoinette's "let them eat cake." He eyed Marcus and Jeremy behind the buffet table and something I couldn't read registered in his eyes.

I plowed on. "But there's no regulation at the ranch. Most single adults can look out for themselves, but at Saint Pat's, we take families and children."

His aquiline nose twitched like a rabbit's. "We'll discuss it at the appropriate time."

I got the message. I'd heard it, or words to that effect, often enough in religious life.

He rose and once again stared hard at Marcus and Jeremy. "Now I must go and mingle." He walked toward the two men as Mike and I exchanged a relieved look.

* * * * *

After dinner, a fifty-fifty drawing and reuniting two lost children with their frantic parents, Mike and I found ourselves a hidey-hole near the stage. We drank directly from the bottle of

Cabernet, passing it back and forth, and observed an agreeable husband-and-wife silence as we watched the Grunge Dogs, a local group, set up for the dance that would greet the New Year. Despite their name, the band consisted of middle-aged, mainstream accountants, lawyers and merchants. Several gave lip service to the word "Grunge" by sporting anemic pony tails.

"Mike, what the hell's happenin'?"

I turned, surprised and dismayed, to see Marcus. He acknowledged me with a nod, and he and Mike immediately started talking "guy." The ranch owner still wore his signature dark blue Stetson on the crown of his large head. I'd been taught it was rude for men to wear hats inside, a tenet of my Midwest upbringing that seemed downright quaint in this western culture.

"How are things at the ranch?" I asked by way of inserting myself into the manly conversation.

"If you mean is 'County' still trying to shut me down, the answer is same-ol, same-ol," he growled, using the popular term for our local government.

I nodded like I understood, but I didn't. Marcus took all-comers, no questions asked and this drove county regulators crazy. Also, the property sprouted old iron vehicles like dandelions, angering the owners of expensive homes overlooking the ranch. Marcus taunted them with the reminder that the Blue Stetson was there first, adding fuel to the flames of discord.

"You could get County off your back by checking your guests more carefully and cleaning up the place."

He held up his hands, palms outward. "Don't go there."

Mike gave me the evil eye and I backed off. Then, in a miracle of good timing, Jeremy entered stage left and Marcus made introductions. The two men each had their own, very different, style. Marcus wore a western red and black striped shirt with a bolo tie. Wranglers bunched below a midsection that while afflicted with middle-aged creep, still looked in pretty good shape.

Jeremy favored classic slim Levis with a long-sleeved black cable-knit sweater that rode easily on his slim frame. He was smaller than his benefactor, with a heart-shaped face and liquid brown eyes that sloped at the corners like a cocker spaniel's.

But it was the hair that set him apart. Blunt cut, it swept back from a dark widow's peak to fall in perfect waves around the nape of his neck. For a fleeting moment, I imagined that hair blown forward by winds on an English moor, or spread across a lover's satin pillow.

A silly grin plastered itself across my face. "Jeremy," I asked "do you live around here?"

"Actually, I lived in Tucson most recently." His voice was soft, seductively warm and I wondered what he did for a living.

As though tapping into my thoughts, Marcus said, "Jeremy was a Tolosa County fireman before he upped and moved to Arizona a few years ago." His eyes reflected the pride he felt in his nephew.

He looked more like a cellist in a symphony orchestra. "Did you fight fires in Tucson?" I asked.

Jeremy's eyes flickered. "Actually, I was a PI and bodyguard there."

"How interesting. I'd like to hear about your experiences sometime." *Now what made me say that?* It sounded like I was coming on to him.

"Happy to oblige, Bella." The spaniel eyes indicated my slightest wish was his command. Maybe it was the eyes, or the way his upper lip kissed the lower one when he said my name, but this guy was charming the pants off me. Figuratively speaking, of course.

"What will you do now that you're back?"

Jeremy made an easy, rolling motion with his hand. "A little of this, a little of that. For now."

"Jeremy's gonna help me out at the ranch," Marcus interjected. He turned to Mike. "By the way, I hear you're takin' the Polar Bear Dip tomorrow morning."

"That's right," Mike said, "and Bella's coming with me."

I tossed him a look. I hate water except to make tea, shower in or maybe admire from the beach, but I had to do this for Mike.

Marcus clapped Mike on the shoulder and turned to me. "You take care of this guy, hear me Bella? I don't want to have to haul his ass out of the ocean."

"Marcus is on the rescue swimmers' team," Mike explained.

Rescue swimmers?

A line appeared between Mike's eyes. "You *are* going to be there, Marcus?"

Oh dear Lord, he's worried too.

"I said so, didn't I? Never miss it." Marcus inclined his head toward Jeremy. "This lug will be on board, too."

"Uh, why do you need rescue swimmers?" I asked.

"A precaution," Jeremy offered, "in case someone gets in trouble."

"But people don't normally go in far, do they?"

"Not normally," Marcus said. "It's so damn cold most people pop in and run right back out. But we always have one or two who test their limits and need to be rescued." He patted my shoulder. "Don't worry. Never lost a Polar Bear yet."

6

"H...hey, Bella."

I turned, expecting a volunteer with a problem, and encountered the round face and small, bright eyes of Walter Lubek. A high-functioning Down syndrome man in his mid-thirties, Walter does odd jobs around Saint Pat's. "Hey Walter, having a good time?"

"Not, really, I don't like the music and there's no pizza." His freckled forehead creased in a frown. "You're my best friend, how come you didn't have pizza?"

A lump formed in my throat. I had no idea Walter thought of me as his best friend. We'd only spoken a few times.

Jeremy smiled, and threw his arm around Walter's narrow shoulders. "Opera and pizza are my bro's favorite things," he said. Walter gave him an adoring look, then returned his gaze to me.

"Walter's your brother?" I asked Jeremy, trying not to let my surprise show.

Marcus interjected, "It's complicated. I'll tell you sometime."

Walter still waited for my answer as though his future depended on it. "Of course, we're best friends and we'll have pizza next year. I can't promise opera though, it doesn't lend itself to dancing," I said, wondering what I'd just committed to.

"Take-out pizza for next year sounds good to me," Mike said, an understandable statement after all the work on tonight's Polish food.

"All right!" Walter thrust out short, freckled arms and moved to encircle my waist.

Marcus grabbed his arm. "Walter, we've talked about this before. What do we do before hugging?"

In answer to my questioning look, Marcus explained, "Walter lives at the ranch with Jeremy and me and works for us when he's not busy at the church. We both keep an eye on him."

Walter stepped back, tugged at the front of his T-shirt—was that Pavarotti on the front?—and looked up at Marcus. "A...as...ask?"

Down syndrome folks love to hug, sometimes inappropriately. "It's fine," I said to Marcus and pulled Walter into a tight squeeze.

We stepped apart and Walter's grin stretched from dimple to dimple. "A...are you staying safe, Bella?" he asked, the grin fading to a shadow.

What a strange question. "Of course I am, Walter. Why do you ask?"

His forehead puckered. "I wo...worry about you a...a...after last summer."

I nodded. Chris, my nephew from Cleveland, and I were nearly killed when we became entangled in the Connie Mercado murder investigation. My heart still fluttered when I realized how close we'd come to dying.

"Don't worry, everything's fine. All the bad people are gone." I didn't mention they had joined a growing cadre of personal ghosts that included my sister Bea, Connie Mercado and now, Loreli Sereno.

"Do you still write about dead people?" Walter asked.

"The *Central Coast Chronicle's* best obituary editor ever," Mike said, somewhat impatiently, I thought.

Walter stared at Mike, considered what he'd said, then turned back to me. "Wha...what do the d...dead people tell you?"

His words caused my heart to lurch anew. I do talk to the portrait of Emily Divina, the windmill's resident ghost. I'm convinced she saved my life last summer. But I wasn't about to tell him that. "Walter, I don't actually talk to dead people. Their friends and relatives give me the information I need for my obituaries."

"Bella?" Walter's small eyes danced. "I *know* you don't talk to dead people. I was kidding." He gazed up at Jeremy. "Wasn't I?"

Jeremy again ruffled Walter's fair hair and turned to me, giving me his killer smile. "Walter likes to joke around. Sometimes people take him too seriously."

"I understand, Walter. It's okay," I said.

The band began its first number. I invited Mike to dance and received a stony look in return. He never learned and it's a sore subject with him.

Saying he had a headache and needed Tylenol, Marcus steered Walter toward the kitchen after hearing they'd find pills on top of the fridge and a frozen pizza inside. Halfway across the room, Walter looked back and finger-waved to me. I waved back, wondering what his life was like. The Blue Stetson was almost twenty miles from Saint Pat's. How did he get back and forth? On the bus? Unlikely he'd have a driver's license and he hadn't arrived with Marcus and Jeremy. He was here when I arrived. Maybe Father Burton picked him up.

"Care to dance, Bella?" Jeremy smiled at me, arms outstretched.

"Oh." I glanced at Mike and noted his clenched jaw. I started to say no and decided that was silly since I'd already asked him. "Sure." I stepped into Jeremy's waiting arms. It was awkward at first; I danced the boy part at the convent's Saturday night dances.

After a couple false starts I got the hang of moving backward and we glided around the floor. *Slow, slow, quick, quick.* Soon I didn't have to count.

Jeremy smelled like a mixture of expensive wool and fresh-squeezed limes. My body tingled. *Down girl.*

He glanced over my shoulder. We twirled around and I saw what he saw—Mike standing like an Easter Island statue. I knew that stance. Little, if anything, would be said. Mike's people came to Chicago from Nebraska, where lots of Polish people settled in the 1800's. Talk of feelings was considered frivolous among those plains-hardened people.

But he'd get over it, later on, safe and warm in our windmill house under the down comforter. Suddenly the idea of a naked male body seemed very appealing. Jeremy twirled me again and I caught a glimpse of Mike's stiff back as he strode toward the kitchen. I felt a twinge of guilt and started to break off the dance and follow him.

No, let him stew over a pile of dirty dishes. Do him good.

"Another?" Jeremy asked when the music ended.

"Thanks, that was fun, but I need to help Mike with the cleanup."

"A good little woman follows her mate." His eyes mocked me.

"That's not true." *Or was it?* "It's just that I want to be sure we get all our utensils back. Mike doesn't know a spatula from a serving spoon."

"I know my way around the kitchen, so let me help." Jeremy took my arm in a way that was casual and yet preemptory. I allowed myself to be led.

A few minutes later, surrounded by volunteers rushing back and forth with pans and trays and with my hands in a sink of sudsy water, wearing blue rubber gloves three sizes too big, I couldn't get the man out of my mind.

Dangerous territory, Bella. What Mother Superior termed "an occasion of sin." Now there's a quaint term.

What was there about him that attracted me? More than his amazing good looks, he carried with him an air of intrigue, but he also seemed a caring individual in his obvious affection for his brother Walter. *Out damned thoughts.*

Scrubbing away at a pan of crusty sauerkraut, I forced my mind to Walter, deciding to invite him for coffee, or maybe pizza, next week. We'd never had a real conversation despite his claim that we were best friends. I wanted to find out more about his life.

Sure I'm nosey, that's a prerequisite for being a nun, but it's more than that. No doubt about it; the mothering instinct still beats within my breast. I'd spent twenty-five years listening to my biological clock tick as I helped homeless Detroit kids build a better life. Now the clock needed a new battery it was not likely to get and I still felt a strong empathy for young, vulnerable people like my nephew Chris, and now Walter. And joke or not, Walter's remark about talking to dead people made me wonder about his grasp of reality.

7

By the time The Grunge Dogs played *Auld Lang Syne,* Mike and I had morphed into zombies. Jeremy proved incredibly helpful with the remaining cleanup and we finished in just under an hour. He'd be a great asset to Marcus around the ranch, maybe get the place spruced up, and talk turkey to him about vetting his homeless guests.

My husband and I stood alone in the Community Center parking lot. Amber haze from the lot's single light shone on Mike's truck and my old Subaru. I'd insisted we bring both vehicles so Mike could leave if he got tired. He'd groused, but agreed in the end.

Besides our cars, only a beat-up white van and a silver SUV remained. They lay in shadow at the end of the lot near the darkened tennis courts. The storm had passed, leaving behind an arctic stillness. Behind the library across the street, the moon played hide and seek with some bad-tempered clouds.

I placed my hands on the front of Mike's jacket, surprised at how cold the leather felt. "See you at home in a few."

"Forget the market," Mike said. "Drink your tea without milk for once. Just follow me home."

"It's only a few blocks and we need bagels and cream cheese for tomorrow. They'll be out of those *bialys* you love by the time we get back from the Polar Bear Dip." The thought of dipping even one toe, much less my whole body, in the ocean at dawn made me shiver all over.

Mike sighed heavily, sending little clouds of steam into the night air. "Okay, okay, but make it quick. I took a sleeping pill and I'm gonna be out cold in half an hour."

"Was that wise?" I glanced at my watch. "We have to be up in five hours and you had—how many beers?"

Mike's palms shot up. "Bella, stop. What's done is done. I'll leave the gate open so you can drive right in, but hurry up."

"Okay." I understood what he was saying. Take-down gangs had invaded several Central Coast homes recently. An open gate offered an opportunity to make trouble.

"Got your cell?"

"In the car." I concentrated on twisting the key in the Subaru's sticky door lock.

"Bella?"

I turned. "Hmm?"

He gripped my wrist, his eyes narrowing with concern. "Be careful. What Walter said about you staying safe gives me the willies."

I started to say "He's a kid" and realized that wasn't true. My mind leapfrogged to the person who eavesdropped as Magda and I talked. Was he—or she—still out there? Maybe in one of the cars by the tennis courts?

"I'll be careful." I danced my fingertips along the back of Mike's hand. He shivered, either from renewed passion or my cold hands, probably the latter. "Warm up our bed, will you?"

"You bet. Let me open that door for you."

I handed him the key and batted my lashes. "My hero."

We pecked and climbed into our separate cars. Mike drove off without waiting to see if my old car started. Honestly, the man was so inconsistent. Or maybe he was tired. Maybe he wasn't feeling well. Maybe...

Maybe you should put a sock in it, Bella. I turned the key in the ignition. *Click.* Tried again. *Click, click*—and then *click, click, click.* The starter again? We'd gotten a new one last summer after problems at the LA airport.

I took a deep breath and tried again. Okay Bella, what's plan B? Call Mike, of course.

I reached for my cell on the console. Not there. Of course not. I'd walked Sam and left it in the pocket of my padded vest. I stared at the two empty vehicles in the lot, my earlier anxiety returning with a vengeance.

The Community Center lay in darkness behind me. Saint Pat's church and rectory slumbered beyond the tennis courts. To get to the rectory and call Mike, I'd have to walk alone and in darkness by the white van and the silver SUV.

No thank you.

I blew on cold hands and considered my next move.

Mike's always football-talking about Hail Mary passes. Can't hurt, might help. I pushed in the clutch and turned the key, steeling myself for another click of death.

The engine turned.

Wahoo! I slammed the Subaru into gear and shot out of the parking lot before Mary changed her mind. Gliding down the steep drive, I heard the sound of another engine starting. I floored the gas pedal, barely slowing down to hook a left off

Community Drive onto Los Lobos Road. The white van followed. No turn signal or lights, sure sign of a drunk driver. Or our eavesdropper. I sped up; so did he.

Should I pull over and let him pass? No, I'd wait and see what happened after the next turn. Without signaling I veered left on Ninth Street toward Bay Oaks; the van dogged me around the corner. My stomach clenched into an iron fist. The events that led to last summer's murders began with a Hummer trying to run me off the road.

I stole a peek at the rearview mirror; van too far back to see driver. Still, something told me it was a man. Without thinking, I groped on the console for my cell phone and, swearing softly, came up with a gas receipt.

The van edged closer. *Bialys* be damned. I wheeled onto the shoulder, downshifted and made a quick U. Passed the van heading the other way. It was unmarked and had solid white panels, the driver a dark profile against the dim light. Something strange about that outline. Too busy to focus. The race up Ninth Street felt like all the demons in hell were chasing me. Sure enough, when I reached Los Lobos Road, the van clung to my tail.

I whipped right on two wheels and a prayer, smelling my own sweat. Three blocks to go. How could this happen? Again. To the same person, driving the same car, in the same town? I bumped onto our dirt access road, past the row of mailboxes standing like darkened sentinels and watched out the side window. The van continued west on Los Lobos Road, a silent ghost in the night.

* * * * *

Thursday, January 1ˢᵗ, early morning

The man stood by the road, watching a lamp flick on in the bedroom window of the apartment, then off a moment later. Was the couple inside making love? Despite his hatred and fear of the woman, he felt a stirring in his groin. Who'd have thought she'd be there tonight? Because he'd listened at the door of the bathroom, and because of the earlier anonymous call, he'd need to improvise, something he was loath to do. The man liked order and was used to being in charge. If only he had the Valium he'd used on the first woman, he'd have more control. He'd have to rely on his wits instead.

8

Thursday, January 1ˢᵗ, 7:06 AM

A pale winter sun winked over the eastern hills as Mike, Sam and I arrived at Cuyamaca Beach. I opened the truck door and wound the scarf I'd just finished knitting around my neck, and buried my nose in it. If the air felt this cold, what would the ocean be like?

Oh God, I wanted to be home in bed. I hadn't slept well, or nearly long enough. I considered telling Mike about being followed last night, but when I entered our bedroom, he didn't even stir. He lay sprawled across the king-size, sawing logs and blowing gas in the darkened room. Sam and I retreated to the living room sofa, with Sam blowing doggie breath in my face until I banished him to the kitchen.

In the cold light of day, last night's following incident seemed illogical, silly even. Was Mike right? Did I blow things out of proportion? Maybe so, but I had this strange sense of foreboding about today. I'd be so relieved when we were finally back home.

Even though my trusty (and waterproof) Timex showed nearly an hour until start time, cars sat door-handle to door-handle in the pier lot. We parked several blocks away. Hiking down the hill toward the ocean, I saw hundreds of people milling around the pier. "Look at those idiots," I mumbled through my scarf to Sam who turned and cocked his head at me. I'd be one of those idiots in less than an hour. The thought of stripping to a swim suit made me want to turn tail and run.

You can do it, Bella.

Mike quickened his step and Sam, not to be outdone, pulled ahead. He strained at his leash, dragging me along. Pretty spry for an old dog. He'd made a good recovery from last summer's ugly knock on the head with a gun butt.

As we got closer, Hawaiian music and the voice of a DJ drifted toward us. The beach had assumed a carnival air despite the temperature. Many "Polar Bears" were in costume: Robin Hood and his merry men and women, clowns in floppy shoes, Indians in full face paint, George Bush and Dick Cheney rubber masks. No wetsuits were allowed and several women toughed it out in bikinis. More power to 'em.

We found a postage-stamp-sized space near the band at the south end of the lifeguard station, spread our towels on the sand and eyeballed the spectacle. Nearby, the DJ held forth on an impromptu stage. No wonder we got this space; the music had switched to rock, the hard kind that assaulted eardrums and battered conversation.

I tapped Mike on the arm and pointed out a man close to eighty wearing a plastic shower cap. He was trying his best to hit on a goose-bumped young thing sixty years his junior. A group of older women sported T-shirts proclaiming themselves to be "Polar Piddlers."

Mike grinned, taking it all in, loving every minute; I was miserable.

During a blessed lull in the music, one of a phalanx of life-guards grabbed the mike and shouted a thirty-minute warning to the few intrepid surfers catching waves south of the pier. Magda and her friend must be out there, but they all looked alike from this distance.

The pace quickened: Fire trucks pulled into a roped-off parking area, a Coast Guardsman barked into a radio, likely to three Harbor Patrol boats hovering beyond the breakers. I relaxed; safety was a big priority.

The music resumed at an intolerable decibel level. It hurt Sam's ears. He whimpered and pulled away.

"Mike," I shouted, "I'm taking Sam for a walk. I'll be back in a few minutes." Mike nodded, busy watching the scene. We had almost half an hour.

Sam and I slogged through soft sand toward the water, finally finding a path apart from the fray. Down the beach a stretch, I couldn't believe what—or rather whom—I saw. Magda.

"Magda!" I called, pulling Sam along.

No sign that she'd heard me and no wonder. Her energy was concentrated on doing a little run in place while struggling to pull a wetsuit over three triangles of scarlet spandex. Mission accomplished, she turned and lifted her hair off the nape of her neck. Martin Tanner, Tolosa County's only African-American sheriff's deputy, pulled up her zipper with one hand while keeping the other planted in that intimate spot between her waist and rear end. Magda had called him a friend last night; that gestured implied more.

Good for her. I was glad she had someone in her life. Still, I was a little puzzled that she'd put yesterday's events behind her so easily. It meant something; I wasn't sure what. She might not have money of her own, but she still lived in her brother's house, which was no-doubt luxurious, and he'd probably ponied up for that Lexus. I felt a pang of envy. If our septic pumping business got in trouble, no one would bail us out. Magda at least had a safety cushion.

Come on Bella, there's no safety cushion against murder.

The couple yanked on black hoods, grabbed their boards and sprinted toward the waves. "Don't let them go out there," warned a little voice inside me.

"Magda!" I shouted, louder this time. "Come back." They hit the water.

Sam whined and pulled back on his leash. The next thing I knew, I was staring at an empty collar and leash, with Sam galumphing toward the waves. "Come back here you crazy dog!" I shouted. I concentrated on coaxing Sam back to the sand, soaking my sweats in the waves. Despite near-hypothermia, I removed my shirt and dried the shivering dog, leaving myself in wet pants and a swim suit top. Sam's tail wagged his thanks.

"You *should* be grateful, you bad dog." Sam gave me a look that said he was only doing what dogs do.

A voice behind me said, "Can't keep a good Lab down." I turned to see the smiling face of Kathy Tanner, our head librarian and Martin's mother. She wore a purple and green African print skirt and an orange parka. Exotic? Perhaps, but on her ample frame the outfit looked good. But she could wear a grocery bag and look good.

"Hey Kathy, long time no see, at least twelve hours."

She smiled and Sam's tail nearly wagged itself off his body. Kathy kept a jar of dog biscuits on the checkout counter and Sam always charmed her out of an extra one or two on our weekly trips to the library. "Doing the Polar Bear Dip?" I yelled over the cacophony of sounds.

Kathy laughed, a deep throaty guffaw. "Be serious." She leaned toward me, holding a hand over her mouth. "I was hoping to catch a glimpse of Magda, Martin's new woman."

So I was right about them being more than friends. "They're out in the surf."

Hmm. Had Kathy recognized Magda last night in that brief period after she opened the bathroom door? Did she double back to eavesdrop on our conversation? "Kathy, I need to ask you something."

At that moment the music screeched to a halt and a lifeguard grabbed the mike. "All surfers out of the water now." He repeated it twice more.

I glanced at my watch. 7:45 exactly. "I need to get back to Mike. We're doing the dip."

"No kiddin'? What about Sam?"

"He's going in with us."

Kathy looked around. "In this crowd? An old dog like that? No way."

The crowd now resembled a Mongolian horde. "Oh God, you're right. What were we thinking?"

"You weren't, Hon." Kathy grabbed Sam's leash. "Go! I'll keep the dog. We'll meet up afterward."

"Thanks, Kathy. Owe you big time." She and Sam walked off, with Sam nosing the pocket of her parka for dog biscuits. Neither gave me a backward glance.

I hurried back to Mike, almost running head-long into the Rescue Swimmers. They charged the water like the Oakland Raiders entering the field, swam out beyond the breakers and took up stations approximately twenty feet apart, bundles of energy in identical black wetsuits and hoods. Impossible to pick out Marcus and Jeremy.

"Where the hell were you? We've only got a few minutes. And where's Sam?" Mike stood in front of me, stripped to geezer trunks. His goose bumps were even bigger than mine, but I was relieved to see him with good color and normal breathing. I told him about Sam and Kathy. He nodded his approval, turned and yelled over his shoulder, "Take off your glasses. We need to get up front."

"Why?" No answer. He was already sprinting toward the water. I tossed my glasses on a towel and took off after him. We squeezed into a place close to the pier, earning dirty looks from other Polar Bears. The DJ yelled the two-minute warning and an invading army of dippers surged forward. The noise plugged my ears and, without glasses, everything looked fuzzy.

"You okay?" Mike shouted, grabbing my hand.

"I guess."

"Go!" The gun sounded and the crowd gave a mighty roar. Mike pulled me along and we dashed toward the water, fighting to keep people from breaking through our locked hands. Let me tell you, I have never felt anything so cold as that ocean— like plunging into a bath of ice water. Waves surged around my ankles, my knees, my waist and suddenly I couldn't breathe.

I yanked on Mike's hand. "That's far enough." I had to force the words out. I froze, afraid to go forward because of the depth, and afraid to turn back because of the encroaching mob. This was so much worse than I'd imagined.

Mike looked at me, I swear for the first time since we entered the water, now lapping at my chest. I clutched his hand in a death grip. "What's wrong?" he asked.

While I fumed over the question, a breaking wave knocked me sideways. Our locked hands broke apart. I flailed about, unable to see or get my bearings; I felt a tug on my legs, pulling me out to sea. Now pounding waves covered my head and water rushed into my mouth. The briny liquid scalded my nose and throat and froze the breath in my chest.

This is what it's like to die.

And then, strong arms were scooping me up, steadying me. "You okay?" Mike repeated over and over, his eyes dark with concern.

I could manage only a dumb nod.

"Maybe we should go back a bit," Mike allowed. We again joined hands, turned and waded toward shore, encountering little resistance from the Mongolian horde. In less than a minute, most had retreated to the safety and relative warmth of the sand.

We settled in water up to my waist and turned to face each other. Hands intertwined, we jumped up and down in the waves like idiots in a Monte Python movie. I relaxed a bit. Moving around definitely made me warmer.

"Oof." Something hit me, sending a sharp pain into my side. I released Mike's hand and turned, wobbled slightly and then righted myself. A red surfboard bobbed beside me. The top sported a dark mountain logo. My heart skipped a beat, then another. Sereno Cellars used a black mountain against a red background on their wine labels.

"What the hell?" Mike asked, staring at the board. I grabbed it, uncertain of what to do next.

I squinted toward the beach. Even with limited sight, I could see that a restless, unsettled feeling hovered over the beach. Onlookers huddled in small groups. Lifeguards leapt from their stations. Whistles shrilled as they bolted toward the water.

"Shark!" The lifeguards shouted, and then again. And again. "Everyone out. Now!" Sirens erupted from the patrol boats stationed beyond the breakers.

Mike pulled me toward shore. Other people in the water ran clumsily toward the sand, in some cases colliding with gawkers moving in for a better look.

"Blood!" Someone yelled. Sure enough, foam on waves near the shore took on a pinkish tinge. A great commotion began next to us, someone in a wetsuit and hood struggling toward the beach half-dragging, half-carrying another person identically clad. People ran out to help and only got in the way.

I screamed and couldn't stop. Time blurred. We splashed and fought our way the short distance to the sand at the foot of the pier, somehow eluding sheriff's deputies cordoning off the area.

Magda lay there, head to the side, eyes open, seeing nothing. Martin stood nearby for a moment, then fell to his knees beside her. The lump in my throat threatened to choke me.

Mike knelt beside Martin, saying something that I didn't catch to the lifeguards and paramedics. They moved as one to comply. My husband must have been one heck of a take-charge cop.

No one told me to leave and so I stayed, dimly registering Jeremy in a dark wetsuit, his face pale, and Father Burton in a windbreaker, administering last rights. I had no idea how they got there.

Martin looked at Mike with eyes dulled by shock and shook his head. "The shark got her femoral artery. She bled to death before I reached her." He pointed to a huge laceration, like a giant scar, on the inner thigh of her wetsuit. There was no blood. Mike reached across the body and traced his finger above the ripped suit, not touching it, the gesture strangely intimate. "This isn't a bite, son. Looks more like a cut."

Overhead, I heard *thwack, thwack, thwack* of helicopter blades.

9

Sick at heart, I gazed up at a rescue chopper arriving too late to save Magda. With a punctured femoral artery, no one could have saved her. She was dead before the crew lifted off.

Was Mike right? Did someone attack her with a knife? The same person who killed her sister? Someone who didn't want her to find out how—and why—Loreli really died.

I scanned the shocked and silent crowd for a chance glimpse of a killer and spied instead two familiar figures who calmed my heart. Sam, collar intact and leash dragging, sat lonely and forlorn beside a group of teens with ears glued to cell phones. Kathy, looking stunned, stood next to the dog.

I made my way to her and gently took Sam's leash. Kathy and I hugged. Her body shook with grief, and I was finally able to cry. We stood that way for a few moments, then she stepped back and pressed her palms against her eyes, willing away the tears. "I was just curious about her, that's why I came today. I didn't mean her any harm."

"Of course you didn't—"

"Mom!" I turned and saw Martin running toward us, his boyish face gray with pain and sorrow. She reached out her arms and he ran into them.

* * * * *

The sharpened abalone iron concealed next to his skin, the man walked quickly toward the deputy's personal car. The couple had been late and left it unlocked—a break for him. Another break—everyone watching the spectacle at the pier. He opened the door and, holding the knife in a piece of newspaper, slid it under the passenger's seat.

* * * * *

Driving home, Mike allowed Sam to sit between us in The Beast, his beloved Ford 250. He wouldn't worry about hair on the upholstery after what we'd experienced today. Sam did what he did best, offering a warm and comforting presence. I fingered one of the dog's silky ears. "Did Martin say any more about what happened?" I asked.

Mike stared out the windshield at the Coast Highway. "He was pretty incoherent, kept insisting Magda was an experienced surfer."

"Both Loreli and Magda were into water sports. How tragic they both died doing what they loved."

"Isn't it? This is going to be hard on her brother."

I thought about Dominic receiving the sad news, perhaps as we spoke. I'd call later and offer condolences, which seemed little enough to do. "Mike, all surfers were supposed to be out of the water. Why were Magda and Martin still there?"

"According to Martin, she wanted to watch the dip from the other side of the breakers. In their dark wetsuits, they eluded rescue personnel who would have insisted they leave."

Magda was a risk-taker. Besides surfing, she was into sky diving and parasailing. Did her behavior contribute to her death? If she'd been sitting on the beach would she have been killed anyway? Sooner or later, if indeed she was targeted. "Martin stayed with her?"

"Tried to. They got separated. The leash of his board got caught on a piece of seaweed and by the time he untangled it, she was several hundred feet away. He saw her thrashing, knew she was in trouble. By the time he got to her she'd been hit."

"So someone was out there, underwater, waiting for them." I said. "Maybe he wrapped the seaweed around Martin's leash, then stabbed Magda while Martin was distracted."

Mike whistled. "Sometimes you scare me, Bella. Sure you weren't a serial killer in a former life?"

I laughed a little, though Mike's observation sent chills down both arms. "Loreli's death was ruled accidental after they found

Valium in her system. Before that, authorities thought it might be murder."

Another whistle. "They'll want to reopen the case after what's happened."

"Where was Marcus? As a rescue swimmer he was supposed to be there. Jeremy was."

He turned toward me. "I thought the same thing."

All of a sudden a truck loomed on the horizon. "Watch the road. There's a semi coming."

"Yes, Mother." The lines around his eyes constricted as he focused on the road. Mike was a good driver, able to handle any emergency. Once again I checked his color and breathing. Normal, despite the morning's trauma and a dip in freezing water. Maybe I worried about him too much, but it was hard not to.

"Anyway," I said, "If Marcus called Magda to extort money from her, it makes no sense that he would kill her. On the other hand, if he killed Loreli, and got a call threatening to blackmail him, he'd want Magda out of the way."

"That makes sense," Mike said. "But what's his motive for killing Loreli? They were engaged."

"Maybe he was tired of her, maybe she cheated on him. There was that twenty years difference in their ages."

"Good point. Let's talk about this after we have showers," Mike said, slowing down. "Ah, home at last." He turned off Los Lobos Road onto our access road. A few seconds later, we pulled up to our gate. It stood open, swinging in the wind. I thought about the white van following me home and currents of alarm ran through me.

"Did you lock the gate?"

His eyes widened. "Dear God, I forgot. We're losing it, Bella."

"*We* need to be more careful." We'd installed a combination lock after the troubles last summer. Only the two of us and Chris, my nephew, knew the code. "Drive through. I'll close the gate after you."

I snapped the hasp into place and stole a moment to collect my thoughts after the tragic morning. If anything was amiss inside, I'd tell Mike right away about being followed. If not, I'd wait. I climbed back into the truck and we wended our way up the gravel drive. As always I was struck by the sight of our windmill home, especially when I remembered that Loreli and Magda found us this perfect spot. A new wave of sadness washed over me.

That's how it's going to be for a while, Bella.

The four paddles atop the mill formed a huge X in a sky of cornflower blue. Last night's storm had crawled back to sea. My heart lifted a little. A gloomy day would have been tough to deal with after Magda's violent death.

Mike swung a wide left into the parking area in front and stopped next to my old Subaru. "Everything looks normal," he said. "Ready for *bialys* and football?" He grabbed my knee. "And maybe a game of hide the salami later?" He squeezed my kneecap and treated me to his I'm-in-the-mood-for-love look.

"I never got the *bialys*, remember? And how can you think of football and sex after this morning?" Was it me? Was there something in my persona that attracted murder? I was a former nun for cripe's sake and yet I seemed to lug around this sack of bad karma like some kind of evil Santa. I wanted to go back to bed, yank the covers over my head and sleep all day.

I buried my nose in Sam's neck, taking comfort in the familiar smell of slightly damp dog. Sam wanted none of it. He started to squirm and whine as Mike said, "We've got company."

Oh, no. Not company. Not now, not after this morning. I raised my head and watched a blue-jeaned young man saunter around the side of the house. He carried an oversized skateboard. A black watch cap all but swallowed Chris's yellow hair.

10

A large backpack rested against the front door. My nephew wasn't in Cleveland any more, and he wasn't in Kansas either. I opened the truck door and Sam bounded out like he couldn't believe it. Frozen in our seats, and shivering in wet clothes, Mike and I exchanged looks. We couldn't believe it either. "So much for hiding the salami," Mike said with a sigh.

"What are you doing here?" we asked at almost the same time and winced when Chris told us he'd used college savings to hop a Greyhound to California after a dust-up with his parents.

Inside, Mike and I changed into dry clothes while Chris played with Sam. Then my husband busied himself making a fire and I hastily brewed slow-roasted for the guys and my strongest English Breakfast with three sugars for me. No way could we face this family crisis without a jolt of caffeine and sugar.

"Chris, what's this all about?" I took a seat on the sofa and set my cup on the coffee table for easy access. I was going to need it.

Across the room, Mike added another log to the fire. Chris perched on the edge of the armchair seat next to it. I was tempted to say something about him having the "hot seat" but decided to keep my lip buttoned. Sam lay with his chin on top of Chris's outstretched feet. He gave a long dog sigh and closed his eyes. All was right with his world, but ours had just gotten considerably more complicated.

"I thought you were getting along okay with the folks," I said. "The Folks" being Ed, my sister's husband, and Janet, the woman he married shortly after my sister Bea died. Janet and Chris have a troubled history to say the least, but things seemed to smooth out as Chris settled into his senior year with plans to return here for college next fall. "Have you called them since you left Ohio?"

"Left a message."

"Did they call back?"

"Didn't check."

"Maybe you should."

"Okay." He pulled a generic cell phone from his pocket and flipped it open.

"What happened to your Blackberry from last summer?" I asked.

"Janet took it away when I flunked calculus."

"I see." What else was there to say?

He checked the phone's face and looked at me. "Battery's dead."

"There's a cure for that."

He shrugged. "Forgot my charger."

"Okay, we'll deal with it later." I remembered similar exchanges from last summer. Perhaps a deep breath would bring patience. It didn't. Tried a gulp of tea. Better. "Let's start at the beginning. Why'd you leave?"

Chris stared into the flames. He made a fist, brought it to his mouth and blew into it, a sign of unease, or to gain think time.

Maybe both. "They said that, like, if I don't go to John Carroll they won't pay for college."

He still had a habit of punctuating sentences with "like." *Watch it, Bella.* Don't be judgmental. Hear him out.

"That's why you left?"

"Part of it," Chris said, shaking his head. "Remember last summer, they were fine with Tolosa Tech? Then they do a complete one-eighty and say I have to go to John Carroll."

John Carroll was an expensive school so it wasn't cost that had driven the mandate. Maybe they wanted him to get a Jesuit education. I searched for a neutral reply. The last thing Chris needed was ammunition in this latest disagreement with his folks. "John Carroll's a good school. The news commentator Tim Russert went there," I added, apropos of nothing.

Chris gave me a blank look. "Totally bogus. Miranda goes to Tolosa Tech."

Aha, this was about Miranda, his girlfriend from last summer.

"It's probably too late to apply to either John Carroll or Tolosa Tech for next year," Mike interjected, sinking down next to me. I pointed to his coffee and he took a sip, watching Chris over the rim of the mug. "You'll have to settle for junior college the first year."

"Way cool. At least Miranda and I will be in the same county."

"What does she say about all this?"

Chris sighed and hung his head. "She doesn't. Changed her frigging cell number. She even unfriended me on Facebook."

The ultimate insult for a seventeen-year-old.

"That pretty much says what she's thinking."

I glared at Mike. How could he make such an insensitive remark? Chris was a teen and these affairs of the heart were life and death. Let's face it, affairs of the heart are life and death for everyone.

"If I'm here, I can see her and...and we can, like, maybe talk about it." His blue eyes held a pleading look that tugged at my heart. "Can I stay? Please?"

Feeling myself weakening, I sneaked a glance at Mike who suddenly found his mug's Chicago PD logo the most interesting thing in the room.

"Chris," I said, "the new high school semester starts Monday and I doubt if we can enroll you halfway through senior year. What would your folks say?"

"They don't give a crap." Chris gulped coffee, his Adam's apple moving up and down.

"Language, son," Mike warned.

"Sorry." He looked at us and his eyes were wet. His Adam's apple continued to work, though the cup now sat on the hearth. "They're just so into themselves they don't give a...don't care what I do."

"I doubt they feel that way," I said, although privately I thought he'd nailed it. "Surely they want you to finish high school in Cleveland. Look, stay the weekend and fly back Sunday night. You won't miss even a day of the new semester."

Chris studied his upturned palms as though they contained the source of all wisdom. "I'm not going back to school."

A quick intake of breath from Mike and I almost dropped my cup. "You're going to quit?"

"I can work for Uncle Mike and get my GED easy. Then next fall I'll go to JC." He'd given the matter some thought.

"We can't let you quit school," Mike said with quiet authority.

Anger erupted in Chris's eyes. "You can't stop me. I'll be eighteen in two weeks."

Mike and I exchanged glances. What he said was true, but no way could we let this kid bully us. We needed to rethink our strategy. "Chris, Miranda is the first person in her family to go to college. She values education. Do you think quitting school is the way to win her back?"

His blue eyes widened like he hadn't thought of that. "Well, uh, we may not get back together right away, but at least I'll be around."

"Be careful, son," Mike said, using his cop voice. "Don't press her if she doesn't want to talk to you."

"How could this happen?" Chris held his head in his hands. "We were so tight last summer."

I wanted to tell him that in college Miranda had entered a whole new world, a world where a small difference in age—and a big difference in maturity—did matter.

"People often, er...change when they first start college." I said, trying to let him down easily. The stricken look on his face told me I had only made things worse.

"Big friggin' deal!" He jumped from the chair, fumbled in his pocket and extracted a Camel. "See ya."

"I thought you quit," I said in my tight little nun voice.

"This is, like, a crisis." He bolted for the hallway, Sam at his heels.

The front door banged shut behind them. I turned to Mike. "What now, *Kemo Sabe?*"

Mike ran his fingers through his buzz cut. "Beats me, Tonto."

"Okay, Lone Ranger. How 'bout I take a shower while you call the parents?"

"Maybe if you get on the line with Ed, he'll suddenly grow a backbone."

"Nope." Mike shook his head. "I'm not joining the cast of the Ed and Janet Show. Or should I say the Janet Show, with Ed as dogsbody." He gave me a lopsided grin. "Go ahead, you handle it. You've had lots of practice with those two."

"Coward." I said to his departing back. "I'd help if they were your relatives."

He turned with a stricken look. He didn't have relatives. His first wife and only son dead in an accident.

* * * * *

"Hello Ed? It's Bella in California."

(Silence.) "I know where you live. Janet's around somewhere." More silence, then Ed hollering. "Janet, it's you know who."

And Happy New Year to you dear brother-in-law.

A door banging, then Janet's voice, "Chris showed up yet?"

At least they noticed he was gone.

"Happy New Year. Mike sends his best regards." *Liar.* "Chris got here about an hour ago."

"Good."

Good? That's it?

"So, so how are things in Cleveland?"

(Sigh.) "Don't ask. Economy's in the toilet, snow's awful this year and Ed can't shovel because of the lumbago. Mom's dementia is worse and we might have to put her in a home. Medicare don't pay and, I ask you, how can we afford that? And once that tax-and-spend Democrat takes office in three weeks..."

"Janet, let's concentrate on Chris. I'm sure you're anxious to get him back. We'll put him on a plane Sunday and he won't miss a day of school. We'll even pay his fare."

Did I just say that?

"No."

"No?"

"What about 'No' don't you understand, Bella? We ain't ta-kin' him back. The kid acts up at school, stinks up his room with those cigarettes and mouths off if I as much as look at him. I've got The Change big time and his attitude gives me hot flashes you wouldn't believe."

"Oh yes I would, Janet dear. I think he's just a typical teen. Plus he seems to have a bad case of Senioritis."

"That's *his* problem. I'm takin' him outta school Monday. He shows up around here, he gets his own place. And how's he gonna pay for that slinging burgers at Wendy's?"

"It's only until he graduates in June. Surely he could pay you room and board and keep a low profile."

"Too late. We're adopting a couple of Korean orphans through the church. They'll get his room." *(Silence.)* "Or maybe I'll make it a sewing room and have Ed fix up a place for them in the basement. How about you, Bella? If you're so anxious to help, why don't you and Mr. Law and Order keep him?"

"Janet, we may just do that. Have a nice day."

* * * * *

"The nerve of that woman!" I fumed to a bathroom full of steam.

Mike poked a head foamy with shampoo out from behind the shower curtain. "Things went that well, eh?"

"She says she's withdrawing Chris from school Monday and if he comes home he'll have to get his own place. If he's failing in school, no way could he get into a private university like John Carroll and she knows it. I think she set him up to leave."

"Vindictive bitch." Mike snapped the washrag against the tile. "What's her trip anyway?"

"She has more problems than we can solve, but her biggest one is Janet. Mike, we have to let Chris stay. If he lives on his own he could get in all kinds of trouble. I saw it all the time at Holy Name, immature kid, bad company, drugs, prostitution to pay for drugs. Kicking a kid out is the dumbest thing a parent can do."

"So let's keep him."

I looked at him wondering if I'd heard right. His eyes twinkled. "Don't say that unless you mean it, Mike. We're not talking about a puppy."

"Good thing. At least Chris won't pee on the carpet."

My heart did a dancer's leap. "You're serious?" Somehow I didn't expect it to be that easy.

"Of course. I said I was, didn't I?"

"What about getting him in school?"

"Got a plan."

"That figures."

Mike shoved the curtain aside and thrust out steam-reddened hips. Water poured onto the floor and I grabbed a towel to sop it up. "Never mind that. Lock the door and hop in. I'll wash your back and tell you my plan."

Never could resist a naked cop.

11

"Cornmeal mush with spaghetti sauce? You expect me to eat that? Whatever happened to spaghetti and meatballs?" Mike stood in the kitchen doorway, fists glued to the same hips I'd ravished an hour ago. Now the hips were clad in old sweats. Chris and I had just told him the menu for New Year's Day dinner.

"Polenta only sounds gross." Chris rolled his eyes at me. Uncle Mike was stuck in the '50s gastronomically. "It's baked with, like, herbs and cheese and served in a light marinara sauce."

"Hah! Now you sound like a waiter in an overpriced *ristorante*. Mike gave Chris an eye-roll of his own. "Where'd you learn to make something like *that?*"

"In my Skills for Living class."

Mike feigned a slack-jawed Archie Bunker look. The clueless mid-life male was an act he assumed when it suited him. Trust me, it was a act. "Skills for Living? Maybe you *should* quit if that's what they're teaching you. What about English, math and science?"

"Skills for Living is an elective," Chris explained as though to a two-year-old. "Got an A."

Janet said he was failing. Not everything, apparently.

"Stop it, both of you." I grabbed the marinara sauce I'd fortunately whipped up on Tuesday, and slammed the fridge door closed with my hip to express my aggravation. Succeeded only in hurting my hip.

Chris finished arranging sliced polenta, hastily garnered from Spencer's, our local independent market, on a baking sheet. He looked first at me, and then at Mike while he crumpled the cellophane wrapper in his fist. "So, what's, like, going to happen?" He tossed the wad in the air and caught it. Did it again. And again.

"Stop that," I said, feeling my temple begin to throb.

Mike's grin got the better of him. "Guess you're going to have to put up with us for a while, buddy."

"All right!" Chris shot his fist into the air and he enveloped his Uncle Mike in a most unmanly hug. I set the pot on the burner and wiped away a stray tear using the corner of the leather apron that Mike and I found useful in places other than the kitchen. *Oh, Mother Superior, if you could see me these days, you'd have a hemorrhage.*

"You're not home free yet, Chris," Mike said. "We'll talk after I work out the details with your Aunt Bella." He shook his head at the kitchen, which resembled a crime scene.

Bad metaphor, Bella.

"While you and Chris make like Rachel Ray here, I'm gonna watch football." He did his Jack Nicholson grin imitation. "Keep those chips and dips coming."

"Chips and dips nothing," I countered. "You expect to eat, you do your share. Record the game and clean those." I pointed to two bunches of greens on the counter.

"Yes Ma'am." He did a mock salute, but I knew he was happy to be included in the dinner preparations. Mike in his grousing mood was just being Mike. It was when he retreated into that dark shell that I couldn't...

I'd think about that later tonight when the ghosts of the murder victims crawled from the closet to ruin my sleep.

The kitchen soon filled with the aromas of polenta topped with Parmesan cheese and a sourdough baguette browning in the oven. The simmering marinara, into which I'd tossed the last of the garden zucchini, plus a handful of Greek olives, added sass to the bouquet.

While I stirred, I reflected that within the course of a single day, one in which a friend was murdered, I'd made love to my husband, cooked dinner, and offered shelter to a kid in trouble. Maybe that's what life was all about—striving for normality in the midst of chaos. Once again I found myself grateful, this time for Mike and Chris, the two people I loved the most, and the food we were about to share.

The sense of tranquility might not last, but right now I'll take it, I thought, sipping Cabernet from my half-full glass.

* * * * *

"Good evening, Sereno residence." *(Female voice, chilly.)*

"Hello, this is Bella Kowalski. May I speak to Dominic Sereno please?"

(Hesitation.) He's not taking calls. Are you from the media?"

"No, no, I'm a friend of Magda's. To whom am I speaking, please?"

(More hesitation.) "This is Angelina Minetti, Dominic's aunt."

"I'm sorry for your loss and I wanted to express my deepest condolences to your family. Would you tell Dominic please?"

"I'll relay the message." *(Click.)*

I held the dead phone in my hand. Not a very friendly conversation, but maybe I was expecting too much from a grieving aunt.

12

Friday, January 2nd, 7 PM

"So here's the deal," Mike said, setting his fork down with a clatter. The plate before him was empty save for a few grains of brown rice and a smear of Chris's special yellow curry sauce. This despite before-dinner grousing about the "manliness" of tonight's dinner menu. Might spinach quiche be the next frontier?

"Your Aunt Bella and I have talked it over and she'll enroll you in school first thing Monday. If you quit anytime before June, you're on the next plane to Cleveland. Deal?"

Chris nodded like he couldn't believe his good luck. Mike picked up his fork, noticed he'd eaten everything on the plate and set it down again. "You can work in the shop weekends and after school."

"Awesome," Chris finally managed to say.

"Exactly. It's called a win-win." Chris darted me a look at the latest "Uncle Mike-ism." My husband didn't seem to notice. "We can use another hand. Looks like the shop'll be busy for a while."

He was right. The latest site for the wastewater treatment plant had been rejected by a citizenry looking for the perfect sewer solution, though "perfect" was open to endless debate. This state of affairs existed despite the state water board's threat of steep fines for delays. Worse, with the second site rejected, there didn't seem to be a Plan C. The good news, I reflected, was that Mike's septic tank pumping business was secure for now.

"Can I, like, sleep in the barn again?" Chris stood and began gathering plates.

"Leave those, Chris," I said. "And it's January, you can't sleep in the barn."

"Don't see why not," Mike interjected. I knew what he was thinking; his study, where Chris bunked the last two nights, was sacred territory. Dubbed the East Wing, it sat above our bedroom in the main part of the house.

Last summer after starting out in the East Wing, Chris had migrated to Mike's barn office. The arrangement provided privacy all around and Sam loved it. He was able to sleep on Chris's bed without getting busted by his "people."

Forks and knives clattered as I loaded them in the dishwasher. "The barn's too cold this time of year. You'll get pneumonia."

"I can, like, get a couple of space heaters, the kind that look like radiators. They're not dangerous," he said, launching a preemptive strike against my standard safety admonition.

"Sounds like a plan to me." Mike picked up the newspaper and snapped it open to the crossword puzzle. Next, he rummaged in the desk drawer for a pencil. My heart stopped in mid-beat. The letter from the credit card company was in there.

"What's this?" Sure enough, he pulled it out and began to read. He looked up, his eyes blazing like six-shooters. "How long have you had this?"

"Only two days. It came New Year's Eve. I didn't want to worry you."

A muscle twitched in his jaw. "How the hell can we pay this off?"

A fair question. I hadn't a clue.

* * * * *

Sunday, January 4th, 3 PM

The man dialed the number from a pay phone and waited for the operator to say, "Tolosa County Sheriff's Office. How may I direct your call?"

"Detective Darrell Vader, please."

"He's off today. Would you like his voice mail?"

"Yes, please." He'd been hoping for that. He listened to the message, and after the beep, said, "This is a concerned citizen. I saw a certain black deputy, whose girlfriend was murdered at the Polar Bear Dip, hide a knife under the passenger seat of his vehicle New Year's Day. Thought you'd like to know."

* * * * *

Monday, January 5th, 8:10 AM

Detective Darrell Vader listened to the message and set the phone down, smiling. Uppity bastard, that Tanner. He had him now. The detective got up and strode toward the office of Tolosa County Sheriff Duane Whitley.

* * * * *

Tuesday, January 6th, 7 AM

"Here." Chris thrust the *Central Coast Chronicle* at me. He turned and plodded down the driveway for his first reluctant ride on the bus. The pack of newly-acquired books strapped to his back made him look younger than almost-eighteen. Like virtually all teens on the planet, he was angling for a car, but we couldn't afford it, and he certainly couldn't. So it was the bus or a long walk to school.

After much cajoling, threatening, and more faxes than you would think possible, Mike had managed to enroll Chris in school the previous afternoon after Stepmother Janet backed down and agreed that finishing high school was in his best interest.

Hers too, with Chris two thousand miles away.

I peeled the plastic wrapper off the paper, stared at the headline and blinked. I bolted up the steps, pushed open the front door and shouted, "Mike, they have a person of interest in the murder."

He didn't hear, the reason being the sound of a jackhammer in the kitchen. Well, not a jackhammer, but the electric coffee mill doing a pretty good imitation. After swearing by 1950s percolated brew, he'd recently converted to fresh ground beans. And like all converts, nothing stood in the way of his mission, in this case that first cup in the morning.

I pulled on his sleeve, earning sudden silence, a frown and grounds spewed all over the counter. "Dammit Bella, look what you made me do."

"Never mind that." I held up the paper so he could see the headline.

He grabbed it from me, sank heavily into the nearest chair and read the story. "Well, I'll be dipped."

"What does it say?"

"Not much actually. Just that the sheriff's office has a person of interest and apparently they're sitting on some evidence for now."

"Why don't you call Ryan Scully?" He was the sheriff's detective who saved Mike's life last summer. They'd become regular racquetball buddies.

Mike glanced at his watch. "Too early."

"No, it's not. You know he'll be up."

"Okay. I'll try his cell."

I took the seat opposite Mike and watched while he punched numbers.

"Hey Scully, it's Kowalski. How's it hanging?"

"Yeah, yeah, me too. Say, '*he-he*,' I know it's early, but Bella wanted me to call."

I gave him the finger.

"Yeah Ryan, it *is* about what's in the paper. What's the deal?"

"No shit? That really sucks."

In between the various expletives coming from my husband's mouth, I strained to hear Scully's end of the conversation.

"Really?" Mike whistled and his eyes widened. "When's he gonna call?" More expletives, then, "You too, buddy. Keep me in the loop."

He set the phone down and heaved a deep sigh.

"What did he say?"

He hesitated. "Uh…"

"What did he say?"

"Look Bella, this is for your ears only. No telling anyone, especially Amy." The *Chronicle's* managing editor was way beyond nosey.

I put my hand to chest. "Would I do that? What's going on?"

"Apparently the sheriff's office got a phone tip that Martin Tanner had planted a knife under the passenger seat of his car after the Polar Bear Dip. They offered to accompany him while he looked. Martin thought it was some crank call bullshit and agreed, then guess what? They found a sharpened abalone iron! It could be the murder weapon and they're running tests. In the meantime they've designated him a person of interest and he's been put on leave."

"That's silly," I jumped up, unable to contain my frustration. "Why would Martin do that? If he had the murder weapon, he'd hardly keep it in his car."

"That's what Scully said too. But—" His voice trailed off.

"But what?"

"It's more than that."

I felt a sudden chill as though I'd walked on someone's grave. "What's this really about?"

"According to Scully, certain people are unhappy that Martin was hired as a deputy, especially when he took up with a white woman—"

"You mean someone's out to get him?"

Mike nodded. "Probably several someones."

"In this day and age."

"Especially now. One good thing. They're definitely taking another look at Loreli's death."

"About time."

Another nod. "In any case they have a big caseload right now and they're thinking of contracting out some cold case work."

Why was I not liking where this was going? "How does that apply to you?"

Mike drummed his fingers on the table, something he does when he's about to deliver news I might not like. "Sheriff

Whitley's going to call sometime tomorrow to see if I want to take it on."

"And that, of course, is nothing you're interested in."

Mike stood and grabbed his lunch and truck keys. "For Christ's sake, Bella, let's wait until I hear from the man before we decide. It's not like we don't need the money. If nothing else, we can pay off that damned credit card."

13

Wednesday, January 7ʰ, 6:30 PM

"Hey, you clean up pretty good," I said to Mike as he came through the kitchen door. Instead of his usual dirty work clothes, he had dressed in casual-nice attire for his earlier interview with Sheriff Whitely: a blue and white checked shirt open at the neck, the navy cardigan I'd knitted him for Christmas, Dockers instead of Levis, loafers from which Mike had removed the tassels.

We smooched, something usually deferred until after he'd showered. "How'd it go?"

"Pretty well," he said, peering into the pot of red sauce bubbling on the stove. "What's for supper?"

"*Pasta Puttanesca*," I said. "Is wine in order?"

"You bet." Mike headed for the pantry, calling over his shoulder, "Can't have "bad girl" spaghetti without red wine."

"I mean, is wine in order because of the interview?"

Mike uncorked the bottle. "You tell me, Bella."

He knew I had mixed emotions about him taking the contract cold case work. On the plus side was the promise of extra money, but I worried about the effects of extra stress on his heart. He reached into the cupboard and grabbed two everyday wine glasses. "Let's talk about it over dinner."

And talk we did, over the peppery dish flavored with a couple of anchovies, the absolute only way the slimy critters will ever pass my lips. When he mentioned his hourly wage, I set down my fork. "Wow."

"Wow is right. Should help pay off our debt. Then we tell them to put their card where the sun don't shine."

I raised my glass. "I'll drink to that."

Mike sipped his wine. "Let's not talk any more about money. I'm enjoying this meal too much. Where's Chris?" He looked around as though noticing his absence for the first time.

"I let him use the Subaru. He went to a basketball game at school."

Mike in turn hoisted his glass. "And I'll drink to that. Two days in school and he's getting involved."

I hoped he was right. Chris seemed moody when he left. I was beginning to realize that my nephew was actually quite a shy person, and not at all confident in his new school environment. And why should he be? He had lots of friends at home because they'd all known each other since kindergarten. Here, he was starting from scratch as the outsider, not a great place to be in the middle of senior year.

I turned my attention back to Mike. "So tell me, what are you going to do in your new job?"

"I've got two cases, the death of Loreli Sereno—"

"Magda would have been so pleased."

He nodded. "I'm also going to work on identifying remains just found near Salinas. The person might have a connection to this county from evidence found on the body. Been out there at least five years, so we're going to have to rely on dental records for an ID. That case is a lower priority than the Sereno case."

"Same timeframe as Loreli's death. Could the two deaths be related?"

"There you go again, jumping to conclusions."

"Of course I jump to conclusions. That's what makes me a good sleuth."

"Okay, Nancy Drew, have it your way. The answer to whether the two deaths are related is, 'highly unlikely.'"

"So, what are your everyday tasks?"

His forehead creased. "Tasks?"

"What will you do every day?"

"Well, I'm not a sworn officer so I can't make arrests, but they want me to dig into the written evidence and re-interview people. Basically grunt work."

"Mike," I said, putting down my fork, "reality-check time. How are you going to do this and run the business without giving yourself another heart attack?"

He took his time over the next sip. "Of course I've thought of that. Little Mike knows the ropes and he wants extra hours because Kaitlyn is pregnant, and with Chris working after school, those two can take up the slack. A lot of the cold case stuff is computer work I can do here at home."

I stared at him, slack-jawed. "You're hopeless with computers. How are you going to work that one out?"

Mike gave me a crooked grin. "That my dear is where you come in."

He couldn't be serious.

"Mike, that's crazy. They're not going to give me access to their files. And it wouldn't be ethical for me to look at them under your ID."

"You've got it all wrong. A lot of the work is just looking up stuff on, what do you call those things?"

"Search engines?"

"Right, and reading old newspaper files and interview reports. "And"—he pointed toward our laptop sitting on the kitchen desk— "you can tutor me on the computer in your spare time."

"Like I have so much of that." But I had to admit the idea of being part of an investigation appealed to my inquisitive tendencies.

"And Bella..." Mike's voice took on an urgency. "This will be a chance to add to the positive side of the ledger."

I reached across the table and gripped his hand. "I understand." His law enforcement career ended on a sour note after being forced to retire early when a suspect died while being arrested. It was an election year and Mike and his partner were hoisted on a political petard.

The phone chose that moment to ring.

"Hello, Mrs. Kowalski? It's Tillie Gonzales."

"Hello, Mrs. Gonzales, how are you?" To Mike I mouthed, "Miranda's mother."

"Frankly, I am worried, Mrs. Kowalski."

"What about, and how can I help? Something you need for the new store?" Mrs. Gonzales had taken over the late Connie Mercado's thrift shop, renaming it "Domatilla's Treasures."

"Chris came to our home tonight, bothering Miranda."

"Tonight? Bothering? In what way?" I glanced at Mike who looked alarmed.

"Yes." She made a clucking sound. "Saying he loves her, that she must give him a chance, even after she tells him it's over. It's making her so she can't study. He just left."

He lied about going to the game. Now Mrs. Gonzales wasn't the only one worried.

"And you will talk to him? Tell him this is upsetting Miranda?"

"Of course, Mrs. Gonzales. I'm so sorry. We'll get it all squared away, I promise. Chris is a good kid, but he's a little confused right now."

"Our family," here she hesitated, "cannot have this kind of trouble."

"I understand." Miranda had hinted some of the uncles and aunts were undocumented.

We said terse good-byes. I hung up, returned to the table and reached for my wine before sitting down. "Chris has been hassling Miranda."

* * * * *

Mike was loaded for bear when my nephew came through the front door half an hour later.

He began casually enough. "You're home early." We sat on the living room sofa watching a nature program on PBS. I tried to concentrate on the program and let Mike handle the situation.

"Yeah," Chris said, handing me the car keys, He kept his eyes averted.

"How'd the game go?"

Chris turned and gave Mike a surprised look. "Game?"

"The basketball game?" Mike said slowly.

Chris snapped his fingers. "Uh, oh fine."

"Win or lose?"

"Won…no lost."

"What was the score?"

"It was—"

"Look son," Mike said. "Miranda's mother called. You weren't at the game."

"I don't have to tell you where I go," Chris said, deciding the best defense was a good offense. "I'll be eighteen Saturday."

"You may be celebrating in Cleveland." Mike cupped his hand to his ear. "I hear that plane warming up."

14

Friday, January 9th, 7:36 AM

Things were still tense at the breakfast table next morning, especially after Mike insisted on dropping Chris off at school. Deciding the joys of motherhood were at times overrated, I grabbed a third cup of tea and retreated to my West Wing office in the old windmill.

I sat at my computer, aware of Emily Divina keeping a darkly-opaque eye on me from her position on the wall behind my desk.

I turned in my chair. "Hey, Emily, how's it going? Did you ever have kids?"

Emily gave me an inscrutable stare, as I expected. With her middle-parted dark hair, high collar and scrimshaw broach, she reminded me of Queen Victoria. All I knew about Emily was what I'd gleaned from the Los Lobos Historical Society. She killed herself after her lover, a fisherman, drowned at sea. The miller, her cuckolded husband, turned her portrait to the wall, and there it remained until Mike and I turned her to again face the world.

My mission today concerned more than conversation with Emily. Mike had asked me to look up the *Chronicle's* coverage of Loreli's death five years ago.

I brought up my favorite search engine and entered "Loreli Sereno." An easy hit: *January 12th, 2004: At a hastily called news conference, Tolosa County Sheriff Duane Whitley announced the discovery today of the body of Loreli Sereno, thirty-eight, a member of the prominent Dos Pasos Sereno Cellars family. "Ms. Sereno's body was found in four feet of water near the sandspit that divides Mariposa Bay from the ocean. Cause of death appears to be an accident that resulted in a broken neck, but we have not ruled out foul play."*

As Magda said, there was no mention of Sadie, the dog. I took a reflective sip of tea, thinking of Loreli with her waist-length braid, escaping tendrils of copper curling around her face and the nape of her neck. Loreli would be how old now—forty-three? Some of the copper would have turned to pewter, but she'd still be the spirited woman I remembered. What a waste.

Her last moments must have been horrible. Did she have time to reflect on the irony of her death, an expert swimmer, dying in four feet of water? If she was murdered and, there now seemed little doubt she was, did she lash out at her attacker? Did the dog, perhaps inflicting some lasting damage?

Choking back tears, I studied the accompanying photo, a grainy image probably taken with a telephoto lens from Bush Lupine Point directly across the bay. The Search and Rescue team huddled over a dark form on the sandspit, the kayak barely visible in the background. How ironic that such a peaceful spot would provide a backdrop to murder.

I continued the search and found a follow-up story:

February 20, 2004: After a ruling of accidental death in the investigation involving Loreli Sereno, winery owners Dominic and Magda Sereno released this statement: "Our sister Loreli's death was not an accident. If there were drugs in her system, she did not take them voluntarily. She had conquered her demons and was ready to resume a productive life." No further details were released by the coroner's office, but in a later interview, Ms. Sereno's fiancé, Cuyamaca ranch owner Marcus Daniels, urged the Sereno family to support the coroner's ruling.

Marcus's reaction got me wondering about his relationship with Loreli. Mike, in his new capacity as cold case investigator, should talk to him. Despite Magda's doubts, Marcus might have been the anonymous caller. Mike should also interview her brother Dominic and Aunt Angelina on the off-chance they received calls.

Memo to Bella: Remind Mike to make those calls. He'll so appreciate the advice.

I printed the stories and sat there, palms pressed to cheeks, staring at the computer monitor as though it might give up more secrets. "Not bloody likely," as my late English grandmother would say. An idea began to take shape; Sam and I should visit Bush Lupine Point and view the murder scene from where the newspaper photo was taken, the closest place we could get to without a boat. I don't do boats.

The Point is part of the Small Wilderness, a preserve of unique, dwarf California live oaks that hug the bay at the north edge of Los Lobos. It's one of Sam's favorite walks with lots of good smells, only a mile from the house. We were due for a hike anyway. A glance at my desk clock showed four hours before my stint at the paper.

Feeling eyes in the center of my back I turned and stared at Emily who returned my stare as though asking what I really hoped to find.

"Not really sure Em, but it never hurts to check." I like to think Emily helps me on these quests, but I'm practical enough to realize this could be wishful thinking.

I hurried down the narrow winding staircase to the main part of the house. At least a walk would help me think through events of the past few days. Lord knows there was plenty to think about: renewed interest in Loreli's suspicious death five years ago, Magda, her sister's murder eight days ago, Martin, Magda's boyfriend, a person of interest in the case, the complicated relationship of Marcus and Loreli, and of Marcus to the only remaining remembers of the Sereno family, Dominic and his Aunt Angelina.

I removed my key from a hook by the front door and locked the dead bolt, noting angry clouds drifting in off the bay. I shrugged off my feeling of displeasure. If I waited for good weather to hike in Los Lobos, I'd spend most of my time indoors.

Went looking for Sam. Didn't take much looking, he was snoozing on Chris's futon in the barn office. My nephew had left the electric heater on. I snapped off the switch, wishing I could switch off my irritation at Chris's carelessness. Who did he think was going to foot the bill for heating empty space all day long?

"Come on Sam. Can you wake up long enough to take a hike? We have much to talk about."

Sam's raised his head at the word "hike," rose and stretched. He hesitated before jumping to the floor, and as he headed toward the door, he favored his left rear leg. "What's wrong, boy?" I patted the mattress. "Back up here. Let's have a look."

A quick exam revealed dried blood on one pad, and he flinched when I examined others on the same foot. "Sorry, boy." Sure enough, a couple slivers of glass had imbedded themselves deep in the flesh. I stroked his head, receiving a "poor me" look. "Stay put. I'll have you fixed in a jif."

I gathered tweezers, antiseptic and rolled gauze from the bathroom cabinet. Sam remained stoic as a monk while I cleaned the wound and removed the glass. When I'd bound the foot with gauze, I again stroked his head. "Now you stay here and rest while I walk. And don't chew the gauze."

I looked back from the door frame and noticed him shivering. "Okay, okay. You win." I did a one-eighty, snapped on the heater, turned the dial to High. "Just this once, hear?"

* * * * *

I grabbed my bike, now exhibiting signs of winter neglect, from a corner of the barn. I planned to ride it to the east entrance of the Small Wilderness to get my heart pumping, then follow the boardwalk. First, I detoured to Saint Pat's to drop off the final figures from the fundraiser. I thought they would make Father Burton smile. Wrong. Even Walter looked uncharacteristically gloomy when I mentioned my hiking plans. Guess the weather had everyone grumpy.

A few minutes later, as I peddled uphill toward the preserve, the dark clouds made good on their promise of fog and drizzle. Anyplace else on the planet these conditions signaled real rain. Here they just signaled more fog and drizzle.

I left my bike unlocked behind the interpretive sign welcoming visitors near the Fifteenth Street entrance, then struck out on foot up a dune of shifting sand to the boardwalk. After stepping onto the raised planks, I paused to catch my breath. The damp air carried a heady fragrance of California Black Sage. Coastal dune scrub covers this part of the preserve. Like the dwarf oaks, low-growing Coffeeberry, Mock Heather and Silver Lupine have their own beauty. Hailing as I do from the rain-soaked and intensely-green upper Middle West, the muted colors of the California palette took some getting used to. But I've learned to love them.

I started toward the bay wishing I'd remembered to look up Aunt Angelina's address in the phone book. Magda said she lived on this street, and a walk-by might be a pretty good idea. Without the address I couldn't do it today.

I walked on, my footfalls the only sound in a cocoon of silence. My heartbeat quickened. There were usually more people around. No doubt the weather had kept them away. I switched to an aggressive stance, head up, arms swinging at my sides, eyes fixed on the horizon.

Clomp, clomp, clomp. Footsteps behind me. They reverberated with a different, heavier, cadence on the boardwalk's planks. I turned, seeing only the side of my windbreaker hood.

Come on Bella, it's just another idiot hiking in the drizzle.

I forced myself into forward momentum with the footfalls still behind me. The person didn't seem to be gaining, but that wasn't surprising. I can really hustle when the spirit moves me. And right then, it moved me a lot.

Unable to stand the suspense a second longer, I stopped and turned my whole body. My follower either anticipated the action, or had reached his destination. He veered off the boardwalk at one of several exits to what we called "the numbered streets." I watched the retreating back of someone dressed for Alaska in a lumpy gray jacket, his head completely covered in a black watch cap.

I forced several deep breaths through my diaphragm to slow my heart, and continued downhill toward the bay and Bush Lupine Point. Approaching the overlook, I saw the bay at low tide. The sight was unsettling, like coming upon someone naked. A fishy, fleshy odor filled my nostrils and roiled my stomach.

I leaned my elbows on the guard rail and squinted into the fog, barely able to make out sailboats moored in the marina across the bay. Behind them, gigantic Mariposa Rock stood guardian over the bay's entrance. Today, fog shrouded its craggy outline.

I stood on tiptoe and surveyed the rich estuary, rippled from past tides. At low tide, the barren flats provided a feast for birds including ducks, mud hens and snowy egrets. Their world was as it should be, at least this corner of it. The Chumash must have looked out from this point and observed the same tableau.

Still, five years ago a terrible murder had shattered the tranquility of this place, and now the sheriff wanted Mike to re-investigate it. Perhaps I'd have a different perspective on the sandspit from the bottom of the point. I studied the steep, twisting path below me and felt the nervous tingling in my legs that precedes vertigo. Could I do it? And what did I hope to see after all these years?

No way. I turned, took three purposeful strides back the way I came, and stopped. Had to tackle that path, if nothing else to conquer my fear.

The beginning proved easy. I found a gap at the end of the railing and slipped through, clinging to the orange plastic netting that bordered the upper part of the path. When the path ended, things got tougher. With nothing to hang on to, I grabbed a bush. Came away with a handful of nettles. Ignoring my now-shaky knees, I made it almost halfway, then paused. The path, such as it was, disappeared into dense underbrush some twenty feet in front of me.

From where I stood, I still had a view of the bay. What would it have looked like that January morning five years ago—sunny, rainy, perhaps foggy like today? Magda's theory was that someone in scuba gear swam behind Loreli and chose an opportune moment to reach up and pull her under. A risky maneuver with the dog in the kayak, but perhaps the murderer didn't know it was there. If he'd been lurking where she launched, he'd have seen the dog.

Maybe he knew her routine, waited until he saw the kayak, then slipped into the water from a well-hidden place. The bay was fairly well exposed, with houses on the bluff to the south, the open sandspit on the west, and the marina and State Park on the north. The dense brush here at Bush Lupine Point would have provided the perfect concealment for a killer-in-waiting to enter the water.

Perhaps one of the locals had noticed a scuba diver entering or leaving the bay early on January 12th, 2004. Would anyone remember such an insignificant detail five years later? Scuba divers were almost as common as sand fleas in this beach community. Still, it wouldn't hurt to canvas the locals who frequented Bay Oaks two coffee shops.

The sounds of birds rustling in the brush interrupted my deliberations. Something dark caught my eye and I looked up.

Someone, a man I thought, leaned on the railing, watching me. A black balaclava covered his face and head. He wore a lumpy jacket.

15

Desperately, I searched for an escape route—seeing nothing but impassable underbrush between me and the bay. I'd need a machete to hack through it. Not that way, and certainly not up the path in his direction.

The man continued to stare. I took a deep breath to calm my heart. Maybe if I ignored him, he'd go away. I counted to ten and looked up. The man stood there and, as I continued to stare, he waved to me.

What the—?

I looked again and he'd disappeared. Did I just get lucky? I waited a few minutes and started back up the path, expecting any minute to be thrown to my death. At the top, there was no sign of him.

At that point, I did what any sensible person would do—ran like hell up the boardwalk, panting from fright and the steep uphill climb to the Fifteenth Street exit. I took an Olympian leap off the boardwalk, feet barely touching sand as I bolted past my bike to the safety of the first house I came to.

And a very elaborate house it was, Spanish, with the obligatory red tile roof and a fountain on the capacious front lawn. A spit-and polish black Lexus sat in the driveway. I leaned on the door chime with one hand and pounded on the heavy oak panels with the other.

A slim woman in her sixties answered, her skin stretched taut over prominent cheekbones, the hair like cotton from decades of bleach. "Yes?" Brown eyes were sharp and questioning. An image flashed across my mind and then was gone.

"What do you want?" she asked coldly.

I couldn't say a word. What *did* I want?

The woman peered around the half-open door. "Well, speak up. Is something wrong?"

"Uh..."

A look of impatience crossed her face. "Good day." She began to close the door.

"Sorry, my mistake," I said as it shut in my face. What did I think I was going to say? Someone in a black ski mask stalked me, and, oh, by the way, he *waved* to me. She'd think I was crazy. Who was this woman, anyway?

Halfway down the drive, I had a pretty good idea: the proximity to Small Wilderness, the blonde hair, the Lexus in the driveway, the planes of the face so like Magda's. I'd just met Aunt Angelina.

I backtracked to the interpretive sign, maybe 300 yards. Out of breath and shaking, I stepped behind it. My heart gave an 8.5 jolt. The balaclava covered my bike seat like a shroud.

* * * * *

At work that afternoon, I started to call Mike at least three times and was interrupted each time I pressed the send button.

Filling him in on the morning's events would have to wait until supper. I finished my work early for once, and to get my mind off Balaclava Man, I forced myself to think about possible solutions to our credit card problem. Even with Mike's extra income it would take a long time to pay off our balance at the new rate of interest. Extra income? He wasn't the only one who could provide that.

I marched across the newsroom to Amy's office. "Got a sec?"

Managing editor Amy Goodheart shifted her eyes from the computer monitor. While she supposedly maintained an open door policy, there was an unwritten rule that you planted yourself at the entrance until beckoned into her personal space.

"I can come back later…"

A gleam of elliptical blue eyes behind tortoise shell frames. "Bella, how many times have I told you? Quit being so damned deferential."

"Sorry, I was just…"

She lifted her eyes toward the stained ceiling tile. "Hopeless, absolutely hopeless." A hand waved in my direction. "Come in, park it, I can give you five."

"What's up?" She asked when I'd perched on one of two chairs opposite her desk. Whether by accident or design, they sat lower than hers. The staff called her "Queenie" behind her back; the name fit. Amy was a force of nature and everything about her was larger than life. Big, hair, strong jaw, the physique of a Minnesota Methodist. Today, as usual, she displayed enough cleavage to shame a romance writer.

Amy tapped her Brighton watch. "Four minutes."

Talking way too fast, I started to ask her if I could work more hours. I'd spit out maybe two sentences when Ben Adams poked his head in the door. "Amy, the suits from Chicago are waiting for you in the conference room."

"Okay, okay, Hon. Tell them not to get their Jockeys in a knot." She turned back to me. "Okay, I get your drift, but there are issues. Let's continue this later."

Issues. I was afraid of that.

She grabbed a mirror and checked her teeth for lipstick, then rose, picked up a manila folder and snugged it under her arm. "Let's meet at Lockhart's tomorrow morning. I'm coming your way for a garage sale." Amy's passion for collecting old perfume bottles was legendary. "Around ten?"

"Sure. I need to pick up a cake for Chris's birthday while I'm there."

"See ya." She and her four-inch heels clattered out of the office.

* * * * *

"He's messing with you."

I'd just told Mike about Balaclava Man. Also, my suspicions that he'd followed me New Year's Eve.

"You think so?" I asked, relief flooding through me. We sat at the kitchen table, dishes cleared, Sam sleeping by the still-warm oven, hurt paw thrust out like a badge of honor. Chris was doing homework in the barn, an activity unheard of on a Friday night.

"Why didn't you tell me about New Year's Eve?" Mike asked.

"Well…" I thought a moment. Why hadn't I told him? Because I didn't want to be accused of over-reacting, but that's not what I said. "You were out cold when I got home, and the next day Magda was murdered, and besides, the guy stayed on Los Lobos Road when I turned off. The next day his behavior seemed like either a coincidence or a sick joke."

"And now it's not." It wasn't a question. The ski mask lay on the table between us. My husband grabbed the mask and fingered the knitted ribs, then pulled his hand back. "What am I doing? This will most certainly have hair and fibers." He got up, moved across the room and grabbed a paper sack from my "bag" drawer. "I need to start thinking like a cop again. This should be kept in case we need it as evidence later."

"Evidence?" I croaked, pulling a loose thread from my "therapy" place mat, the one I'd practically shredded in the past six months due to the trauma in our lives. "I thought you said the guy wasn't dangerous."

Mike stayed my hand over the place mat. "I said he was messing with you. I don't know if he's dangerous or not."

"So we report him?" I asked.

A flicker of hesitation in the gray eyes. "Not yet. Let's see what happens."

He's being too cautious in this new job, I thought. Doesn't want his colleagues to think he's got a Nervous Nelly wife. I should challenge him on this, but in some crazy way I understood. Mike and his partner made an error in judgment and someone died on their watch. This was a chance to wipe the slate clean, to rebuild his lost confidence. I was a big girl, I could mind my own Ps and Qs, as my English grandmother used say.

"*The good little wife always follows her mate.*" That's what Jeremy had said, and the mockery still stung. Was I being the good little wife at my own peril?

"In the meantime, keep your eyes open." Mike said, derailing the thought.

"Don't worry, I will." Feeling a sudden chill, I pulled my sweater close around me.

"Tell me what you did after you found this." Mike held up the bag with the mask, then tucked it in the desk drawer and sat back down.

"I stuffed it in my windbreaker pocket and rode home."

"Straight home?"

"Yeah, but I haven't had a chance to tell you—before I found the mask, I was so scared I ran all the way to the first house off the Fifteenth Street exit. I was going to ask the owner to call the sheriff, but I changed my mind."

Mike nodded like he understood and I continued: "Here's the thing. I'm almost sure it was Aunt Angelina's house."

Mike's forehead creased in a frown. "Aunt Angelina?"

"Magda, Dominic and Loreli's aunt. Magda said she lived right off the Small Wilderness Preserve."

My husband gave me a "there-you-go-again" shake of the head. "Several streets open onto the Preserve. What makes you think you got the right one?"

"The house was fairly affluent and there was a Lexus like Magda's in the drive. And she had Magda's cheekbones."

Mike cocked his head. "Not bad. Let's look her up in the phone book."

"Can't. She has a different last name and I can't remember what it is."

He patted my hand. "I'll ask around and get her name, though at this point I don't know why it's important."

"I also climbed down the path from Bush Lupine Point to the spot where the underbrush begins. If Magda was right and Loreli's murderer swam behind her, snapped her neck and swamped the kayak, he'd need a well-hidden place to enter and exit the water."

Mike again patted my hand. "Good observation, Doctor Watson."

"I'll bet Holmes didn't pat Watson's hand," I said and he had the grace to grin. "You should ask the locals if they remember seeing a diver around the bay the morning Loreli was killed."

"Unlikely five years later, but a good idea. I'll check the coroner's report for the time of death and ask around. Think I'll keep you, Doctor Watson. Now how was the rest of your day?"

"Busy." I didn't want to mention the possibility of extra hours until Amy gave the okay.

16

Saturday, January 10th, 10:30 AM
"The guy in the mask is ringing your chimes."

"Mike said almost the same thing," I replied. "He doesn't think the guy's dangerous." Amy and I faced each other across a small table at Lockhart's Bakery. I'd just finished telling her about yesterday's misadventure in the Small Wilderness Preserve and how I'd been tailed New Year's Eve. I'd ease into the issues involved in me working more hours a bit later.

"You *did* make a report to the sheriff?"

"Of course," I lied.

"Good. Can't be too careful." The managing editor took a bite of Russian Tea Biscuit. "Yum." Crumbs landed on the front of her purple velvet warm-up jacket. She brushed them off with a manicured and be-ringed hand. Gold hoop earrings dangled beneath a pouf of copper-wire hair; gold tennis shoes and a gold lamé handbag with a serious case of hardware overload completed the shopping-channel outfit.

"I mean first the guy waves to you for Chrissake, then he leaves the ski mask on your bike seat," she said.

I took a sip of white tea, and decided it was overrated compared to its green and black cousins. "Yeah, it was strange—and spooky."

"By the way, where was the Great Protector while all this was going on?"

"Sam? Home with a cut paw."

"Give the old fella a love pat for me." She shivered. "Why'd you pick the Small Wilderness for a solitary hike? All that underbrush gives me the creeps, especially on a foggy day."

"I wanted to visit the murder scene."

Amy's well-moisturized forehead creased in a frown. "What murder scene? The Sereno woman was killed at Cuyamaca Beach."

"Magda Sereno was, but her sister Loreli died five years ago kayaking in the bay below Bush Lupine Point."

"Ben's story said the death was accidental."

"That was the official verdict, but law enforcement at first considered foul play. It's in the original article."

"That's incredible! I don't f"ing believe this. How come that background wasn't in Ben's stories?"

"Better ask him. I mentioned it to him last Friday. Mike's looking into Loreli's death as part of his cold case assignment."

She shoved aside the remains of her biscuit. "Swell. Seems like everyone knew but me. I wish you'd come to me directly."

"Amy, I didn't think it would be appropriate to go behind Ben's back. After all, he's your friend." Amy had confided to me earlier that they were "seeing" each other, whatever that meant. I personally thought Ben couldn't write, much less research, for— to borrow one of Mike's more colorful phrases—sour owl shit. But who was I to stand in the way of true lust?

Not wanting to meet Amy's eyes, I let mine drift across Los Lobos Road to the thrift store Amy's late friend, Connie Mercado, once owned. The current proprietor, Miranda's mother, Tillie, had re-christened it "Domatilla's Treasures." After our terse conversation Wednesday night, I assumed Chris was keeping his distance from his former girlfriend.

As I watched, a familiar red sedan pulled into one of the parking spaces in front of the shop. Miranda got out and disappeared inside.

"Probably works weekends," Amy said, mirroring my own thought. She sniffed and I realized her eyes were brimming with tears. Must be tough to see her friend's shop run by new owners.

"What happened at the meeting yesterday?" I asked, hoping to distract her.

She reached under the frames of her glasses and wiped her eyes with a napkin. "Same-ol, same-ol. Have to keep the stockholders happy so they want us to make cuts."

Little currents of alarm chased each other up and down my spine. "Define 'cuts.'"

She gave a simultaneous shrug and sigh. "The usual."

"*Staff* cuts?"

Her mouth made a tight line. "Over my cold, dead body. But the short answer to your question yesterday is 'No, I can't offer you more hours right now.'"

"Oh." I swallowed my disappointment, and Amy's eyes focused on the entrance behind me. She leaned across the table. "Kathy Tanner just walked in."

Upon catching sight of us, the librarian's face registered dismay. She recovered quickly, waved and became engrossed in a shelf of wrapped breads opposite the serving case, probably to avoid us.

"Should we ask her to join us?"

"I don't know," I said, then, "well sure."

Amy got up and spoke briefly to Kathy, gesturing toward our table. In a few minutes, they joined me, Amy with coffee for the librarian, Kathy holding aloft a chocolate cupcake.

"Hey Kathy." I half-stood and tried to give her a hug while avoiding a baptism of fudge frosting. "Are you keeping busy?"

Oh dear, how dumb did that sound?

Kathy smiled, letting me know it was okay. "Tryin' to stay that way."

"Would it help to unload on two nosey women?" asked Amy, who's not famous for her tactful beginnings—or endings. She set the coffee down and dragged a chair over to the table.

"Can't think of anything better, Hon." Kathy lowered herself into the seat and sighed. "Well now." She bit off a hunk of cake and closed her eyes. "Um, um. Comfort food. Better than a dose of greasy greens anytime."

We sipped and munched in silence. "I know y'all were talking about the murder," Kathy blurted without preamble. "Everyone in town is."

"Actually—" Amy started to say.

Kathy held up a hand. "It's okay. Just want y'all to know I didn't like the idea of Martin bein' sweet on Magda. But he's a big boy. I know my son, and he would never kill her."

I put my hand over hers, ignoring the threat of frosting. "Of course, he didn't kill her. Do you know what this is really about?"

Kathy lowered her head. "It's a race thing."

"That's what Detective Scully had told Mike."

"Especially now. Make no mistake, there's some ol' white guys just itchin' to bring back the 1950s."

Amy snorted. "Like that would happen."

Kathy put a hand on her chest. "I know that, and y'all know that, but do they?"

Without a good answer, I gazed across the street at Domatilla's Treasurers, just in time to see Chris, on foot and wearing a backpack, enter the shop.

What did he think he was doing?

Amy reached across the table and put a hand on my arm. "Bella, let the kid fight his own battles. He's eighteen, after all."

But...but he's got a backpack and it's Saturday," I sputtered, shaking off her hand.

"What do you think? He's got a gun? Maybe he wants Miranda's help with his homework. Maybe she called *him*. Maybe he wants to buy you a present."

I sank back down. "I hope you're right."

17

Amy was wrong. The sheriff's deputies arrived a few minutes later.

"Best go, Hon," Kathy said to me as we witnessed the scene unfolding across the street.

The managing editor's cell chose that moment to chirp. She glanced at the face and swore, then pushed the talk button and said, "Amy Goodheart."

I sat paralyzed, watching her.

"Never mind that," Kathy said. "Go!"

Risking imminent death from heavy traffic, I dashed across Los Lobos Road to the thrift store. Just as I hit the sidewalk, the deputies emerged with Chris wedged between them. He looked young, vulnerable and ready to cry.

"What's going on?" I demanded.

Chris hung his head.

"Are you the mother?" Deputy One asked.

"Aunt," Chris mumbled.

The deputy pushed his glasses up with his index finger. "We have to take him in Ma'am, and book him. He's an adult."

"What's the charge?" I asked, trying to sound in control and succeeding only in showing my panic.

Deputy Two turned to Chris who studied the backpack at his feet. "Miranda says I hassled her. I only wanted to bring back the stuff she gave me last summer."

Oh dear Lord. "And did you, hassle her?"

"He's been read his rights, Ma'am," Deputy One interjected.

My nephew's frightened eyes belied his no-big-deal shrug. "I suppose, but I didn't mean to. Look, this is all a big misunderstanding."

"It's not that simple, son. The girl and her mother are pressing charges." Deputy One gave Chris a look I interpreted as sympathetic, then turned to me. "We have to take him in, Ma'am. You can follow in your car."

"To where?" My mind refused to function.

"County jail, Ma'am. It's out on—"

"I know where it's at," I snapped.

"Let me drive you." I spun around to see Kathy. She'd followed me across the street. How long had she been standing there? Long enough, obviously.

She handed me my purse. "You call Mike while I drive." I took it, grateful for the kindness of friends. Speaking of which, I looked across the street in time to see Amy's SUV fishtailing out of the parking lot.

"A press crisis," Kathy said, anticipating my question.

I nodded. Failure of the outdated equipment was a fact of life at the *Central Coast Chronicle*.

* * * * *

Soon we were headed toward the county jail twelve miles east in Tolosa, with Kathy expertly running through the gears of her Mini Cooper. I'd called Mike, who set a new record for swear words delivered in ten seconds. After he ran out of steam, he promised to call our attorney and meet me at the jail.

It had started to rain and a gray drizzle ran down the windows, blurring images of the winter-brown fields that hugged the road. A desolate scene that matched my spirits. What possessed Chris to do what he did? And on his birthday, yet.

Kathy turned the wipers to high and the blades whooshed across the windshield like stick-men on steroids.

"Haven't seen y'all since New Year's Day, and now this," she said.

"Can you believe it?"

"Not hardly." She pulled out and passed a truck. "Lot of weird things happenin'. Did I tell you I got caught using the men's bathroom New Year's Eve?"

Whoosh, whoosh.

My mind snapped to attention. "Caught?"

"Yeah, some guy grabbed the stall door just as I was coming out."

"What did he look like?"

Kathy smiled. "I was so embarrassed I didn't look at his face."

"There must have been something. Think Kathy, think."

She did, and shook her head. "Sorry."

"That's okay. I need to ask you something else."

"Fire away."

"Two somethings, actually. I was talking to Magda in the women's that night. Did you recognize her when you opened the door?"

"Not 'til later."

"So you didn't try to listen at our door after you came out of the men's?"

"Girl, if I'd realized it was her I would have. But no, I didn't. Why?"

"Someone fell against the door while Magda and I were talking. I opened it and saw the door to the men's open, and a leg disappearing inside. Think Kathy, do you remember anything at all about the guy?"

Whoosh, whoosh.

"Now you mention it, there was something. He had his left hand on the handle of the door and I saw a small scar on his wrist—like he'd tried to slit it at some point." She downshifted to second gear and pulled into the parking lot of the Tolosa County Jail. "We're here."

I brushed aside thoughts of the New Year's Eve interloper in the immediacy of Chris's problem.

* * * * *

The business of booking, bail bonding and release took forever; the day had disappeared into winter dusk by the time we finally arrived home.

"What now?" I asked Mike after Chris had slunk off to his hidey-hole in the barn, the ever-faithful Sam at his heels. A good thing. He would need the comfort of the dog tonight. His hearing was on Monday, the twenty-sixth, two weeks away.

"What *now?*" Mike dropped his keys on the counter with a loud clunk. "He goes back to Cleveland after the hearing, that's what."

"We can't Mike, they don't want him. You know that."

Silence while Mike pondered the truth of that statement. He gazed at the small photo of Ethan. Was he thinking that his dead son, who'd also be eighteen, would be a better kid, or at least less trouble, than Chris? I felt a familiar pang of anger and jealousy. I'd had this thought before.

But Mike surprised me. "If he stays squeaky clean between now and the hearing, we'll talk about him staying."

"That's great. Maybe I should go to Miranda and Tillie, and see if they'll drop the charges," I said, opening the fridge and staring at the bleak prospects for dinner.

"Bella," Mike said, "don't even consider it unless you want to make things worse."

* * * * *

Somehow we got through the rest of the weekend, with Mike watching a lot of basketball and Chris remaining out of the firing line in the barn. At his insistence, we refrained from calling his parents. He was now eighteen, a legal, if not emotional, adult.

The rain lingered like a house guest overstaying his welcome. I spent Sunday doing a budget for this year's homeless program. Thanks to the benefit, we were in good shape for our February care-giving duties.

18

Monday, January 12ᵗʰ, 2:47 PM

The first day of the week found me in the midst of an attack of *Chronicle* crazies. The Grim Reaper had a busy three days and I was on deadline to write and edit several obituaries.

What a way to make a living.

"I'd like to do an obituary." The man standing beside my cubicle had dark, haunted eyes. A thin and narrow face matched his gaunt body. Tufts of hair sprouted like gray seedlings from his pale scalp.

The body might be infirm, but the tanned and callused hands gripping his walker spoke of a lifetime in the fields. A battered shoe box rested on the seat of the walker, a deluxe model painted a spiffy electric blue.

"Of course," I said, a bit surprised. I don't get many visitors these days as the paper now encourages obituary submissions via e-mail, a policy that should mean less work for me. The reality is quite different.

"I...I'm Dominic Sereno." His eyes filled with tears. "Magda is...was...my sister."

"Yes, I knew her," I said, deciding to leave it at that. I stood and took one callused hand in both of mine. "I'm Bella Kowalski, and I'm so sorry for your loss."

Familiar words, but delivered from the heart. My job was always sad and sometimes heartbreaking. Magda told me her brother had inoperable cancer. "Thank you," he said simply, his voice breaking. "Please call me Dominic." He indicated the chair beside my desk. "May I sit, Bella?"

"Of course. Forgive me. Let me close the file I'm working on and we'll get started."

Ben Adams stopped tapping away on his computer in the next cubicle.

"Have you written something?" I asked when Dominic seemed comfortable. He was dressed simply in a flannel shirt, Levis and boots rundown at the heels. I thought about what Magda had said about him. He certainly didn't look like a man bent on retribution.

"Written something?" he asked as though he'd failed to do his homework.

I nodded. "Not a big deal, but often people put thoughts down on paper and we use those to get started. Sometimes they want nothing changed, in which case I correct only spelling and punctuation. We now accept e-mail submissions."

He smiled, revealing the tiny laugh lines of better days around his eyes and mouth. "Online assistance for the bereaved?"

"Something like that," I said, surprised at his drollness.

He pulled the walker closer and with shaking hands grabbed the shoe box and placed it on my desk.

Seeing tears, I offered him a tissue. "Take your time. We have all afternoon."

I heard the click of heels outside my cubicle. Amy stopped, eyeing both the shoe box and the weeping man. She didn't point to her watch, but the message was clear: we didn't have all afternoon, I was on deadline.

Fortunately, Dominic noticed neither Amy's presence nor my anxiety. After a few moments he regained control, wiped his eyes and patted the box. "This contains all I have left of Loreli and Magda. They called it their "Secrets Box.""

"Secrets Box?" Seemed a bit juvenile until I remembered that Bea and I kept an old suitcase stuffed with our own treasures. We took turns hiding it under our side-by-side single beds, one week hers, and the next, mine. If Mother was aware of it, she never let on. I hadn't thought about that suitcase in years and wondered what happened to it.

Dominic's next sentence jerked me back to the present. "Not all that secretive really, except to my sisters when they were young. Mementos from school, snapshots, those kinds of things. I thought perhaps we could use these to put together the obituary." His voice broke. "Not much to show for two lives."

Feeling a sob rising in my throat, I leaned over and grabbed a form from my side drawer. "I'm sure that will be useful when we work on the details," I said. "First, let's start with some basic information. Have you planned a service?"

"Yes," he said, "the coroner finally released the body." His voice broke once more, and we waited a bit. "The service will be Saturday at 2 PM at the winery." He fished in his shirt pocket and handed me a business card with the address. "Father Burton will officiate."

"A mass?" I asked.

"No, Magda wasn't a practicing Catholic, nor was her late sister." He gave me a slight smile. "Aunt Angelina insists we have a priest and she's a hard person to say no to. Father is her confessor."

"And she lives in Los Lobos?" I asked.

From Ben's cubicle came familiar sounds of a drawer opening, a pad slapping the desk and a ballpoint pen clicking.

"That's true." He shook his head slowly. "How did you know?"

"I think Magda mentioned it."

"Of course."

Dominic removed the lid from the box and that simple act began a new round of weeping. My heart ached for him. Here he was facing cancer that would most likely be terminal with only an old aunt left. His partner, Vito, left when his health broke, his parents were long dead, both his sisters gone. I felt a surge of anger. This gentle man had worked hard all his life and deserved a peaceful death. Murder had cheated him of that.

With the box open and snapshots, prom programs and other mementos strewn across the desk, he tried to go on, but was too grief stricken to continue.

"We don't need to finish this today. Why don't you come by tomorrow?"

"No, no," he said, "this must be in tomorrow's paper. Magda has many friends. They keep calling about the service. It's very hard on me," he finished, the first note of self pity I'd heard.

"I'm afraid it's already too late for Tuesday's paper," I said, feeling like a heel.

"Is there anything you can do?" His eyes pleaded with me to say yes.

"Um, I'll ask my managing editor for an extension, but it's really out of my hands." I glanced at the remnants of two lives spread before me. "Why don't you leave the box with me, and I'll stay late and finish the obituary. I can fax or e-mail you the draft, and you can correct any errors. Maybe, just maybe, we can make the morning edition."

"Thank you," he said, pushing the empty box toward me. Except it wasn't empty; there was a video tucked away at the bottom.

"Don't you want this?" I asked, holding it up.

"No, I might misplace it and it's too precious to loose." His eyes filled again. "Just keep it in the box. Please call me when you finish and I'll go down to my office and retrieve the fax." He smiled and I saw traces of the robust man he must have been before illness eroded his body.

"Do you want to pick up the box, perhaps tomorrow?" I asked.

"Or you could come to the funeral on Saturday," he said. "Magda would like that. She told me New Year's Eve after she returned home that you and your husband were going to help us."

"*Us?*" I asked, the word out before I realized it.

He nodded. "I too received a phone call from someone wanting to sell me information about Loreli's murder."

"And you didn't pursue it?"

"I thought it was a hoax, that is, until Magda told me she received one, too."

"Do you think it was Marcus?" I asked. "Loreli's fiancé?"

He shook his head. "We haven't spoken since she died five years ago, but I'd know that sandpaper voice."

"Did your aunt receive a phone call as well?"

"Not that I'm aware of. I didn't ask because I didn't want to upset her. Her emotional health is fragile and seems to get worse as she gets older, so much so that she hardly ever visits her second home in San Francisco." He paused. "Will we see you on Saturday?"

In the next cubicle, a pen scratched frantically. "You bet," I said, reaching out and shaking Dominic's hand. "May I bring my husband?"

"Of course," he said. "I'll expect you both. The more the merrier."

The more the merrier?

He noted the look on my face. "I'm sorry. Irreverent humor helps me through the day. I forget that sometimes people are offended."

"I'm not offended. I understand completely."

He smiled. "You are most kind, Bella Kowalski."

* * * * *

Dominic left bearing a receipt for the box and I hoofed it to Amy's office and begged for a deadline extension. She promised to arrange it. Sereno Cellars is a big advertiser and their interests must be catered to. I like to think that compassion played a role as well.

I phoned Mike and told him I wouldn't be home until ten at least. He wasn't thrilled, but he wasn't as grumpy as he might have been. Around eight, I hit the print key, sat back in my chair and read what I'd pieced together from the Secrets Box and from what Dominic had related:

Magda Elena Sereno, 1964-2009

Dos Pasos resident Magda Elena Sereno died in a tragic surfing incident on New Year's Day at Cuyamaca Beach. A member of a founding family of Central Coast vintners, Magda attended school in Dos Pasos, and later graduated from Tolosa Technical College, where she performed with their celebrated dance troupe.

After graduation, she attended the NY-UP Dance Academy in Manhattan. At the time of her death, Magda had just moved back to the Central Coast. Besides spending time with her brother and aunt, her passions were dancing and water sports.

She was preceded in death by her parents Giuseppe and Mary Sereno, who emigrated here from Bari, Italy following World War II. Giuseppe apprenticed at local wineries and the couple opened Sereno Cellars in 1952. A younger sister, Loreli, also preceded Magda in death. She is survived by her brother, Dominic, and her maternal aunt, Angelina Sereno-Minetti of Los Lobos and San Francisco. Services will be held at the Winery at 2 PM, on Saturday, January 17th. All are welcome. In lieu of flowers, the family requests donations to the Surfrider Foundation, of which Magda was an active member.

Stiff and sore from sitting, I made my way to the only fax not spewing paper, inserted the obituary and entered the number on Dominic's card.

While the machine sucked in the paper, I stretched my tired arms behind my back and over my head, staring across the newsroom into the darkened confines of Amy's glass-fronted office. Someone moved in the shadows.

My heart gave a little knock against my ribs. Movement again, Ben Adams emerging from the office and hurrying down the corridor. He couldn't get out of there fast enough.

Back at my desk, I stuffed things in drawers. I started to put the shoe box away, then hesitated. Ben knew I had it and I didn't trust him. The man was what my late English grandmother termed "shifty."

19

The hand-held camera shook, giving the black and white frames the herky-jerky look of an old-time film, the aura enhanced by the lack of sound. The group of people gathered around one end of the baronial table were decked out in 1920's attire. Dominic sat at its head wearing a raccoon coat.

"Must be hot in that," Mike said from his place next to me on the sofa. He leaned forward, eyes glued to the TV, slurping decaf.

"Gross," I said. "Watch the film."

The date-stamp on the video from the Secrets Box said April 2003, happier days at Sereno Cellars. Dominic's hair still grew thick and dark. He wore it slicked back like The Godfather. That and his black mustache gave him a rakish air. A large heavyset man of about the same age, good looking in a Mafioso kind of way, whom I took to be Vito, the former partner, graced the other end of the table. Dressed as a Capone era mobster in a light fedora with a dark band, he made an arresting presence as he waved to the camera.

The camera panned back to Dominic. Magda sat to his left, decked out in something glittery and tight, a rhinestone (possibly diamond) band around her head. She'd painted her lips into a cupid's bow. On Magda's left, a younger Marcus wore a dark cowboy hat with a ridiculously wide brim. A white bolo tie contrasted with his black cowboy shirt, which was piped in white. He repeated Vito's waving gesture. What is this thing about waving to video cameras?

"Wonder who the photographer is?" I asked and received a shrug for an answer. The lens again panned the length of the table, which was huge and old and may have begun life in a Tuscany castle. A tall vase, alive with tulips and willow branches, dominated the center of the table. Like an unseen visitor admiring the view, the camera zoomed to a view of the hills beyond the huge oval window that served as a backdrop to the table.

"Must be the winery," Mike said.

"Brilliant. You should be a detective."

"Smart alec."

The camera found Aunt Angelina and an almost-unrecognizable Father Burton sitting across from Magda, Angelina to Dominic's right, with the priest next to her. Dominic's aunt was dressed in a chemise way too revealing for her scrawny frame and Father Burton had cast aside clerical garb in favor of a white robe and flowing headdress. He looked like a Bedouin.

"Who's he supposed to be?" Mike asked.

"Looks like Rudolf Valentino in 'The Sheik.'"

Father and Angelina leaned toward each other, faces almost touching. They shared a single glass of wine from a stemmed glass. Father whispered something and Angelina threw back her head and laughed.

"Pretty chummy for confessor and confessee," I said.

Mike shook his head. "Weird."

"Weirder and Weirder."

At that point Loreli swept into the room, Mary Pickford curls loose around her shoulders and streaming down her back. Her hair provided a sharp contrast to something that looked like a black snake wrapped around her neck. "What's that?" I leaned forward and decided it was a boa made of dark feathers. Still, thinking of how she died just a few months later of a broken neck, I shivered.

She slithered into the seat next to Marcus, planted a smooch on his cheek and pointed to the wine bottle. Marcus poured her less than half a glass and handed it to her. She tossed him a pout, reached for the bottle and filled her glass. Marcus frowned as she gulped half the wine and raised her glass to the camera in a "so there" salute.

The screen went blank for a few seconds, then Jeremy dashed into the scene and stood behind Loreli.

"Aha, the photographer revealed," Mike said.

"What's he doing there?"

"Beats me."

Marcus's foster son grasped Loreli's shoulder in the same proprietary manner I remembered from his grasp of my arm New Year's Eve. He'd parted his chin-length hair in the middle and swept it back over the ears, where it refused to stay. He was decked out in old-timey tennis whites, shorts that came almost to the knee and a cabled V-neck sweater banded with dark stripes. Jeremy squeezed her shoulder slightly and she set the glass down.

Hmm.

Two servants entered bearing gigantic platters of what appeared to be prime rib to be carved at the table. Others followed with large bowls of side dishes. I imagined the aromas of garlic mashed potatoes, Italian salad, perhaps fresh spring peas with mint and chanterelle mushrooms. Despite being fed two hours before, my stomach rumbled.

Jeremy moved back behind the camera and the screen went blank.

"So what did we learn from this video?" I asked, pushing the eject button on the DVD.

"That Jeremy plays tennis?"

"Not necessarily. Would a serious player play in a sweater? He'd melt. This video reminds me of the old movies they show at the Hearst mansion. Come on Sherlock, give me your assessment."

"Well," Mike said. "The partner Vito looks like a gangster, Angelina and Father are way too chummy, Loreli likes the sauce and Marcus ain't happy about it." He paused and scratched his chin, which bore a late-day shadow.

"What about Vito?" I said. "He could be the murderer."

"Unlikely. What's his motive?"

"He and Dominic were together for a long time, he may still be an heir in the will."

Mike considered. "Presumably Dominic is an astute business man with at least one lawyer. He'd have changed the will by now. On the other hand, that guy Marcus sure is a puzzle. I've been asking around town. He's obviously dedicated to helping the downtrodden, and his land has been in the family for generations. Why risk all he's doing, and has, with all those code violations? What drives the man?"

"Lack of money? Pure cussedness? He's an enigma, all right. And I sure don't see him and Loreli as a couple. On the other hand, Jeremy seems to have had a lot of influence over her.

Notice she put the glass down when he squeezed her shoulder? What should we take from that?"

Mike drained his cup. "I have no idea at the moment. Got ice cream?"

* * * * *

Tuesday, January 13th, 12:30 PM

I sat in my cubicle, staring at the remnants of my egg salad sandwich, a half-drunk café mocha, and a pile of papers waiting to be filed. The phone rang.

"Hello, Bella? It's Jeremy."

"Jeremy?" I repeated, like a ventriloquist's dummy.

"Jeremy Beamer. From New Year's Eve?"

"I know who you are," I said, more sharply than I'd intended.

"Bella, I was wondering, would you like to meet for coffee?"

"Coffee?"

"Maybe tomorrow morning, around ten. What time do you go to work?"

"Wednesday's bad," I said, trying to decide if I wanted to do this. Casual acquaintances who suddenly issue invitations for coffee often want more than Java. "I go in early."

"How about Thursday?"

"That might work," I found myself saying. A meeting would provide an opportunity to question him about his relationship with the Serenos, especially Loreli, and also find out more about Marcus. "Shall we meet in Tolosa?"

"I can't get too far from the ranch Thursday," Jeremy said without explaining why. "Do you mind driving to Cuyamaca Beach?"

"Um, I guess not. Where and what time?"

"How about the pier at ten? We can decide where to go from there."

"Okay."

"And Bella," Jeremy continued, "I've been thinking about you a lot since New Year's Eve."

Oh dear. "Mike and I have a very special relationship."

Hesitation and a nervous laugh. "Sorry, that came out all wrong. What I mean to say was that I've thought of you *two* often. Most of my friends have scattered since I left here five years ago and I'm looking to make some new ones. If you're uncomfortable, bring Mike along."

Yeah right. "Mike's busy during the day."

"So you're still okay with getting together?" Jeremy asked.

"Sure. I mean, I guess so."

"Good, I want to talk to you about some plans I have for the ranch. They involve you, Bella."

20

Thursday, January 15th, 9:55AM

I parked the old Subaru in the small lot off the Cuyamaca Beach boardwalk, still not sure I wanted to meet with Jeremy. But I was curious about his plans for the ranch and my part in them. I also intended to prime the pump a bit and find out more about him and Marcus and their relationship with the Sereno family.

Also, how Walter came to live at the ranch and whether he was happy there. Call it nosey and interfering, but the young Down syndrome man had touched my heart.

How different the beach looked today from when Magda was murdered two weeks ago. Gone was the hard-edge brilliance of New Year's morning; today the ocean wore a thick blanket of fog. A few intrepid surfers clung to their boards, waiting in vain for a good wave. Freezing mist prickled my skin.

I windmilled my arms to stay warm as I walked along the narrow boardwalk, spotting Jeremy near the bathrooms at the foot of the pier. A dark watch cap and a bright blue parka gave him the look of a mountaineer. He carried a large picnic hamper.

His dark eyes lit up as I came closer. "You look great," he said, extending his free hand and holding my proffered one a second too long. His hand radiated heat into my freezing palm. Why hadn't I brought gloves?

I extracted my hand. "Uh, what's in the basket?"

His smile widened. "A surprise picnic."

Stranger and stranger. I eyed the fog, felt the dampness on my face. "You're kidding."

He opened the hamper lid and brought out a pair of mittens and a scarf. "I came prepared. Come on, it'll be fun. He held out the basket for my inspection. "There's fresh-brewed coffee and hot Swiss cocoa. And—" he pointed to a foil wrapped package, not that he needed to, a heady fragrance escaped from it— "cinnamon buns baked fresh this morning by my own hands. They're a big hit with our homeless guests."

"Yum. I'd do almost anything for a cinnamon roll." "Almost" being the operative word. I stared at the ocean, calm, gray, hungry for the next victim, remembering Magda dying out there. "I'm not sure I can stand to be here long."

Jeremy said nothing, but handed me the mittens and, before I could protest, wrapped the scarf around my neck, staring deep into my eyes. As I stood there, feet nailed to the planks, he took my arm and propelled me forward. "Look at it this way, Bella. Here's a chance to replace a bummer experience with a good one. Let's tap some of the adventurous spirit lurking behind those big brown eyes."

"I guess."

I removed my arm from Jeremy's grasp and scrambled in double time to keep pace with his long strides. The effort made me dizzy. The planks swayed slightly and, despite my best efforts, my eyes kept returning to the black water below.

I paused halfway. "I think this is far enough."

Jeremy halted mid-stride and stared at me. "You look pale. Is something wrong?"

I leaned against the rail and put a hand to my forehead. My knees shook. Gulls perched on the rail eyed me with avian curiosity. "I have a bit of vertigo."

Jeremy smiled as though that were no big deal and again made a hostage of my arm. "Allow me, Madame. Keep your eyes on the horizon and you'll be fine."

After what seemed an eternity, we found a bench at the end of pier. Jeremy was right, the vertigo retreated to its own corner if I kept my eyes on the horizon and concentrated on the gentle lapping of waves against the pilings. Gulls screamed overhead and again several perched on the railing, eager for a handout.

Jeremy set the hamper between us and undid the wooden pegs that held the lid down. Tucked inside were two stainless steel thermoses, yellow crockery cups and plates with napkins to match. The aromas of cinnamon and sugar wafted toward me as he tore open the foil package, placed a bun on a plate and handed it to me. He shook out a napkin and tucked in my lap. The intimate gesture made me squirm.

I turned a bit, so that Jeremy's hand fell away, and bit into a roll, the dough warm and sweet and overflowing with cinnamon and butter. "Yum. This is to die for." A nearby gull apparently agreed. He looked ready to pounce and I put up my hand to ward him off.

"Thank you," he said and we were silent, lost in the moment. Without warning, the gulls stirred, and then flew away. Jeremy's eyes followed them. "Maybe better food down the road."

As he said this, the entire pier shook like a creature fending off a predator. My heart lurched sideways in my chest. "What was that?" I asked, almost choking on a bite of roll.

Jeremy surveyed the scene, which now looked peaceful enough, except for the absence of birds. In fact things were eerily quiet. "Probably a small earthquake offshore. Happens all the time."

In a flash I was on my feet. "Let's go. If we have another one I want to be on terra firma."

"Stay a few more minutes, Bella. Chances are that was it."

"But what if it isn't?" Even as I sat back down, I heard my voice rising. "We don't have earthquakes in Michigan and I can't get used to the ground shaking with no warning." I shivered. "It's so biblical."

"But you have tornadoes and the chances of being hurt or killed in them are much greater."

"That's true, but at least we get warned. The randomness of quakes scares me. I can never really relax."

"I've spent my entire life along the Pacific Rim. Trust me, that little shaker was just a blip on the Richter scale."

"Easy for you to say," I remarked, irritable now and off balance at being forced for politeness sake to stay in a place that made me uneasy.

"You're right," he admitted. "Forgive me?"

"Of course." I took a bracing sip of hot coffee and then one of cocoa. Not able to make up my mind, I'd opted for a cup of each. They provided warmth and relief from anxiety. He was right about earthquakes. Since changing the subject was one way to get my mind off them, I held up the sweet roll. "I take it the food at the Blue Stetson has improved since you arrived."

He nodded and pressed his palms together. "Sure has. Marcus is a great guy and I owe him everything, but cooking is not one of his talents."

Aha. A chance to prime the conversational pump. "How did you two hook up?"

Jeremy removed the watch cap and combed his fingers through his hair, sweeping it back from his brow. "Marcus took me in after my parents—my adoptive parents, the only ones I ever knew—died when our house caught fire."

"And you got out okay?"

His eyes met mine and his voice caught. "I was spending the night with a friend. I was thirteen."

"I put my mittened hand over his bare one. "What do you know about your birth parents?"

He hunched his shoulders. "Only that I was born in Oakland. My adoptive parents, the Beamers, told me my birth parents lived on the Central Coast somewhere." His other hand found its way into mine and he squeezed it. "A year after the fire I...I ran away from my foster home in Shasta County and hitchhiked down here, trying to find them. Found Marcus instead and that turned out to be the luckiest thing that ever happened to me."

"Do you have a birth certificate?"

He shook his head. "Burnt up in the fire."

"If it was a closed adoption, and it probably was in those days, only your adoptive parents' name would be on the certificate. You could petition the courts, have the records opened and find your birth parents."

Again his fingers slid through the dark hair. "Not interested. They gave me away, didn't they? Marcus and Walter are all I have, all I need." He turned to me. "Though I would like to have a woman in my life."

Here we go again. "How did you come to stay with Marcus?" I asked to steer the subject away from his love life. Strange that an attractive guy had no girlfriend. Forty-plus and living with his guardian? He even came to the New Year's Eve benefit with him. What kind of life was that? For both of them.

"Well, I met Walter at the foster home and we ran away together and made our way down here to Marcus's. We heard about his place from some people we met on the road. That was in the late '70's."

"So Walter's not your real brother?" He shook his head. Something didn't compute. "Wait a minute. That was thirty years ago. Walter's only in his mid-twenties."

"He's forty-one, two years younger than me."

"Really? I'm amazed." I thought about it for a moment. "I guess Down syndrome folks often appear younger than their age."

"I never really noticed." Silence settled between us and I conjured up an image of Walter's face: Small crows' feet radiated from the corners of his eyes and under his chin sat a pad of soft flesh. He could be forty-one, but the idea took some getting used to.

"Marcus has been sheltering the homeless for more than thirty years? Certainly commendable, but why so long?"

Jeremy took a long pull on his coffee. "He was only twenty-seven when his older brother, a hippie type, was murdered sleeping under a bridge near San Francisco. Marcus was devastated, and decided to do something for the county's homeless to honor his brother's memory."

"I had no idea." So Marcus was more than an angry curmudgeon obsessed with fighting local government. He'd been helping people down on their luck for most of his adult life.

Jeremy drained his cup. "When he inherited the ranch from his parents, he turned it into the *de facto* shelter we have now, a bed for the night and breakfast—drop in, stay a night or a year, help with chores, no background checks, no red tape."

"Sounds good, but we both know that can lead to problems."

He set down the cup and raised his palms in an "I-know" gesture. "The Daniels were always a bit different than their neighbors, and never known for their tidiness. The property was a mess when his parents had it, and it's even worse now. Building codes and permits are against Marcus's religion. He added several buildings for guests to sleep in and a cook house, none of it to code, of course."

"And you didn't try to stop him?"

"Might as well try to stop the tide. Marcus does what Marcus does. Besides, I was a single man living the good life as a fireman. Had my own apartment until I quit and moved to Tucson several years ago."

I glanced at my watch; later than I thought. I'd have to leave in half an hour. "On the phone you mentioned plans for the ranch. Surely you and Marcus would have to bring the property and buildings up to code before doing any expanding."

"That's true." He turned to me. "Here's the deal. I came into some money quite by accident a few years ago and decided to get out of the rat race at the fire department."

I refrained from asking how and why so as not to derail his train of thought.

"Bummed around Tucson for a few years, body-guarding. Long story short, I found out it's a sleazy profession and decided to come back here."

"Was that a good decision?"

He shrugged. "Too early to tell. I finally figured out a man has to take pride in his profession, and neither the politics of the fire department nor babysitting spoiled rich kids gave me much satisfaction. Marcus has spent most of his inheritance and helping him out was one way to pay him back for all he's done for me. We can get a construction loan and fix up the place. The property's divided into two parcels, as you may know."

I didn't, and he continued: "A great old house sits on the part of the property I plan to use. Maybe we can open a half-way house for incorrigible juveniles whose parents are well-off. Trust me, I've had plenty of experience with those as a body-guard. We can charge big bucks, several thousand per month is the going rate and many facilities get more. Marcus doesn't charge his guests, except for sweat equity work. This facility would bring in enough income for both of us. A win-win so to speak."

"Sounds good, but surely you can't just hang out a sign and call yourself a halfway house. The state must have stringent requirements."

"Not as many as you might think. I've been talking to people and reading up on it on the Internet."

I had a hard time believing it would be that easy. "Wouldn't you need a counseling background to get a state license?"

"Not as an owner, and I can hire the talent. That's where you come in."

Okay. "I don't see how. I have no formal training in counseling, and I only manage the Saint Pat's homeless program for one month a year. This is my first stint."

"Not a big deal. I'd like to hire you as manager. There's a potential for big bucks, Bella."

It bothered me that Jeremy seemed more interested in "big bucks" than helping disadvantaged kids. But maybe that was unfair. He had a special bond with Walter, and he was certainly disadvantaged. They'd been together a long time, Jeremy looked out for him, and Walter called him "Bro."

"What would I do?" I asked, buying time to think about his offer.

"Take care of the day-to-day running of the facility, drive clients to meetings, counseling and maybe AA or Narcotics Anonymous, and to medical and legal appointments, do the bookkeeping, and update the website."

Sounded like a tall order.

"Can you create a website?" he asked.

"Sure, with a little help. I can at least find my way around a computer keyboard."

Jeremy lifted his cup in a salute. "There you go. Interested?"

Was I? "I'll talk it over with Mike."

A knowing smile: *The good little woman always follows her husband's advice.* "Of course. Take your time. With the licensing and bringing the property up to code, we can't open 'til fall, even if we started tomorrow. I need someone reliable like you, Bella."

"How do you know I'm reliable?"

"Simple. I'm a good judge of human nature. Will you think about it?"

"Sure," I assured him, wondering what Mike would say. With budget cuts, my job at the paper might not last, but this new opportunity hardly represented a bastion of security. On the other hand, people weren't beating down the door with job offers.

I polished off my second cinnamon roll. With all the calories I'd consumed, I could have only yogurt or a salad without dressing for lunch. But the feast had been worth it. "I can't get over how good these rolls are."

He grinned his pleasure at the compliment.

"You said Marcus can't cook. Did Loreli prepare the meals when she lived at the ranch? 'The good little woman' and all that?"

He didn't react to my jab. "I didn't live there when she and Marcus were engaged, but, let me tell you, she did her share. She was a real sweetheart."

"Loreli was that," I agreed, priming the pump some more. "And Magda as well."

"How do you know them?" he asked, sparks of curiosity in his eyes.

"They sold us our house eight years ago. You know how it is, a short but intense relationship during escrow, and then only casual meetings afterward. I hadn't seen Magda since before Loreli died—until New Year's Eve."

He gulped coffee and stared at the flat horizon. "How did she end up helping out New Year's Eve? That doesn't seem like something she'd do. I didn't know her well, but she always acted like a princess."

Should I tell him we'd met earlier that afternoon at her request? No, he'd ask why and I had no intention of telling him about her anonymous phone call. "We ran into each other on the street. She seemed at loose ends, it was New Year's Eve and I ended up asking her to help out as bartender."

His laugh sounded more like a bark. "Ha, I'll bet she was upset after Marcus and I showed up."

You don't know the half of it. "What would you expect, considering the bad blood between Marcus and the Serenos?"

"Dominic's screwed up too," he muttered, seemingly unaware of the *non sequitur,* but unable to let go of his hostility.

"Whoa," I said. "Let's not go there. We're not going to find common ground discussing the Serenos." As I said this, I eyed the water below the planks. It seemed to be rising. The tide coming in, probably.

"Well, I could tell you some tales that—" He stopped. "What the hell?"

First came a noise like a giant slap. The boards clattered and banged and the entire structure shuddered as water poured over the planks and swelled around our ankles.

"Rogue wave!" Jeremy shouted. "Hang on."

No way. I jumped up and prepared to run for it. Strong arms held me back, but they couldn't protect me from the sudden terror that swept my body. Once again the wave surged. Jeremy lifted me into his arms as though carrying me across some unseen threshold.

Time blurred, changed shape, and moved backwards. A long buried memory stirred in my brain: Uncle Jimmy throwing me off a dock at Lake Erie.

"Jeremy, put me down," I panted.

He did, saying, "What's wrong? The wave was probably caused by a little aftershock."

I shook with terror. "No, you don't understand. I can't stay here any longer. I hate earthquakes, I hate piers. My uncle threw me off one when I was a kid." I looked down at my wet shoes and pant legs. "I want to go home and change, I want to be away from here." I didn't add, "I want my mommy," but I might as well have.

My clogs sloshed and squeaked as I scurried off the pier leaving behind a perplexed Jeremy.

21

Saturday, January 17th, Midnight

Exhausted, I pulled myself up the stairs to my office in the old windmill. Mike and Chris were snugged up in their respective beds. With the earthquake and rogue wave on the pier, plus work, it had been an exhausting couple of days, but I needed to accomplish one more thing before Magda's funeral tomorrow.

I opened the door, warming to the glow of moonlight streaming through the sliding door. The room smelled of new-cut wood from the paneling that now lined the walls. This remodel had been such a good idea. As always when I entered my office, Emily Divina made her presence known and my eyes were drawn to her portrait on the west wall. "What do you think of our decorating, Emily?" I asked, admiring the new (to me) desk and chair, the chintz sofa, the hardwood floor and ash paneling. Did a twitch of approval pass those arrow-straight lips?

I lit my desk lamp, reflecting that Emily and I never failed to communicate when I entered her presence. She never responded verbally, but her spirit was present. We held our own silent, private ritual, something shared across space and time.

I eased my tired body into the chair and dragged the Secrets Box from my bottom drawer, along with the bag containing the video, and the copy I'd made of it. I hadn't asked Mike about reproducing it because I wasn't sure what his reaction would be. Or Dominic's, for that matter.

After dumping the contents on the desk, I began sorting through the sad items one more time. Was there something here that might provide a lead? The snapshots of endless football rallies and proms weren't helpful at all.

I dreaded tomorrow, but something in me needed to attend the funeral, for myself and for Dominic and his aunt, a strange woman to say the least. The day would be very hard for both of them. I was grateful that Mike—and a reluctant, but anxious-to-please, Chris—were going for moral support.

Attending funerals is something one does both for the living and for ourselves, I reflected. Tomorrow should provide me some closure with Magda, and perhaps, by extension, with Loreli. But finding their killer, or killers, would be the best closure.

Wondering what I hoped to discover, I sifted through the sad trinkets: a broken rhinestone bracelet, an orphaned earring, a dog-eared bookmark. Where was the special insight I prided myself on? There were scraps of paper that looked like pocket trash: a grocery list, four gas receipts and a list of what looked like last names.

I gathered up the gas receipts and studied them, amazed at the low price of gas in the fall of 2003. The fuel was purchased in town and paid for in cash, leaving no trace of the buyer. Were they in the box because they meant something, or were they just carelessly filed? I often leave things in some pretty strange places.

I put the receipts aside and picked up the list, crumpled and dusted with ash as though someone had thrown it in the fireplace and then retrieved it. The heading across the top proclaimed in green Arial script: ClearChoice, with a local phone number. On impulse I dragged the phone across the desk and dialed.

"Sunshine Dry Cleaners. Our hours are—" ClearChoice was now another business. I studied the list. Eight surnames marched down the page in no apparent order. They were scrawled in Loreli's distinctive wide backhand script that I remembered from our real estate documents: Stryker, Smith, Hackman, McGarrity, Winfield, Dryer, Adams and Enfield. Smith and Adams stood out only because they're common names. I turned the list over—nothing on the back.

I had no idea why the gas receipts and the list were in the box, but it wouldn't hurt to make copies. I ran them through my fax-copier, added them to the bag with the reproduced video and stowed all in my bottom desk drawer. After tucking everything else into the Secrets Box and replacing the lid, I carried it downstairs and set it on the front hall bench so I wouldn't forget it tomorrow.

The bench had taken on the look of a garage sale display since Chris's arrival, with books, sneakers, backpack and parka competing for space. Wearily, I hung the parka on an overhead hook, rousted Sam off our bed and onto his own, and called it a night.

* * * * *

Saturday, January 17th, early morning

Reporter Ben Adams dialed the number of Saint Patrick's rectory. A sleepy voice answered: "Father Burton here. Please state your business and it had better be urgent this time of morning."

"My business is urgent, Father. I'd like to discuss Loreli Sereno's death with you this afternoon."

Dead silence on the line, then, "Not today. We're holding Magda Sereno's funeral."

"So much the better, Father. I'll see you there. Look for the orchid necktie."

22

Saturday, January 17th 1:45 PM

Mike expertly guided the old Subaru up the winding road twenty miles east of the Coast Highway, deep in the heart of the Central Coast wine country. "Some spread," he remarked as Sereno Cellars swam into view, shimmering in the early afternoon sun.

"Right, and this car is *so* disgusting," Chris said from the back seat. "Couldn't we just rent a car for today?"

"You paying?" I asked.

"Auntie Bella, you know I'm broke." Complaining, whining, calling me "Auntie Bella" again, Chris was more like his old self, a normal teen. It would be such a relief to get his hearing over with a week from Monday. Our attorney thought since Chris had no record, he'd be sentenced to community service hours rather than a fine, or God forbid, jail time. If so, he could work off some of his hours during Saint Pat's upcoming "House the Homeless" month, now only two weeks away.

"We're not exactly rolling in dough either," Mike said, his eyes never leaving the road.

"Image isn't everything," I added. We were starting to sound like typical parents, not a bad thing.

A huge sigh from the back seat. Chris didn't agree. Oh, to be eighteen again and know what I know now. Another parental platitude. I glanced over my shoulder at my handsome nephew, corn silk hair blowing in the breeze from my open window. He sat staring a hole through the back of Mike's seat. His arms were crossed over the chest of the thrift store sport coat purchased for Connie Mercado's funeral last summer. Suddenly I was filled with dread. This would be my first since hers, and the images of that day still clung to my insides like spider webs to attic rafters.

I turned and studied the scene outside. God had provided a glorious day for Magda's sendoff. The midday sun shone on my face, and on close-cropped grape vines, which stood in undulating mahogany rows as far as the eye could see. Hundreds of pruned rose bushes lined each side of the road. "This must be gorgeous in mid-summer when the grapes ripen and the roses are in bloom," I observed.

Silence from the men in my life. Chris maintained his funk and it seemed Mike and I shared the same foreboding about today. In fact, his own angst might be worse. Connie had been his friend, not mine, and he'd been so overwrought he hadn't shown up for her funeral. At least today I'd been able to get him into the car.

We entered a sweeping circular drive and passed the family home on the left, a glaringly white two story Spanish-style hacienda nestled within a copse of old oaks. Dominic had chosen to hold the service in the winery tasting room, a wise decision considering the expected crowd. We approached this immense building, also white, flying a flag with a black-mountain logo against a backdrop of red like Magda's surfboard. I swallowed back the lump in my throat. Two huge domed windows dominated the front of the building. They flanked a massive oak door, now open in welcome.

"I'll pull up and let you guys out," Mike said.

"No way," Chris muttered. "I don't want anyone to see us getting out of this old clunker."

"Nonsense." Mike stopped at the front entrance and turned off the engine, which bucked and sputtered before it died. Several yuppie types stared at us and I longed for a bag to cover my head.

"We'll wait here," I said, opening my door. Chris slouched against the back seat. "Come on, out you go."

Mike said, "Go on in and save me a seat." He started the engine, which thankfully turned over the first time, and headed for the gravel parking area.

"Ohmigod," Chris whispered as we entered the tasting room through the massive doorway, "Awesome!"

His teenage hyperbole said it all. Were it not for the floor-to-ceiling glass, we might have been in a cathedral. Everything in this room was on the grand scale: a high and very white plastered ceiling lacking only a resurrection fresco, the wide center aisle, now cluttered with folding chairs. The aisle ended in a magnificent marble staircase leading to a mezzanine that looked out over the tasting room where we now stood. The room exuded a fragrance of fermenting grapes and old oak common to wineries everywhere.

Two long and narrow oak tables flanked the center aisle. Each held tall bouquets of white calla lilies in vases of the finest porcelain. From the video, I recognized the tables, one was now set with dozens of long-stemmed wine glasses, like crystal roses refracting light from the windows into hundreds of tiny rainbows.

Pausing to admire the scene, I realized I'd left the Secrets Box in the back seat. Hopefully Mike would bring it, or at least lock the car. But then no one would steal an old shoe box.

Chris and I took seats near the front on the left. We saved Mike the aisle seat because he fidgets. Saving a place for him was hardly a problem. So far there were fewer mourners than I expected, maybe twenty, dressed in black, mostly men, but a few women, sitting together and speaking in a soft Spanish cadence. Many wiped their eyes with handkerchiefs clutched in work-worn hands. Most likely employees of the winery. Dominic would need a large staff for an operation this size.

Near the back, Martin Tanner sat alone, staring into space. It took guts for the deputy to come today, but I was proud of him for doing so.

The immense building housed the processing operation as well as the tasting room. I peered down a long, narrow hall to the right of the staircase. Toward the back stood immense steel tanks next to a glassed-in room that looked like a laboratory.

Mike came in and took his seat. "Not many people here," he said, forgetting to use his church voice.

"Shh!" I looked around. No one had noticed. "I wondered about that myself," I whispered. "Dominic said Magda's friends were calling about arrangements, but so far there don't seem to be many here."

"She was in Colorado a long time. Friends drift away," Mike said, leaning forward and looking to Chris for confirmation and receiving a stony stare in return.

"I know, maybe…" I left the observation unfinished, that perhaps the friends' phone calls were wishful thinking on Dominic's part.

A burst of energy radiated from behind us. A large group of men and women streamed through the door, strode down the aisle and took seats around us. Tan and fit in black Surfrider T-shirts proclaiming "Hang Ten for Magda," they represented all ages. Chris grinned and my heart surged; Magda would be so pleased.

Dominic and an older blonde woman I recognized as Aunt Angelina from that day near the Small Wilderness, entered from a door to the left of the staircase. Magda's brother, his pallor heightened by the red necktie knotted against his scrawny throat, sat hunched in a wheelchair pushed by Angelina. My own throat tightened. His condition had deteriorated since Monday. He held a red lacquer box on his lap as through it were a small child. Angelina, dressed in filmy and flaming scarlet, wheeled him in a no-nonsense fashion to a low table by the lectern. Red must be the signature color of the Serenos, I decided. I also decided to cut Angelina some slack. People often express grief as anger.

Dominic reached toward the table and set the box of Magda's ashes down with utmost care. He moved it this way and that until he was satisfied with its positioning, then waved Angelina off and sat close to the box, as though he couldn't bear to be separated from his sister. Angelina pointed to two seats on the aisle in the front row, and when Dominic shook his head, she turned her back and took one of the seats. We had a good view of both from where we sat a few rows back

Father Burton appeared at the top of the staircase. He descended slowly, making the most of his grand entrance. Instead of flowing vestments or black clerical garb with a Roman collar, he wore a white linen suit with a red and black flowered Hawaiian shirt. "White buck" shoes, a relic of the 1950's, and a white

Panama hat with a band that matched the shirt made him look like fugitive from a Tennessee Williams play. Strange choice for a funeral, especially for the officiating priest. But then Father Burton was a strange fellow. Mike and I exchanged glances, and I resisted the urge to roll my eyes. Chris appeared wide-eyed and interested, if a bit puzzled.

Father set the Panama hat to one side and held up a hand for quiet. He coughed and sipped from a bottle of water that appeared from nowhere. His hands shook ever so slightly and he gripped the edges of the podium to steady them. Another shared glance between Mike and me. Father Burton was nervous.

"Today we are here to mourn the tragic loss of our dear sister, Magda Elena Sereno, tragically taken from us on New Year's Day. Magda began life—" He stopped, eyes focused like a blue spotlight above our heads to the entrance. I turned—as did others. Marcus and Jeremy were now seating themselves in an otherwise-empty back row.

"The plot thickens," Mike whispered.

After some murmuring and foot shuffling by the attendees, Father Burton droned on for a while longer, then finished his eulogy, said a brief prayer and shook incense over the box with Magda's ashes. The smoky, sweet smell filled the air. Dominic bowed his head and crossed himself.

I glanced over my shoulder at Jeremy who was giving bad eyes to Martin. If the young deputy was aware of it, he gave no sign. What the heck was that all about? He had a perfect right to be there. So many currents of emotion ebb and flow around the living at funerals.

Father invited people to share remembrances of Magda. I hoped people would be respectful. Sometimes these turn into inappropriate "roasts" of the bereaved.

I needn't have worried. Several Surfriders told of Magda's commitment to their cause, preservation of the health of the world's oceans. In halting English and mopping her eyes with a handkerchief, Magda and Loreli's nanny shared stories of childhood pranks played on their older brother. Dominic's thin shoulders shook at her words. My heart ached for him. Angelina stared straight ahead, her back ramrod straight. I changed my opinion of her to "cold cookie."

"I'd like to speak," boomed a male voice from the back. Father Burton's eyes widened noticeably as Marcus ambled down the aisle and took his place behind the lectern. I hoped he wouldn't say anything that would blight this day.

He was bareheaded—the blue Stetson left behind. He reached out to grab the lectern and his hands trembled. Like Father, he was nervous. He looked directly at Dominic, sunlight glinting off his granny glasses. "I'll be brief. I just want to say that I was wrong, wrong, and wrong about Magda, hell about the whole family." He stopped and looked at Father Burton. "Sorry about the cuss word."

He turned his attention back to Dominic, who listened intently. "I was jealous of your closeness and the way my fiancée Loreli loved you, and wanted to spend so much time with you. Believe me, I've had plenty of sleepless nights to think in the five years she's been gone." He stopped and poked a finger under his granny glasses to wipe away a tear. "Now that I have my foster son Jeremy with me again, I understand what a comfort family can be. If I'd had that knowledge five years ago, Loreli might be alive today."

A shroud of silence enveloped the room. Marcus stepped away from the podium, moved to where Dominic sat and offered his hand. Dominic gripped Marcus's hand in both of his.

Reconciliation. At least one good thing had come from this day.

Father Burton apparently didn't think so. "That concludes our period of recollection," he said abruptly. He raised his hands and made an impatient "up" gesture. "All rise for the Lord's Prayer." Mike and I again exchanged glances. I'd planned to speak, even had my notes ready. I folded the paper and crammed it back in my purse. The nerve of that man. I should report him to the Bishop. What would I say? He's too friendly with a woman he hears confessions from, and he wears funny clothes to funerals?

Maybe not.

"Our Father who art in heaven. Hallowed be thy name. Thy kingdom come. Thy will be—" He stopped dead, and, one more time, his eyes focused beyond us. Seeing outright fear on that imperious face, I turned. Ben Adams stood in the doorway, wearing a garish orchid necktie. He stayed frozen in place for a few seconds, then apparently thought better of coming in, and he and his necktie melted away. What was that all about? I wondered.

Father pulled himself together and began the rosary, undoubtedly wondering who else was going to show up unexpectedly. The service droned on for twenty more minutes, but the day had been so full of surprises I was hardly aware of the Our Fathers, Hail Mary's and Glory Be's emanating from members of the congregation familiar with the traditional prayers. The aroma of food being prepared somewhere close by and mixed with the lingering scent of incense, left me queasy.

"In the name of the Father, the Son and the Holy Spirit." Father crossed himself with his rosary's silver crucifix. The beads clattered as he set them on the lectern. "That concludes the public part of our service." With an open palm he indicated the box next to Dominic. "Scattering of the ashes in the vineyard will be held later for family members only."

I wondered if Loreli's ashes were there among—and now part of—the vines. How appropriate for the sisters' physical remains to be united with the earth, and with each other. I thought of my own sister's body in Michigan's cold ground and shivered. As much as I loved and missed Bea, I didn't want to be buried there.

Servers appeared bearing bottles of wine, large platters and chafing dishes. The scent of garlic and cheese and succulent meats grew stronger. My nausea disappeared, in fact I was starving. I'd skipped breakfast and my empty stomach rumbled in response to the siren song of food aromas. I ruminated, not for the first time, on funerals and the sudden desire for food.

"As with the wedding feast at Cana, Dominic and Angelina invite you to partake of their food and wine before starting on your journey home," Father said in his best priestly voice.

Chris jumped up. "Let's get there before the rush."

"Not so fast. First we have to pay our respects to Magda's family," I said.

"You're kidding," he said.

"Well, well," Mike said, rising and shaking one foot and then the other as though they were asleep, "wasn't that interesting?"

"Sure was," I agreed. "How about getting the box from the car so I can give it to Dominic?"

"You bet," Mike said a bit too quickly. He found it hard to put sympathy into words for the bereaved. I understood. All three of us had experienced the trauma of funerals for close family members. Mike with his wife and son's, Chris with his mom, my sister's memorial, though he was too young to understand its meaning. He'd asked afterward, "Are we going to wake her up now?"

"Can I go with Uncle Mike?" Chris asked, snapping me back to the present.

"No, you come with me."

He looked at Mike for support. "Do I, like, have to?"

"Yes," I said. Chris needed to learn to communicate words of comfort to people who needed them. Today was a chance to begin.

Mike took off like a shot for the car and Chris and I approached Dominic, still seated next to Magda's ashes. Angelina stood beside him. A crowd began to gather around them. We stood in line, fidgeting like everyone else. Just as Mike approached with the Secrets Box, a place opened up before the couple. I stepped into the void, with Chris and Mike behind me. "Someone tried to jimmy the car lock," Mike whispered in my ear.

I turned. "You're kidding!" He shook his head and set the box down beside him on a vacant chair as though it were toxic.

We couldn't say more because Dominic was smiling and holding out his hands, which I took in both of mine. "Bella, you were able to come," he said. "I am so pleased."

"Wonderful service," I said. "Magda would have loved it." And she would have, except for Father Burton's posturing. What possessed the man?

Something flashed in Dominic's dark eyes and he glanced at Father Burton, now deep in conversation with Jeremy at the buffet table. What was it with those two and their serious conversations?

Dominic turned to Angelina who stood beside him like a sentinel. "This is Angelina, our"—he corrected himself—"my aunt."

"How do you do." She gave me a stiff, straight-across smile and a clammy claw. I dragged Mike forward and introduced him. Chris remained a step behind and I decided to give him a moment. Dominic and Mike made uneasy small talk while Angelina fussed with the panels of her dress. I attempted a small-talk moment with her, and when that fizzled, turned in desperation toward the entrance. Anything to avoid staring into those cold eyes.

At the entrance, Jeremy and Marcus talked to one of the Surfriders, then took their leave. Darn. I'd planned to tell Marcus how moved I was by his eulogy. It's unusual to hear someone say, "I was wrong," in public. Or in private.

As for Jeremy, it was probably just as well he'd left. I'd decided to refuse his job offer at the Blue Stetson without even broaching the subject with Mike. Part of me still found him attractive, but another part, the one I listen to, warned me there was something off-kilter about the situation, and perhaps about the man himself.

"And who might you be, young man?" Dominic's words broke into my thoughts. He looked beyond me, smiled and extended a knobby hand to Chris.

Before I could utter a word, Chris grabbed it like he'd been glad-handing all his life. "I'm Chris, and I'm very sorry for your loss." A pregnant pause, then, "Sir."

Did I hear right? So what if the words sounded a bit rehearsed, he still got an A+. "Chris is my nephew from Cleveland," I explained.

Chris grinned and said to Dominic, "I live in California now." He looked to me for confirmation and received an enthusiastic thumbs up.

"I believe this belongs to you, Dominic." Mike reached behind him and handed the Secret's Box to Dominic, whose eyes misted over. Dominic glanced at the other box with Magda's ashes and I considered the irony: one contained the remains of a human being, the other filled with her earthly treasures.

Angelina pounced like a cougar. "I'll take that," she said, reaching over Dominic's shoulder.

Dominic put a staying hand on the box, revealing a flash of the Dominic-of-old. "No need, my dear. You stay here and greet our guests—make sure they get something to eat. I need a break anyway." He made a high-sign Chris's way. "I'll store the box in my office and this fine young man can wheel me there."

Chris glanced at me for a sign that it was okay, and I made a "go" gesture. As my nephew steered Dominic down the long hall to the right of the staircase, Angelina's eyes followed them.

* * * * *

Ben Adams sat at the traffic light, revving his silver Corvette, his thoughts spinning like the engine's rotations. The whole day had gone wrong. He hadn't had any luck retrieving that old box from Bella's car. He knew it would prove useful if he could only get his hands on it. Probably too late now. And who'd have figured that Jeremy and Marcus would be there? He could talk to Father Burton later, but now he had a better plan, one where he would control the action. He punched numbers into his phone.

"Central Coast Development, Jack speaking."

"Jack, this is your favorite investigative reporter. There's some shit going on out at the Blue Stetson that could swing that property your way if it was shut down. Maybe you could put some pressure on Amy to do a tell-all story, you being such a big advertiser and all."

* * * * *

Mike sat beside me in the back seat on the way back from the funeral. He patted my hand for attention. "What did we learn from today?"

"Hmm?" I gazed the window, eyes and brain at half-mast. Another hard day behind us.

"Stay in your lane!" Mike bellowed as Chris took a blind corner from the center line. He'd allowed Chris to drive so we could sit in the back and discuss the day's events. Beside him on the passenger seat was a gift from Dominic, an old globe that looked valuable. He'd also given me a leather-bound edition of "Two Years before the Mast" by Richard Henry Dana, the nineteenth century writer who as a young seaman visited the Central Coast. How generous the vintner had been, despite Angelina looking daggers at us as we left with our gifts.

Now Chris turned and called over his shoulder, "Relax."

"Watch the road!" I yelled, grabbing Mike's arm. Maybe this wasn't such a great idea.

"Will you stop, Auntie Bella?" Chris said, but he did back his foot off the accelerator.

"So, where were we?" Mike asked, shaking his head. "What did we learn?"

"Father Burton looked frightened when he saw Ben Adams at the door. They could be in cahoots."

"Over what?"

"Mike, I have no idea, but I'll never forget the look on Father's face."

"Don't read too much into that," Mike said. "He may have just been surprised. But our friend Ben seems way too interested in the Sereno family."

"That's what I've thought all along," I said. "He could be the one who jimmied our car lock. He was eavesdropping in the next cubicle when Dominic left the Secrets Box with me on Monday."

"An eavesdropper does not a car thief make," Mike said, smiling as he scrambled the King's English.

"Did you see Jeremy give Martin bad eyes?" Mike shook his head and I continued: "Why would he care if Martin came to the funeral? And he and Father Burton held another deep conversation. I'd love to know what they talk about that's so serious."

Mike considered, saying instead, "Marcus gave a great elegy, but it could have been a smokescreen. I still think he's our man. There's something not quite right about that man."

"That's what I think about Jeremy," I replied

"Dominic's aunt—" Chris interrupted.

"Mr. Sereno to you, son," Mike said.

Chris shook his head, the blonde hair swinging around his shoulders, and began again. "*Mr. Sereno's* aunt sure wanted to get her hands on that old box, and he doesn't trust her. He locked it up in his safe. That safe is a big sucker. About this big." He took his hands off the wheel to show us, and when I gasped, put his hands back where they belonged.

"I wonder what she's so interested in." Mike said.

"Probably doesn't want anyone to see that DVD of her and Father playing kissy face," Chris said.

"How do you know that?" I asked.

"You, like, left the video in the player, and I, like, watched it the other day. Except for Dom—Mr. Sereno—those are some weird people."

"Chris, you're too nosey for your own good."

"Guess I take after you."

Mike smiled. "Touché." He scratched his chin. "We may have to ask Dominic to submit that box as evidence somewhere down the line."

"Evidence of what?" I asked.

"I don't know, it's just a hunch, but I think there's something in there, or on the video, that ties together Loreli and Magda's murders."

I lapsed into silence, watching the taupe and gold winter landscape pass outside the window. "Mike," I said, "there's a list of last names in the box. One of the names is 'Adams.'"

Mike clapped his hands together. "Dang! Why didn't you say so sooner? Could be our friend Ben wants to get his mitts on that list." He tapped Chris on the shoulder. "Turn around. I need to take another look at the contents of that box."

I tapped Chris's other shoulder. "Keep going." And to Mike: "Don't even consider it, husband. You're not going to disturb a grieving man on the day of his sister's funeral. Besides, I copied the list, and the video as well."

* * * * *

Saturday, January 17th, 11:30 PM

Flashlight gripped in a shaking hand, Angelina Sereno-Minetti entered the office, closing the door behind her. She made her way to the safe, opened it using the combination she now knew and removed the papers inside the Secrets Box. She carried them to Dominic's desk and played the light over them. A fist tightened around her heart. The most incriminating document of all was missing. She was so sure it would be there. Had that nosey nun kept it? Or did Dominic hide it somewhere else? She had to find it. Everything depended on that piece of paper.

23

Monday, January 19th, 10:37 AM

Engrossed in my latest obituary, I gave a little yip of alarm when Ben Adams' blond head appeared over my cubicle wall.

"You scared me."

"Sorry," he said, though he didn't look it. "Amy wants to you at the Monday meeting. Eleven in the conference room," he added as though, after several years on staff, I wouldn't know when and where the regular meeting was held.

"Thanks," I said, ignoring the putdown. Strange. Normally the obituary editor was not included in these weekly confabs where story assignments were handed out.

I cracked the door to the meeting room twenty-three minutes late thanks to a woman seeking an obituary for her cat. After explaining the *Chronicle* only eulogized humans, she looked so crushed I'd spent an extra few minutes on the Internet locating a pet website that accepted feline obits. Amy always says my primary goal as obituary editor is to provide comfort to the bereaved.

Try explaining that to her and the six reporters whose stony stares greeted me as I sank into the only empty chair, which happened to be next to Ben. I caught a few head-shakes being exchanged around the conference table.

"Shall we move on now that Brenda Starr has arrived?"

Amy's sarcasm didn't spare anyone, including friends. While I considered crawling under the table, Amy consulted her clipboard. "Let's see, all of you have your assignments except Jim, Ben and Bella."

Me?

She fixed her gaze on Jim. "I want you to cover the Redemptor story in Los Lobos."

"Redemptor? What the hell is that?" he asked, tapping a pencil on the table.

Amy waved her hand as though banishing a gnat. "Oh some contraption this guy has invented to extract, that is, *redeem*, drinking water from sewage. He's installing one in his front yard." She stared at a stain on the ceiling. "It's *so* Los Lobos," she said, dismissing my hometown's ongoing sewer saga.

"Wait a minute!" I said, preparing to defend the hometown honor.

"Is this Redemptor thing legal?" Jim asked, cutting me off.

"That's for you to find out," Amy snapped. "We'll run the story on the twenty-first." She turned to Ben and me. "I've saved the best for last. Got a big story for you two."

"Us two?" Ben croaked as I propped up my slackened jaw with a fist.

"That's right. I want you guys to do an in-depth story of the Blue Stetson ranch. Who's there—we've heard rumors of sex offenders—what laws Marcus Daniels might be stretching or outright breaking, building and fire code violations, the whole enchilada."

"How are we supposed to get this information?" Ben asked. I wondered the same thing, but my voice seemed to be glued to my tonsils. True I'd asked for extra hours, but this assignment seemed like a tall order.

"This is undercover." Amy's hands framed a large arc. "We're talking Big Story. You two will spend several nights, as many as it takes, at the ranch as a homeless couple, gathering data, talking to people, keeping your eyes open for hanky-panky. You might even write a book about it later, Ben."

Had she lost her mind? Marcus and Jeremy would recognize me.

Ben looked stunned and, as I gathered my wits to mention this little impediment, he rose to his feet. "If this is such an important story why put the obituary editor"—he fairly spat the words— "on it?"

Amy sputtered something; Ben sailed on. "Why assign a rookie, when Jim or almost anyone else here could bring more experience to the table?" He scanned the room, taking in Joann, Jake, Brian, a very pregnant Lindsay, and of course, Jim. They all stared at Ben as though he'd turned into the Jolly Green Giant.

Amy's voice hardened. "Ben, when you're managing editor you can make those kinds of decisions." She stood. "In the meantime, you've all got your marching orders. This meeting is over. Enjoy your lunch."

As the bewildered reporters filed out of the room, Amy tugged at my sleeve. "Got a sec?"

No one refuses Amy when she asks that question. "Sure," I said, though I longed to get back to the hazardous waste site that was my desk, call Mike and tell him the news.

Amy took off her glasses, closed her eyes and pinched the bridge of her nose. The exchange with Ben had affected her. She blinked and I was surprised to see a tear gathering in the corner of each eye. She caught me looking and slapped the glasses back in place. "You probably wonder why I assigned you to this story."

"Well, *yeah,* that thought did occur to me. Ben has a point. Why not give it to someone with more experience? And what about my duties as obituary editor? Surely you don't think—"

Amy lifted her palms from the table. "No, I don't expect you to do both jobs. I've lined up a temp with obit experience to help out. There's more to this than meets the eye."

"I thought so."

"You're on the story, not as a reporter—though Ben won't know that—but to keep an eye on him and act as fact-checker."

She took a huge, ragged breath as if it hurt her heart. "I'll give him this, Ben is really good at investigative reporting."

"I sense a 'but' coming."

A brisk nod. "Um, this is for your ears only, understand?" I nodded. "No telling, even that sexy husband of yours."

I touched my heart. "Would I break a confidence?"

Amy gave me a "don't go there" look. "I've been keeping tabs on Ben. He's lifted text almost verbatim from different websites."

"Really?" I stared at the managing editor, hardly able to believe what I'd just heard. "How did you find out?"

She took a sip of coffee and made a face. "Cold." She banished the offending mug. "I discovered the rat's dirty little secret rereading his last couple of stories. Unfortunately, they were in print by that time."

"This is serious."

She nodded again. We were starting to resemble those bobble-head dolls in the backs of cars.

"Why would he do such a thing?"

"Ben has a distinctive writing style, but his grasp of technical material is less than wonderful. Also, these 'stars' get so full of themselves they think they can get away with murder."

So she'd finally noticed. I offered a noncommittal "hmm" and she continued, "There were paragraphs in those stories where his writing didn't sound like him. On a hunch, I checked a couple of websites he'd used, and sure enough, he'd done a cut and paste."

"Have you confronted him, or told anyone else?"

She shook her head. "No, and no. It's a big dilemma. On one hand we need him with Lindsay going out on maternity leave. On the other, this puts the paper, and my *tush*, at risk. Remember that reporter from the *New York Times?*"

"When he went down, he took the editor with him."

"Exactly."

"Maybe you should talk to Mister Cut and Paste."

She shook a mane of copper hair, releasing a wave of Obsession, her signature perfume. "No can do."

"Why not?"

Amy pulled the mug back toward her and ran her finger around the rim several times. She reached for a paper napkin and carefully wiped the outside. "Trust me, Bella, I can't."

"Amy, did you sleep with him?"

She balled up the napkin as the room took on an unnatural stillness.

Oh my God. If she had, he could claim sexual harassment. Even if it weren't true, she'd be dead meat as far as corporate was concerned.

I'll say this for Amy; she's an optimist. She looked up and gave me a lips-only smirk. "With a no-nonsense ex-nun partner, he should keep his nose clean."

My first thought was I hated it when people used my former life to make assumptions about me. My second was that I didn't like this one bit. "So I'm a spy?"

"Not exactly, but make sure you double check his sources, and his stories, against any websites you use. Also, make sure his reporting doesn't get creative. Our Ben tends to embellish at times. To keep Marcus Daniels from suing us, this story must be absolutely accurate."

"Amy, another thing, and this is important."

"What's that?"

"I can't go with Ben to the Blue Stetson. Marcus and his nephew will recognize me. I've had a conversation with each of them."

More than one with Jeremy, but that was none of her beeswax.

She raised her hands and spread her fingers. *No big deal.* "Go in disguise. I can fix you up so even Mike won't recognize you."

"What about Mike? He'll have a conniption—"

"What about him? Do you tell him everything?"

Mostly. "Let me think about it." He'd have a fit, but this assignment meant extra hours, maybe enough to pay off the entire credit card balance.

Amy frowned. "Bella, there's something else you need to know. I know how hard you work, but to help meet our budget goals this year, I've been told to cut nonessential hours, including yours."

Nonessential? "You said just days ago staff cuts would be over your dead body."

She shook her head. "I wish."

"Look, the policy of e-mail submissions was supposed to make my job take less time, but instead it takes more. Often I can't open the file and I have to call the sender, and if we can't resolve the problem, I have to take the obituary over the phone. And that's just one of a hundred things that can go wrong from the time the obituary comes across my desk until it's printed in the paper."

"Try telling that to the actuaries in Chicago who come up with these things. But one thing I can do—combine obituary editor with research assistant and make it one forty-hour job."

"You're not going to replace Dawn?" Our former research assistant had recently moved to San Francisco.

"I won't have to if you agree to take on her duties, at least for now."

"So I'm not going to be a 'real reporter' on the Stetson Ranch story."

"That's true, but Ben won't know that. And for this one, you'll share a byline with Ben."

"He'll love that."

She grinned. "Won't he? Are you game?"

Was I? "I guess. But I don't understand why you're taking on this story when Chicago wants you to stick to local stories."

"This *is* local, and we've gotten an anonymous tip that there's lots of stuff going on out there, sex offenders, drug deals, maybe even prostitution. This is a chance to really impress Chicago and save my job."

"Amy, I didn't realize your job was in jeopardy."

She tossed the crumpled napkin into the trash can behind her with the aplomb of an NBA player. "All our jobs are."

24

Monday, January 19th, 4:00 PM

I drove the twelve miles home feeling the gut-wrenching sensation of things slipping out of control. I'd felt this way after Connie's murder last summer, and my instinct had been dead-on. Events after that murder had spiraled downward into a maelstrom of danger, mistrust and more murder.

Now I had a similar premonition about going undercover with Ben at the Blue Stetson ranch. And yet I promised Amy I'd do it. Why? What would happen if I backed out?

I'd put Amy in one heck of a jam, that's what. She'd been foolish getting involved with Ben, but she was human after all. The 'Ben Situation' needed to be handled carefully. If she confronted him with charges of plagiarism, the worm would rat to Chicago about their affair and claim sexual harassment. By watch-dogging Ben's writing activities, I could keep things on an even keel, at least until the Blue Stetson story appeared.

Mike. A big problem. I hung a hard right west onto Los Lobos Road and passed Tolosa's main food shopping center wondering what, if anything, I'd tell him about the undercover aspect of the story. Amy mentioned spending several nights at the ranch. If that really happened I'd have to explain, but I'd worry about it when I had to.

I turned my eyes briefly toward the rolling farmland with its rich, dark soil that lined both sides of the highway. Something gnawed around the edges of my insides. I should be over-the-moon happy that Amy offered me a crack at a real story. But deep in my heart, I felt used. Let's face it, if she didn't need a spy, I'd never get this chance.

If I had an ounce of guts, I'd make a stand for integrity, but, even under the best of circumstances, Amy's a hard person to refuse. And these were not the best of circumstances.

If I refused this assignment, life at the paper would grow difficult. I'd work less and maybe be laid off. Mike's extra money as a cold case consultant wouldn't go far without my income. Amy promised me the job of combined obituary editor/research assistant would be full time. I'd get benefits, including health insurance, no small thing with Mike's heart condition. Ever since last June we'd known our current provider might cancel our coverage at any time. If that happened, with Mike's pre-existing condition, we'd have few options. Employer-provided health care provided more stability.

I downshifted for the light at Foothill Boulevard, which led to the community college Chris would attend next fall. He'd need help with tuition, another expense. That did it, I slapped the steering wheel. I might not like it, but I had a job to do. I'd just suck it up (one of Chris's more colorful phrases) and put one foot in front of the other until I'd completed it. Too Pollyanna? Sure, but Polly, that aging maven of positive thinking, had served me well in the past.

Ten minutes later, when I pulled off Los Lobos Road onto the access road that led to our driveway, my breathing eased and my hands relaxed around the wheel. Our home is our refuge, where we try to leave trouble at the gate.

I spied The Beast, Mike's truck, from the gravel drive. Good. He always started dinner when he got home first. I needed a big hug, a good meal and a glass or two of white wine.

Hopefully Chris was home early too, working on his English paper due Thursday. It would be such a relief to get the hearing over with next Monday. Our attorney was sure he'd receive community service hours and I'd use him at Saint Pat's next month. Most important, we could all move on.

I opened the car door and stepped outside, inhaling the crisp sea air. Sam appeared from one of his hidey-holes and licked my hand, tail wagging the dog as usual. "Life is pretty good, Sam," I said. He didn't disagree, and snugged as close as he could to me without knocking me down as we made our way up the walk. I opened the door and he thrust himself ahead of me, as usual, and bounded for the kitchen and his food bowl.

Standing in the hall, I breathed in, expecting the aroma of warm comfort food, spaghetti sauce or beef stew. Instead, I almost choked on the lingering odor of this morning's bacon. The house felt cold, unused; I reached beside me and cranked up the thermostat.

"Mike, I'm home," I called over the roar of the furnace starting up. "Mike?"

I heard a chair scrape across tile and my husband appeared in the kitchen doorway, his face the color of cold macaroni. Sam's long face peeked out from behind him. "Thank God you're finally home."

"What's wrong?"

"Chris is gone."

* * * * *

It took me a second. "What do you mean, gone? Maybe he made a new friend, and he's out with him—or her. The best way to drive out an old nail is with—"

Mike raised one hand like a traffic cop, fumbled in his pocket with the other and thrust a folded piece of lined paper under my nose. "Here. Read this."

The note made a crackling sound as I shook it open. I held my elbows close to my body and clutched the wrinkled paper in both hands to keep them from shaking. In neat script that belied what must have been a troubled state of mind, Chris told us he just couldn't face the hearing. He planned to "hit the road."

"Why did he do this?" I said, fighting the urge to crumple the paper and toss it somewhere, anywhere, in the fireplace, out the back door. "He'll most likely get community service." I crammed the note in my pocket and pulled out my cell. "We need to call the sheriff."

"Can't."

"Nonsense." I flipped open the phone, stopped when I saw Mike's expression. "Why not?"

He shook his head. "He becomes a fugitive from justice the minute they find out he's gone."

He was right, of course. "So what do we do? Have you tried his cell?"

Mike nodded. "He's not picking up." He put an arm around my waist and guided me toward the living room. "Let's sit down and talk about this like the rational people we're not at the moment."

When we were seated close each other on the sofa, Mike said, "You're right about him only getting community service, but there's more to it than that. He's embarrassed. By acting like a knucklehead, he's lost face, not only with us, but with Miranda and her family as well."

"That's true." Last summer Chris had thought the world of them and the feelings were mutual. The Gonzales family must feel so betrayed.

"Surely..." I stopped, unable to finish. Had we failed to reassure him that, while he'd done something stupid, it wasn't the end of the world, that he could recover from it? Perhaps even be a better person for the experience?

"There are other things involved," Mike said.

"What?"

"For one, I think he's tempted by the lure of the open road. After all, he just turned eighteen, and he got a taste of freedom on the trip out here. I found a well-thumbed copy of Jack Kerouac's novel, 'On the Road,' under his mattress."

My spirits lifted a bit. "Maybe that's not so bad. As you say, he is of age."

"There's something else."

I didn't like his tone. "Go on."

"This is much, much, more serious." His voice dropped an octave. "He could be dealing drugs."

I jumped up, banging my knee against the coffee table. "Mike, I said, rubbing my leg, "that's preposterous. Why would you even think that?" His cop mind must be in overdrive.

He made a steeple of his hands and blew into his fingers. "I found a withdrawal slip he used as a bookmark. I only paid him a couple hundred. Where else would a kid his age get a grand except by selling drugs?"

A thousand dollars. "I don't know, but surely there must be lots of places."

"Name one."

"Uh, not from his folks, that's for sure." Ed and Janet hadn't even called on his eighteenth birthday, and he'd forbidden us to contact them after his arrest. "Uh...?"

"Exactly. I'm not saying it's drugs, only that it's a possibility."

"Mike, if he's got money, he's not going to hang around town or go to a local homeless shelter. We don't have time to waste." I grabbed my coat from the hall bench. "You cover the Tolosa airport and I'll take the train station."

"Good idea."

"Got your phone?"

He nodded, stood up and checked the power level on his cell, then dropped it back in his pocket. "Bella?"

"What?"

"Stay inside the terminal. Take Sam with you. Some pretty unsavory characters hang out on that bridge over the tracks. Remember that university student was murdered there several years ago."

25

Sam pushed ahead of me to get inside the door of the Tolosa Amtrak station. He'd caught scents of things that promised a world of canine delights: two kids munching popcorn, an old man holding a hand out to sniff and maybe be petted with, a teen whose battered pack promised smells of past adventures.

I dragged the reluctant dog toward the counter. "Come on. We don't have time right now."

There was no line and the clerk watched our approach. As I got closer, he called, loud enough for everyone to hear, "Ma'am if that's not a guide dog, he can't be in here."

I turned and watched Sam pulling the opposite way, his blue and white bandanna askew. Obviously not a guide dog. I gave him another good yank and this time we made it all the way to the counter. "I just want to ask a few questions. It will only take a few seconds."

The clerk wasn't having it. He plunked a "Closed" sign in front of me. "Come back without the dog, after my coffee break. I'll talk to you then."

"I'm back," I said seventeen precious minutes later, after I'd locked an unhappy Sam in the Subaru, dug a photo of Chris from my bag, and fumed behind three people who must have been booking world tours.

"Now, how may I help you?" The clerk, if not all smiles, was now at least civil. Amazing the powers of caffeine.

I thrust the photo of Chris under his nose. "Have you seen this young man? He's my nephew."

"Missing?" The clerk asked in a flat voice, like he'd heard it before.

I nodded. "Perhaps you remember him buying a ticket?"

He examined the snapshot which showed Chris in cutoffs beside one of Miranda's surfboards, his blond hair blown forward by the wind.

He shook his head. "Sorry, we get fifty kids a day easy in here lookin' like this."

"He has really blue eyes," I said, hearing desperation in my voice.

He handed the photo back. "Sorry," he repeated, "doesn't look familiar."

"Okay. Thanks." Gulping down my disappointment, I moved away from the counter. What next? Maybe step outside and ask people waiting for the San Diego train if they'd seen Chris.

As I stopped just inside the double doors to button my coat, I heard, "Bella Kowalski?"

Marcus Daniels stood beside me, arm extended to shake hands, a cheroot clamped in the corner of his mouth. I took an involuntary step back, resisting the urge to fan the air. Then I realized the cigar wasn't lit. My eyes must have looked blank because he prompted, "Marcus Daniels? From New Year's Eve?"

"Of course." I took his hand, which was warm and dry. "I didn't expect to see you here."

My insides churned. His easy recollection didn't bode well for disguising myself at the Blue Stetson. On the other hand, it might be a good excuse for me not to go in the first place.

"Going somewhere?" he asked.

"Actually, I'm looking—"

"Sir? *Sir?*" the clerk called, "you can't smoke in here." He abandoned his customer and stepped to one side of the counter. "You can't smoke in here," he repeated.

"I get it," Marcus growled. He yanked the damp cheroot from his mouth, moved across the waiting room and waved it under the clerk's nose. "Ain't lit."

The clerk sniffed and pointed an offended finger toward the door. "Sir, please step outside and dispose of that before approaching the counter."

"What *are* you doing here?" I asked when we'd stepped through the double doors to the departure platform.

Marcus scanned the tracks leading north and south. "I come here every night to find guests to sleep at the ranch."

"Really?" Something didn't ring true. "The clerk didn't recognize you."

"He's new," Marcus said, flicking a nonexistent ash off his stogie. "That's why he's such an officious little prick."

Couldn't quarrel with that.

"It's a lot safer for the homeless to spend the night at my ranch than around these tracks or under a bridge." Marcus eyed the young man with the large pack I'd seen inside, now bent over to tie his shoelace, keeping his distance from the knot of people waiting for the San Diego train.

I realized I had Chris's photo in my hand and held it up with both hands. "My nephew's missing. Have you seen him at the ranch?"

Marcus looked carefully at the snapshot and shook his head. "Sorry, hasn't been around. And I keep tabs on who's there." He watched the shoelace-tier who was now adjusting the pack on his shoulders. "Looks like a potential guest." He turned back to me. "You call law enforcement about your nephew?"

"Can't. Chris is awaiting a hearing for threatening his girl-friend, uh, make that former girlfriend."

Marcus shook his head. "Dumb kid. Does he have a car? Money?"

"No car, but Mike thinks he's got at least a thousand dollars."

He whistled. "How old's this kid?"

"Just eighteen."

"Bad combination, a brand new adult and lots of cash. He's probably long gone. But I'll keep my ears open, let you know if I hear anything. I've also got some ideas about where you could look."

My heart gave a little flutter. "Really? That would be great."

The young man strode toward the open metal steps of the bridge over the tracks, maybe fifty yards south of the platform. "Come on," Marcus yelled over his shoulder, "We got a live one."

I hesitated, glancing around at the gathering darkness. I didn't really want to be on that bridge for several reasons: It was high and probably swayed, and it had been a crime scene.

Another thing. Despite the reconciliation scene with Dominic at the funeral, Marcus could still be Magda's killer. He didn't seem the type, but neither did Sweeney Todd who slashed customers' throats while barbering them.

Marcus tapped the toe of his boot against the platform. "You coming or not?"

On the other hand, he had some ideas about where Chris might be, and that was why I was here. I shouldered my bag. "Wait up!"

He didn't, and stood deep in conversation with the young man by the time I'd huffed my way up the steep metal steps to the bridge. I peered over the edge at the tracks far below. My legs shook and my vision blurred. Height and I have a dysfunctional relationship.

A few seconds later, the young man shook his head, adjusted his pack and took off across the bridge. Marcus turned to me and shrugged. "Probably headed for the bridge under the 101 freeway. Rough crowd gathers there. Hope the kid knows what he's getting into."

I hoped the same for Chris, and made a mental note to have Mike check under the bridge, and take Sam along for protection. I hitched the bag up on my shoulder. "Marcus, I have to go. Can you give me a heads-up on where else we might search?"

"Have you checked the parks? Couple years ago I'd have said the Greyhound station, but that's gone now. Go by the downtown Tolosa library. Across the street is a hub for the city and county buses. And—" He paused, looking over my shoulder. "Here comes Jeremy, he might have some ideas."

My stomach did a little back-flip as Jeremy approached, dressed in tight Levis, a black leather jacket hugging his trim torso. "Bella, what are you doing here?"

Before I could open my mouth, Marcus said: "She's here to check on her nephew. He's missing."

Jeremy's brow creased in a frown. "Alone? Your husband should be with you."

His words implied a lack of concern on Mike's part. My face and neck flamed despite the chill air. "We didn't think we had time to waste. He's checking other places Chris might be."

"We need ideas, Jeremy, not rhetoric," Marcus said.

Jeremy jammed his hands into his jacket pockets. "Does your nephew have money?"

"Yes."

A sharp whistle swallowed the night sounds. The San Diego train, maybe two minutes out. I so did not want to be on this bridge when its lumbering hulk passed under it.

Marcus added, "Maybe a lot of money."

Jeremy turned to me and I was surprised by the cold look in his brown eyes. "Kid's probably long gone. You notify law enforcement?"

His words felt like a stiletto to the heart. "We can't," I said without explaining why.

"Okaay." He drew the word out. "We have a situation. Is Mike checking the park by the ball field? Lots of homeless gather there."

The whistle sounded again, shrill, insistent—and much closer. The sour smell of diesel filled my senses. I thought about running down the steps, but I didn't want to be trapped that close to the train when it passed. Bile filled my throat.

"Good call, Jeremy. Worth a check. Kid might still be around." Marcus yelled over the ruckus. "Come with us and we'll drive you around in the van."

"Well, I—" My cell chirped and I flipped it open.

"Hey," Mike said. "Any luck?"

"No, but I'm here at the station with Jeremy and Marcus. Hold on." I grabbed the railing as the train passed under the bridge, which trembled with the vibrations of the force beneath it. Heat from the engine enveloped me. I tightened my grip on the railing with one hand and hugged the phone to my ear with the other.

"Where are you?" Mike shouted when the screeching and shaking ceased.

"I told you, at the station."

"That's obvious. Tell me you're not on the bridge."

"I...I came up here with Marcus. He and Jeremy are going to drive me around to look for Chris." I looked to them for confirmation.

"Bella, listen to me. Don't do that. Leave now, go home."

"But..."

"Just do it. I'll stay on the line with you 'til you're in the car."

I clutched the phone in my closed fist and turned to the two men. "Gotta go."

"Wait," Marcus said, taking a step forward. "We'll come with you."

"Have to go now," I said, and scurried off the bridge. Pounding down the stairs, I heard no footsteps following. I glued the cell to my ear and spoke into it. "Okay, I'm off the bridge, heading toward the parking lot."

"Good. Stay on the line with me."

I barely heard Mike. Someone parked in a ten-minute spot had cranked the music up and the windows down. As I passed a white van, an aria from "Madam Butterfly," one of the few I recognize, drilled into my chest. I flashed a look of annoyance at the young man behind the wheel. Feet propped on the dashboard, Walter was too lost in the music to notice.

"Mike," I said. "I just passed a white van."

"So?" Mike's question drifted over the ether. I looked over my shoulder at the vehicle and noticed the license plate for the first time. "The plate says "Stetson" and Walter's sitting in the driver's seat." I hesitated, a thought forming. "Do you suppose he has a driver's license, with his disability and all?"

Silence. We'd lost our connection.

Mike called back and I relayed the information about searching under the 101 bridge and at the park by the ball field, as well as Walter's last name. "I'll check with the DMV about a license," he said. "Now get inside the Subaru and take yourself and Sam home."

"We should come with you to check under the 101 bridge. You shouldn't be alone."

"Go home, Bella. That's the most helpful thing you can do. Chris could still come back tonight, and if no one's there, he might leave again."

He was right, of course. I sat in the car, parked kitty-corner from the van. Sam licked my neck, obviously acquiring a taste for the diesel residue I smelled on my skin.

"Cut that out you crazy dog." I wiped my sticky neck and grabbed my keys from the passenger seat.

Movement in the side mirror caught my eye. I paused, keys in hand, and turned to see Jeremy and Marcus climbing into the van on the passenger's side. The door slid shut with a whoosh, taillights came on. Ten seconds later the van backed up and pulled out of the lot. Walter sat behind the wheel squinting into the night. I don't think they saw me.

"What's wrong, Bella? Are you okay?"

I'd forgotten Mike, and now told him what I'd just seen. "Should I follow them?"

"God, no. Go home, try to catch some sleep. Tomorrow could be a busy day. Before you turn in, check the house phone for messages. Call me right away if there's one from Chris. Or if by some chance, the kid's home."

Would that we should be so lucky. "Will do. Be careful. I love you."

"Love you too." Silence. "Bella?"

"Everything's going to be all right."

"I know that," I said, forgetting Mike's distrust of the two men.

26

Tuesday, January 20ᵗʰ, 2:30 PM

"Of course you can still go undercover," Amy said, snatching off my glasses and tugging a watch cap over my cropped hair. I'd been trying to tell her about my encounter with Marcus and Jeremy at the train station, but she waved off my concerns that it could blow my cover. Her attitude didn't seem quite rational, but what else was new?

She plucked a pair of Jackie Kennedy-sized sunglasses from her bag, fitted them over my ears and stood back to admire her work. Ben, standing next to her desk, emitted a mild snort.

Amy ignored him. "A couple layers of sweats, a swipe of grime to the face and hands, a spritz of olive oil for the greasy-haired look, a scarf to hide the mouth. Even your own mother wouldn't know you."

"Amy, I can't see a thing out of these glasses."

"Do you have a pair of prescription ones?"

"Sure, but—"

"There you go." She turned to Ben. "Doesn't she look *great?*"

The snort again. "She looks like Bella playing a homeless person." He studied the ceiling tiles. "This is so hare-brained. Maybe we shouldn't do this after all."

Amy's eyes flashed. She put her hands on her hips and gave him The Look. "Get over it, Ben." She waved the backs of her hands at us. "Okay, kiddies, off you go."

I held back. "Amy, I have to talk to you."

She huffed a sigh and pointed to Ben. "Go," then turned to me, indicating a chair in front of her desk. "Park it. You have thirty seconds."

As I took the seat I glanced through the office's glass wall at the hubbub in the newsroom. Ben watched me from the water cooler.

"Twenty-eight seconds."

"Amy, I have to take myself off this assignment, even if it means my job."

Did I just say that? "Look," I continued before she could interrupt. "Not only have I had close-up conversations with both Marcus and Jeremy, Jeremy offered me a job at the ranch."

Amy uttered the "F" word, slapped her hand on the desk, and rose from her chair. "And you turned it down, of course."

"Not yet, but I'm going to."

"Swell." She sank back down and stared out the glass wall as though for inspiration. "You can't back out of this. Don't ask me to explain why, but all our jobs are on the line. It's too late to get anyone else. Besides, you're the only one I trust around here."

Behind the glasses, wheels turned. "Here's how we'll solve the problem. You can't have the byline I promised you, but Ben doesn't need to know that now. The new job as research assistant stays. Just go out to the ranch tonight and keep your eyes and ears open."

Talk about mixed emotions! I felt a pang of disappointment about the byline, even as I realized the anonymity would protect me if this misadventure turned toxic. "What about keeping Marcus from recognizing me?"

She raised her hand in a gesture of dismissal. "You're a smart woman. Figure it out."

* * * * *

Tuesday, January 20th, 3:17 PM

Back at my desk, I saw a missed call from Mike. My heart drummed in my ear as I waited for him to pick up.

"Mike it's me. What's up?"

Truck noise from "The Beast" in the background. "I'm on the road to San Jose. Chris called half an hour ago."

Thank God. Relief washed over me in waves. "What's he doing there?"

"Called from the Amtrak station. He borrowed some change and called collect from a pay phone. Some thugs took his cell, his money, skateboard and maybe cracked a couple ribs for good measure."

My already-skittish stomach dropped to my toes. "Good, I mean that's awful. He needs to be in the hospital. Did you tell him that?"

"Yes, he does, and no I didn't. If he goes alone as a transient, he risks getting arrested. I told him to wait for me outside by the city bus stop. And for God's sake, to keep moving, so he doesn't get picked up for loitering."

"Moving around will be agony for him with those ribs."

I know, but I can be there in three hours, four if I run into traffic."

"That's a long time."

A deep sigh reverberated in my ear. "Best I can do, Bella."

I thought about tonight's assignment. Should I tell him? No, he'd go ballistic and maybe I'd be done and home before we had to talk about it.

"I'll call when I get there and know something more."

I had another stomach-dropping thought. "Chris has no health insurance."

"You know that for sure?"

"Yeah, Janet told me in one of our friendly phone calls. How are we going to pay for this?"

"I'll put it on the credit card. Don't worry."

27

I tucked the Subaru into a dark corner by the Cayumaca pier, half a mile north of the Blue Stetson ranch. Lights shown on the pier, but the lot itself lay shrouded in darkness. I shivered, again thinking of Magda dying here. What would the night ahead bring?

"Thank God we made it," Ben groused. "Thought for sure we'd end up getting towed."

"This old Subaru is more reliable than she sounds," I said, switching the ignition off.

"Right." He gripped the dash as the car continued to shake from the engine's after-burn. Being transported in a twenty-five-year-old clunker didn't fit with his image of cool. Not that his vintage Corvette was much newer, but that silver bullet he called a car would be a come-hither target for law enforcement and thief alike.

"What is it?" he said, as I looked at him. "Something wrong with my disguise?"

"No, it's fine. I just can't get used to looking at you with dark hair and horned rimmed glasses."

He removed the glasses and slicked back his new "do," looking exactly like the Ben Adams of old, except with darker hair. Startled, I looked again. Without glasses, he looked a tad like Jeremy. "Decided if you went in disguise, I should too."

"The pack with the tent's behind the rear seat," I hinted.

He reached around and rubbed his lower back. "I've got a bad lumbar disk. Afraid you'll have to carry it."

"It's at long way. We can share."

"You can handle it," he said, checking his small backpack. "Okay, recorder, notebook, pencils. All set." With that he hopped out of the car and started off down Highway One at a pretty brisk trot for someone with back problems.

"Wait up!" I called, struggling to pull the straps of the heavy pack over my shoulders.

We moved along, mostly in silence as Ben stayed well ahead of me. Actually I waddled, encumbered by the pack and several layers of sweats and sweaters that gave new meaning to the term "layered look."

I was prepared to do whatever it took to survive the night and hoped for divine intervention with whatever happened after that. Better than staying home and waiting for the phone to ring. Hours had passed since Mike and I last talked. I'd check my cell for messages as soon as I could carve out a spot of privacy.

"Watch out!" I called as an oncoming semi doing at least seventy swerved dangerously close.

"Shit!" Ben exclaimed. We jumped back in time and its bank of taillights disappeared into the ground fog that had appeared out of nowhere.

"The driver must be asleep at the wheel," I said.

We stayed well behind the white line after that. I felt like a target in a shooting gallery every time a car or truck whizzed by. Too many appeared to be playing a crazy game of chicken with us. That and the dampness caused me to shiver despite being suited up like a moon-walker. The pungent smell of wet grasses—to say nothing of my own fear—permeated my nostrils. Bile collected in the back of my throat and I choked it down.

Could I really do this?

After what seemed an eternity, but was probably only twenty minutes, we spied a campfire in the distance. The ranch. Despite my fear of the night ahead, the sight of embers shooting into the night sky comforted my troubled soul.

As we approached, I replaced my everyday specs with the prescription sunglasses. They reduced my vision to images swimming in the night. "Ben," I called, "come here."

"What's wrong?" he asked, doubling back to me.

"I can't see in these glasses with the fog. I'm changing to my regular glasses."

"Bella, you have to leave these on."

"I guess," I adjusted the frames, knowing it was a useless gesture. "Stay close so I don't fall over things."

Ben made a tsking sound, and jerked on my elbow. "Come on, we don't have all night."

Unfortunately, we did.

"Let me do the talking," he said.

Actually Ben didn't have to say much. We were met by Captain and Honker, this evening's guest-greeters. The nearby bonfire threw off enough light for me to see a resemblance to the old-time comedy team, Laurel and Hardy. Captain, who seemed to be the leader, had the same lean body and acerbic manner as Stan Laurel, but in a battered Greek sailor's hat. Heavyset like Oliver Hardy, Honker lived up to his name, hacking and honking into a huge red bandanna pulled from his jacket pocket. He used his damp paw to shake my hand. Surreptitiously, I wiped it against my sweats.

"First names only," Captain warned, and we introduced ourselves as Dick and Jane. This caused some good-natured ribbing from Honker, Captain's more garrulous counterpart. He indicated a group of dark shapes in the field behind us.

"That there's the overflow area. We've got a full bunkhouse tonight 'cause of the cold. But me and Captain snagged us a spot in the barn."

He squinted at me, his face so close into mine I could see his rheumy eyes and smell his sour breath. "You ain't pregnant or nothin'?"

"No," I said, while Ben made choking sounds.

"Good. If you was in a family way, we'd find ya a place in the women's bunkhouse."

An image of Mike and Chris flashed into my mind. I was more "in a family way" than Honker could ever imagine.

"You have two bunkhouses?" Ben asked.

"Sure. One for men, the other for women and kids. Less problems that way."

"I'm sure." The woman's quarters would be a perfect place to gather information. Could I fudge and tell him I might be pregnant? Nah. Better to sneak in later.

Honker kept his face in mine. "Why you wearin' them shades? You high on somethin'? If so, we don't 'low no stuff in here."

"She's got pinkeye," Ben said, while Honker stared at the hand I'd shaken a few minutes ago.

Good one, Ben. You just got us kicked out of here.

Apparently pinkeye wasn't a problem. "Come over closer to the fire, Miz Jane," Captain said. "Ya look cold."

Indeed I was. The ranch sat half a mile from the ocean and its intense dampness. The four of us flowed as one toward the bonfire whose warmth soothed my face and hands, but did little to banish the anxious chill inside me. The fire's light improved my near-distance vision enough to make out eight guests gathered 'round. Most waved a hand in casual welcome. One, a heavyset man, looked vaguely familiar, but I couldn't place him. Thank God neither Captain nor Honker made an effort to introduce us.

Captain picked up a large stick and stoked the fire, sending a storm of sparks into the night sky. "After y'all set up your tent, come on back and sit a spell, have some cocoa," he said. "We got cookies from the weekend."

"You only have cookies on the weekend?" I asked.

"We have cookies every day, better ones first of the week. And sometimes cheese and crackers. People drop off leavings from their weekend book signings and art shows," Honker added. He chuckled. "Yes ma'am, with all the artists and writers in this county, we get plenty goodies. Mr. Marcus loves his goodies, he should be around shortly."

Mr. Marcus. Ben and I exchanged a look—time to set up our tent. Neither of us felt ready to face him.

"Y'all come back now, hear?" Honker called after us. "Don't get too frisky out there."

As if that would happen.

* * * * *

Tuesday, January 20ᵗʰ, 8:23 PM

I exchanged the sunglasses for my regular specs as soon as we'd moved away from the fire. The overflow area contained at least twenty tents in all sizes, shapes and states of repair and dis-repair. They hugged the creek under a copse of eucalyptus heavy with moisture. The trees gave off the strong odor that always reminds me of cat pee.

Anxiety overwhelmed me. How could I get through the next twelve hours? It didn't help that Ben seemed uneasy in a way I never expected. I'd expected his usual cockiness; instead here was a man who kept looking over his shoulder and jumping at every night sound. Was that why he decided on the disguise?

He stopped and stared up at the dripping trees. "Don't those things fall without warning?" he asked. "Let's pitch our tent on the other side of the creek. No trees over there."

"I'm not wading through that," I said. "It's almost sure to have frogs and other slimy critters."

Even darkness didn't hide his shudder. "Okay, okay. But let's move away from the others."

This we did, finding a semi-private spot under one of the larger eucalyptus. Ben stared up at branches so heavy with moisture it dripped in our faces. "These trees sure make me nervous."

I yanked the tent and poles from the pack. "Make up your mind, Ben. Since we can't walk on water, we have three choices: get our feet wet crossing the creek and freeze all night, stick close to the others and hear snores and grunts until dawn, or settle under this tree and take our chances on it staying upright."

"Guess we'll stay here," he allowed, holding a pole aloft and staring as though it were some sort of prehistoric weapon.

Swell. This guy doesn't know a tent pole from a tadpole and he's got as many neuroses as I do.

I did most of the setting up. Once we were huddled under the domed structure, Ben fiddled with his recorder and I checked my cell messages. Three from Mike. Something tickled my nose and I sneezed.

"The damp air getting to you?" he asked as drops of moisture plopped against the tent dome.

"No I'm fine." I glanced at Ben, not wanting to play the messages in his presence. The less he knew about my business the better. Plus, despite being some distance away, sounds from the other campers carried through the tent walls. If we could hear them, they could hear us.

There'd be more privacy in the bathroom. I stuck my head out the flap and saw various structures: two barns and several outbuildings, none with any apparent signage. Which one was the women's bunkhouse? I decided to ask someone sitting by the fire.

"Ready?"

Ben hesitated. "I've been thinking, Bella. You *are* pretty recognizable. Maybe I should go out there alone and you stay here." He indicated the cell phone still in my hand. "You probably have private business to attend to."

I sure do buddy and you're not going to find out what it is. "No way, Ben. I'm going out there with you. We need to wrap this up ASAP. The more nights we spend here, the greater the chances we'll be exposed."

"I suppose you're right," Ben grumbled. He thought a moment. "Let's spend tonight trying to small-talk Honker and

Captain, their backgrounds, why they'd rather be here than in a sanctioned shelter, that kind of thing."

"We can try, but I'm not sure they'll tell us much. The whole idea behind the Blue Stetson is 'No questions asked.'"

"We have to start somewhere," Ben said, and I couldn't disagree with that.

"I need to find the women's bunkhouse, and while I'm there using the bathroom, I can check the condition of the building and maybe engage the women in conversation."

Recalling a constant of convent life, I added: "When people live in close proximity, some pretty intense personality conflicts develop. We can use that to our advantage because everyone loves to dish the dirt on someone who bugs 'em."

Ben shrugged. "You may be right, but that's not going to happen tonight, or even tomorrow. It takes time."

"Yeah, but you said yourself, we have to start somewhere, and we might just get lucky." I flexed fingers still cold and stiff from setting up the tent. "Besides, I want a cup of hot cocoa and a cookie before they're gone."

* * * * *

Tuesday, January 20th, 9:15 PM

"Here come the lovebirds," Honker said as we approached the fire. Several people hooted and shot fists in the air. Missing was the heavyset man who had looked familiar. Good. One less thing to worry about.

Ben said, "Honker, can you tell Jane where the women's bunkhouse is so she'll know where to go when she needs to take a pee?"

Whoa, Ben. Too much info.

Captain spoke up. "Overflow people use the Casey's by the creek. You're not allowed in the bunkhouses."

"That's right," Honker said, pointing a thumb in the direction of the bunkhouse we'd just passed. Captain, taking a sip from something in a paper bag, didn't notice. Interesting. The two played good cop, bad cop. How could that be used?

The others made room and we settled in for a long winter's chat. The fire pit resembled those at nearby Cuyamaca Beach. Midnight requisitioning at work, no doubt.

Honker brought cocoa in Styrofoam cups and peanut butter cookies in a crumpled paper napkin. This is as good as it's likely to get tonight, I reflected, taking small sips of the warm liquid to make it last.

Captain and Honker squeezed in on either side of us. They seemed unduly interested in us, and who could blame them? Maybe they suspected we were up to no good. Both sipped from wrinkled brown bags, belying the ranch's sober living policy. I heard a slight hum from Ben's recorder; no one else seemed to notice.

Captain leaned forward, studying me. Without warning he reached over and tried to snatch my sunglasses. "Why don't you take them things off so we can see your purty face."

I shoved his hand away. "Stop that. I've got pink-eye and smoke makes it worse."

"Sorry, purty woman." He didn't sound it. Talkative now, he turned his attention to Ben. "No offense, sonny, but it's obvious the lady here is somewhat, shall we say, more senior than yourself. She your ma or something?"

"No, she's not my mother and it's none of your business," Ben snapped, brushing back his longish dark hair.

Captain set his bag down and raised his palms in a conciliatory gesture. "Sorry," he repeated.

"He don't mean nothing by it," Honker interjected. "His brain's been pickled in alcohol too long. Right, Captain?"

"You got no reason to talk," Captain said, taking a sip from his bag.

A boy approached the fire at a dead run. "Maw, Skeeter crapped his pants!" He stood rocking on his heels behind a woman sitting opposite us. She got up, said a word no child that age should hear, and followed her son up the path toward the bunkhouse.

"Do you have a lot of children here?" I asked. If so, they hadn't been in evidence.

Honker said, "A few. Only if they're with their mamas. Mr. Marcus don't encourage it. More potential for trouble with kids around."

"How about lone teens?"

"Over eighteen, sure."

"Have you seen any lately?"

Captain narrowed his eyes. "You looking for someone? Maybe a kid of yours run away?"

Ben stared at me with sudden interest.

I shrugged. "No special reason. Just curious, that's all."

"You better take your curiosity up with Mr. Marcus," Captain said.

"Where is, uh, *Mr.* Marcus?" I asked.

"Oh, he'll be around soon," Honker said. "Likes to check out his guests. Nice guy, though. Fair. Unlike that nephew of his." He made a mincing motion with his hands. "Jeremy, what kinda name is that?" He peered at Ben. "With that girly-girl hair, you kinda remind me of him."

I felt Ben fume beside me, while I struggled not to laugh.

Captain chimed in. "Yeah, I don't trust him. Oily, that's what he is. But Mr. Marcus is fine people."

Marcus was bound to recognize me, even with sunglasses and a long scarf wrapped around my neck. I hatched a plan. The minute I saw him coming, I'd pull the scarf over my mouth and hightail it to the bathroom. Same plan with Jeremy, only I'd hightail in double time.

I glanced at Ben, who knew nothing about my relationship with either man. He stared at the fire with a blank look, like he didn't know where to begin. He wasn't the only one. His eyes had the wide-eyed look that fear brings. Did he feel we'd bitten off more than we could chew? The stakes were so high. If we were discovered, the fallout could be tremendous. On the other hand if we got lucky and snagged our story, the fallout would be unpredictable when it was published. A lose/lose. Why did Amy insist on pursuing this fool's errand? At least my name wouldn't be on the byline.

We'd have to stay here every night for a month to get people to trust us enough to open up. The thought overwhelmed my tired brain. I drew my legs up close to my body, adjusted the scarf over my arms for extra warmth and laid my head on my knees. If I just rested my eyes for a moment, I'd be fine.

"You must have had a hard day." Behind the sunglasses, now askew, my eyes flew open. Marcus's sandpaper voice. I kept my head averted, adjusted the frames, and remained silent.

"You deaf and dumb?" he asked.

"No," I mumbled into folded arms. "Just beat."

"If you took off those sunglasses, you'd sleep better," he said.

"She has pinkeye," Tobias interjected.

"Whoa! Let me see." Marcus made a move toward me and I ducked away from him, pulling my scarf over my mouth.

"Be that way," he said. "Looks to me as though you've got something to hide. You'll have to leave. I can't let you stay here and infect everyone else. The health department would be all over my ass." He bent toward me so that I felt his breath on the back of my neck. "You alone?"

A rustle beside me and Ben got to his feet. "We've got our own tent. She won't infect anyone."

"Nice try, but what about using the Casey's? Come on now. Don't make a fuss. I'll give you a voucher for the local clinic and you can come back when you're better." Marcus reached down, took my arm and lifted me to my feet, knocking my scarf askew and the sunglasses off.

He shifted slightly to face me. "Look at me," he said, and when I didn't, "Look at me."

Hoo-boy, it's all over now.

Ben sprang forward and grabbed his arm. "For Chrissake leave her alone. What business is it of yours if she wants to wear sunglasses?"

"This is between me and the lady," Marcus said, shaking off his arm. "And it sure as hell is my business if she's on drugs or a fugitive from justice. I run a clean and sober place here and don't you forget it."

What about Captain and Honker and those wrinkled bags? I wondered, but didn't say.

Marcus glowered at Ben. "You hear me, Junior?

At that, Ben just lost it and shoved Marcus. Surprised, Marcus fell a step back. Empowered now, Ben tried to shove him again, but as Marcus moved to one side, the reporter ended up shoving dead air and stumbled, almost falling. Marcus used the moment to gather strength and advanced, fists at the ready. It only took a few seconds and Ben sat on the ground, legs splayed, and glasses askew.

"Okay, that's it," Marcus dusted his hands together. "You two, out! And don't come back."

The fun wasn't over; Jeremy approached at a dead run. "Marcus, we need you!" He pounded toward us and grabbed his uncle's sleeve. "A man tried to flush a baggie of something down the toilet, and when it backed up, Walter tried to plunge it down, but only made it worse and now—"

Walter. How could I have forgotten about him?

Jeremy stopped and stared at Ben, his mouth agape, his look, if I read it correctly, not just surprised at finding the reporter on the ground, but more like the man had returned from the dead.

Ben sat frozen to the spot and, so intent was Jeremy, he didn't even notice me.

"Shit!" Marcus took off running a nanosecond later. "Move it," he yelled over his shoulder to Jeremy, "Make yourself useful."

28

Tuesday, January 20ʰ, 10:10PM

The resulting confusion enabled us to escape to the relative safety of our tent. I closed and tied the tent flap and we sank down cross-legged on our sleeping bags. "Let's leave while we can," I said, reaching around and stuffing things in my pack. "Jeremy recognized you."

Ben's hands made a dismissing motion. "The dude was just surprised to see me on the ground. I don't know him."

Maybe. "Ben, I still think we should go."

"No way. Look what we've already discovered. Honker and Captain have alcohol and that baggie in the toilet could be dope. That's a lot for just a few hours."

Good point, though I hated to admit it.

"They won't come looking for us till morning and we'll leave before first light." His lip curled. "Thanks to you falling asleep, our cover as a couple is blown to hell, but I can come back tomorrow night alone, with a different disguise. I'll shave my head, and I can sure move a lot faster without you."

Yeah, Yeah. I was too tired to argue.

"I need to visit the little boys' before we turn in." Ben tossed his head in the general direction of the men's bunkhouse.

"Better use the Casey's. Marcus and Jeremy will be busy in the bunkhouse for a while. Time for me to visit the women's."

"Sounds like a plan," Ben said. He untied the tent flap. "See ya."

* * * * *

Tuesday, January 20th, 10:20 PM

I got strange looks from the women and girls in the bunkhouse bathroom, but no one challenged me. The facility turned out to be surprisingly commodious. It featured five small showers in good repair, a row of stalls that actually locked, clean sinks and a large, well-lit mirror.

Probably a zoo in the morning; by that time, we'd be long gone. Keeping my eyes on the scuffed toes of my hiking boots, I headed for an empty stall. When everyone cleared out, I'd play Mike's messages. Maybe we'd have to start texting. Texts were silent. Memo to Bella: Have Chris show us how.

I pulled out my cell, stared at its lighted face and waited. Outside, several kids jabbered and carried on. Pretty late for little ones. I wondered where they stayed when the parents were at work. Not my concern, but still worrisome. I hated to think about a kid spending his or her day alone in a car. Or worse, on the street.

"Hey, you gonna stay in there all night?" A woman rattled the stall handle.

"Give me a break," I said. "I'm backed up."

"Eat some prunes," the woman said. "My kid's gotta go." Two small feet appeared under the stall door. The girl began to whine and jump up and down. She mimicked her mother. "Gotta go, gotta go."

I gave up, flushed for effect. "All yours," I said as she grabbed the open door. With any luck I'd have the tent to myself for a while.

29

Tuesday, January 20ʰ, 10:35 PM
Fat chance. By the time I got back, Ben sat in the middle of his sleeping bag, scribbling with one hand and holding a flashlight

with the other. The beam gave his face a skeletal glow. I leaned over and asked, "What are you writing?"

He turned the page over. "Uh nothing, just some notes."

"Want to share?"

"Not really."

"Okay, be that way." I crawled into my bag to the sounds of humanity preparing for sleep: loud yawns and noses blown, comings and goings, tents zipped. After a few minutes, Ben stashed the notebook in his pack, set the flashlight at the ready near the tent flap, and crawled into the sleeping bag. "Ready to sleep?"

"I guess." The moment I'd been dreading. I didn't want to sleep anywhere near this guy, much less hip to hip. The thought gave me a cold, hollow feeling. Not fear exactly, just creepy. We weren't more than a few inches apart, given the confines of the tent. We lay there for what seemed a long time, but was probably less than half an hour. I could tell by the silence that Ben wasn't sleeping either. Finally, I heard him breathing regularly and then he began to snore. The sounds outside diminished except for background sound of traffic on Highway One. The rhythmic thump, thump, thump lulled me into a pre-sleep state where my thoughts became nonlinear. Finally, I drifted off.

* * * * *

Thursday, January 27th, 2 AM

Knowing what had to be done, the heavyset man hurried toward his meeting with the man who called himself Jeremy. He couldn't afford to be late.

* * * * *

I awoke to absolute silence. My watch face glowed 2:15, we'd been asleep for three hours. The temperature had plunged into the low thirties. The tent walls dripped moisture from our accumulated breath and the air held the stale smell of sleep.

Lying there, I realized I couldn't hear Ben breathing and propped myself on one elbow. "Ben?"

Nothing. I reached over and came away with a handful of empty sleeping bag. He could have left a note, but this was a chance to listen to my messages. I turned on the phone and jumped at the sound of the booming "Welcome" message.

"Turn that goddamn thing off!" someone yelled from a nearby tent. Heart racing, I snapped the phone closed. I'd have to try the bathroom again.

Shivering, I climbed reluctantly from my sleeping bag and crawled to the entrance, grabbing jacket and boots as I went. I shrugged into the jacket, pulled the boots on without lacing them and stood by the tent entrance. The fog had lifted, the sky was awash with stars.

I started along the path to the women's bunkhouse, trying not to let my laces trip me on the rocky path. Coming closer, I spied two men talking by the unlit back corner of the building. I couldn't hear specific words, but the voices sounded male, and one carried a low rumble of anger. I lasered my eyes toward them. Ben? I wasn't sure. The second man was bigger. Marcus? No, this man was heavier. They must have seen or heard me because they stepped further back into the shadows.

I reached the bunkhouse, stepped into the foyer and caught my breath. Double doors in front of me stood ajar and I couldn't resist peeking inside.

Nightlights glowed dimly in the darkened space which looked like it might have started life as a meeting room. Now at least forty women and kids slept in three-tier bunks. A baby cried and its mother made crooning noises. The air smelled of too many bodies in too small a place, like someone needed to open a window. I resisted the urge to do so, stepped back and started down the hall toward the bathroom.

How difficult it must be to sleep night after night in a roomful of strangers. By contrast, spending the night in a tent with Ben didn't seem bad. Well, not *so* bad.

Inside the bathroom, I flipped a switch by the door and reassuring light flooded the room. After heading to the end stall, I slid the lock into place, lowered the seat cover, sank down and played the first message. My hands shook so I could hardly hold the phone.

* * * * *

7:30 PM: "Hi Bella, I'm just pulling into the San Jose train station. I'll call you back as soon as I find Chris."

Five hours to San Jose? Traffic must have been terrible. I hope Mike didn't have truck trouble. Surely he'd call me if he did.

8:02 PM: "Hey Bella, it's half an hour later and I haven't found the kid yet. Don't want to worry you any more than you already are, but I'm trying to keep you in the loop. Sure wish you'd pick up, but you probably turned in early, at least I hope so. (*Little did he know.*) If I don't find the kid in another half hour, I'm going to call the cops."

Oh dear Lord. Where was Chris? Why does everything just keep getting worse?

9:06 PM: "Hi Bella, I've got someone here who wants to talk to you."

"Hi Auntie Bella, it's Chris. I'm okay, but my chest hurts like a son-of-a-you-know-what. Uncle Mike's taking me to the ER. What I did was pretty lame, huh? Love you."

Thank you, thank you. When Chris gets home I'm going to hug his neck—if I don't wring it first.

11:20 PM: "Hi Bella, we found a 24-hour urgent care and, according to the doc, Chris's ribs are only bruised. He taped them up and released him with some pain meds. We're going to find a motel and get some shut-eye. Depending on how Chris is doing, we'll start in the morning, or stay an extra day. Are you okay? Now I'm worried about you. Call me."

Bruised only—another reason to be thankful. And urgent care would be cheaper than an ER. Good thinking, Mike.

12:12 AM: "Hey Bella, were at a Budgeteer. Noisy but cheap. Give me a call on the cell when you get this, no matter what time, because you're seriously starting to worry me."

Okay, time to call Mike and tell him what I'm up to.

As I pressed send to return Mike's last call, I realized something had changed. A current of alarm shot up my spine, and I snapped the phone shut. Two large feet, presumably male and shod in hi-tops with orange Day-Glo laces, stood in front of my stall. "Hey," I said, "what do you want?" The feet stayed put. "If you have to go, use the men's." Maybe it was still closed due to the baggie in the toilet. "There are plenty of other stalls."

No response. The feet took a half-step forward and the door handle jiggled. "If you don't stop right now, I'll call 911 and scream my lungs out," I yelled. The feet turned and thudded from the bathroom, but not before the person they belonged to snapped the lights off.

Damn and double damn. The face of my cell phone gave off some light, but the space beyond loomed like a black hole. Shaken and sweaty, I sat on the stool a few minutes, debating my options. Maybe someone else would come in; no one did. I could call 911, but I'd blow my cover, and I might be dealing only with a prankster.

Finally I reached a compromise with myself, put 911 on speed dial and sprinted back toward the tent. I didn't get far. A crowd now stood near where the two men had been talking. Several of them had flashlights and I heard sirens in the distance. I ran toward them, grabbed someone's light to the sound of an indignant cry, and shoved my way through the mass of humanity around a man on the ground. I dropped on all fours, aware of the unmistakable smell of feces. Ben must be sick. "Ben? Are you okay?"

What a stupid question. The reporter lay there, twisted into a position no living person could assume. A huge wound covered his temple. Nearby lay a broken bottle, half out of its wrinkled paper bag.

30

I remember dropping the light and not much after that. I screamed and the voice that emerged belonged to a stranger. The world morphed into a blank white screen.

When I came to, I heard Marcus say the bottle belonged to Honker. Sheriff's detectives arrived, including Ryan Scully, whose neck I hugged in a most unprofessional way. He didn't object.

While the forensics people did their thing, I gave the detectives my preliminary statement. I confessed that Ben and I were there undercover for the paper, because I couldn't think of a lie they'd believe. I told them about the man in the bathroom with the Day-Glo laces. They speculated his presence was due to confusion over the closure of the men's.

Too numb to argue, I told them about Ben and the angry, heavyset man standing in the shadows of the woman's bunkhouse. They asked if it was Marcus and I answered "Too big." I then described this man, who'd been sitting by the fire when we first arrived. They agreed it seemed likely he was an informant Ben had arranged to meet, but were doubtful he'd killed the reporter.

They drove me home afterward. On the way, I recalled one more thing: Walter standing amongst the gawkers outside the tent before the detectives arrived. Something about his appearance disturbed me, but I couldn't think what. It had been a long, horrible night and I couldn't dredge it up. We agreed that I would make another statement after I'd had a chance to think about the night's events. They were very kind.

* * * * *

Wednesday, January 21st, 10:55 AM

"How could you let this happen?" Amy paced the floor in front of her desk, lifting her glasses to wipe away a tear with a coffee-stained paper napkin. She'd already plowed through a box of Kleenex. She cried at the drop of a hankie and I wasn't sure whether the tears were for Ben, or to express her anger at me. Probably both.

"Amy," I said, trying to keep a lid on my temper, "I know you need someone to blame, but I'm not that person. I could not have prevented Ben's murder." Amy could be unkind at times, but never unfair. Until now.

"What about that guy whose liquor bottle was used to whack Ben?"

"Honker? He gave his statement last night, and several guests saw a bottle in a bag on the floor next to his bed. Anyone could have picked it up. I doubt he's a serious suspect. No apparent motive."

"'Apparent' being the operative word."

"I guess." I rested my elbow on her desk and kneaded my forehead with my finger tips. I'd slept the sleep of the dead for four hours thanks to chemical help, the effects still lingered and I needed to be home in bed.

She stopped mid-pace and gave me a squinty-eyed stare. "Well, how did he seem to you? Nervous? Distracted?"

"Are you asking, did he see this coming?"

"Exactly."

I thought a moment. "Well, he did seem distracted, fearful even. I put it down to the crappy nature of this assignment. He had an earlier altercation with Marcus, and Marcus decked him."

Amy sank back into her chair. "You're kidding? What about?"

I explained about faking pinkeye so I could keep my sunglasses on and Ben's overreaction to the term, "Junior." "Not only that, I'm sure Jeremy recognized him, though Ben denied it."

"So if we leave out Honker, and I'm not saying we should, either Marcus or Jeremy—or both—had some reason to murder Ben."

"The man I saw talking to Ben by the bunkhouse was heavier than Marcus."

She eyed me skeptically, her focus still on Ben. "The bastard sure did a good job of making himself popular in the few hours he spent there."

"That's true, Amy. But you sent us on a fool's errand with a high probability of failure."

Amy flinched but again said nothing. Someone tapped on the glass wall. I turned and saw Eli Schwab, our accountant, making frantic "come here" gestures to Amy. His face was bright pink. She waved him off and turned back to me.

"Did the two men see you?"

"I think so. They stepped back into the shadows as I passed."

"And this was what time?"

"A little after two."

"You think maybe he met an informant, someone he didn't tell you about?"

"Knowing Ben, that's exactly what he did. I heard two male voices, but not what they said."

"Not one single word? Think Bella, think."

I tried, but I was too rattled. "Well, the other man sounded angry."

"Angry how? What did he say?"

Again I wracked my brain. *Something.* I slammed my hands on her desk. "I don't remember."

Amy sighed. "Okay, maybe you'll think of it later. Let's leave the angry, heavyset man aside for the moment and try a different tack. Ben is—was—an investigative reporter. He dealt in information. Ben had something he wanted to either get from, or give to, Marcus, Jeremy or the other man. Does that make sense?"

"Sort of. Ben and Jeremy were both at Saint Pat's New Year's Eve. But if Ben recognized Jeremy that night, would he have agreed to this assignment?"

Amy cocked her head, thinking. "Maybe he didn't see him. Anything else from last night?"

I thought for a moment. "Well, earlier in the tent, he was writing in his notebook, and he didn't want me to see. Could have been a list of questions or observations, or his grocery list for all I know."

Eli appeared at the window again. His face now resembled a boiled beet. Amy ignored him, and he went away.

"How long were you in the bathroom?"

"Maybe ten minutes. When I came out Ben lay on the ground by the woman's bunkhouse." I grabbed the desk, feeling the room swim.

"Did you grab Ben's notebook before the law arrived?"

"Of course not. I was out cold and besides, I wouldn't disturb a crime scene."

"Never mind your scruples, this is the media business. That notebook undoubtedly has information compromising to the paper, maybe even evidence of Ben's plagiarism, and who knows what else?" She dropped her head into her hands for a moment, then looked at me. "You would have nabbed it if you were conscious, right?"

I sighed. "Right."

"Now law enforcement has the notebook and we're not likely to get it back for a while, if ever," she said, reaching for the phone and punching numbers. She grabbed the pencil once again and tapped it against the desk as she talked. "Detective Scully? Amy Goodheart from the *Chronicle*." Pause. "Yes, yes, I understand you're too busy for an interview, but we're missing Ben Adams' notebook, which has notes for stories in progress. We need it back ASAP." Pause. "Really? Thanks, anyway." She thudded the receiver back into the cradle. "They don't have it."

"Maybe saying that was the easiest way to get rid of you."

"Good point, but I don't believe it." Amy's mouth twitched; I took it for a smile. More pencil tapping. *Rat-a-tat. Rat-a-tat.* "Where's the notebook?"

"Still at the scene?"

"Exactly. I want you to go out there and find it."

I'd rather be boiled in hot oil. "Amy, that's impossible. If the detectives didn't find it, how can I?"

"You have to try."

"No, I don't, even if you fire me."

"I won't fire you, Bella. Who would I turn to if you weren't here?"

Right. Who'd do your dirty work?

She pressed her lips together to stem tears that I suspected of being spawned by a crocodile. "Do it for me, Bella. Please. Because if we can't find out what Ben was up to, I am well and truly screwed as far as this job goes."

Amy's job was her life. She sailed through that life dumping her messes overboard, expecting other people to jump in and clean them up. Mostly me. I hauled myself to my feet, overwhelmed with weariness. "I'll think about it."

Of course she took that as a yes.

Okay, Bella, you did it again, let yourself be conned. I'd almost escaped out the door when another thought erupted from the bad-idea factory that passed for her brain. "What does Mike say about this?"

What would he say?

Early this morning I'd finally reached him in San Jose, and told my very sleepy husband a half-truth: I'd been on special assignment and would fill in the details later. Chris was resting comfortably and I ended the call quickly, not mentioning Ben's murder. Mike could do nothing from there, and he had enough on his plate with Chris's problems. I still worried about the effect of cumulative stress on his heart.

"Uh, I haven't told Mike."

"What do you mean, haven't told him?"

"He's in San Jose. For a conference of cold case detectives." That was in Sacramento and not until next week, but she didn't know that.

The explanation seemed to satisfy her and I hoped she wouldn't check on the conference. I took another step and almost collided with Eli Schwab. "Amy, can you wrap this up, and give us a hand out here? Marcus Daniels is in the lobby, threatening suit, and I've fielded sixteen calls in the last half hour. There's just so much I can do to put out these fires." The accountant glared at me like we all knew who had fanned the flames.

Eli was right, the lobby was a zoo. Marcus had disappeared into one of the inner offices, but local media, thrilled with a chance to dig dirt on the *Chronicle*, had pounced on the story like vultures on a carcass. Even the beleaguered *Los Angeles Times* sent reporters to smear the *Chronicle's* reputation all over its front pages.

Stepping outside into fresh air, I took stock: the rehab job with Jeremy was in the tank, nothing else on the horizon work-wise, I'd best accept Amy's assignment from hell. The paper needed that notebook, and I needed their paycheck.

* * * * *

Wednesday, January 21ˢᵗ, 3:05 PM

I skipped lunch to take care of a looming crisis on the obit-uary desk and drove thirty minutes from the newspaper office to the ranch outside Cuyamaca Beach with only a thick knot of anxiety filling my stomach. How would I go about looking for the notebook? What would I say to Marcus, or God forbid, Jeremy that would gain me access to the property? They'd probably run me off with a shotgun.

A half mile south of the pier, I crunched a right off Highway One onto the ranch's gravel drive. I passed the fire pit, now nothing but dead ash in the thin mid-afternoon light. How different the place looked today, another hard-scrabble ranch common as sand on the Central Coast: barns and outbuildings that predated the New Deal, equipment whose sole function was to collect rust, a vintage John Deere presiding over a fallow field.

The absence of people contributed to the dust-bowl aura. Had the murder driven away guests? Or had they been trundled off by county officials?

I stopped the Subaru in the sparse patch of gravel that passed for a parking lot. Where to start? The overflow area seemed as good as any. The tents had disappeared into the night, replaced by yellow crime-scene tape. If there'd been a notebook left behind, law enforcement would have noticed.

Or not. Stranger things had happened, and strange was the only thing I could count on.

Eyes fixed on the ground, I started toward the back of the women's bunkhouse, thinking the notebook might be there. About halfway, I looked up and saw Walter approaching, a sad smile on his round face. "Hey Bella, I'm so glad you came to visit me." He stretched his arms out. "I could use a hug."

"Me too," I said folding my arms around him and squeezing tight. He smelled of a fresh shower.

"Where is everyone?" I asked.

"Well, Marcus took Honker to the sheriff's office for another little talk." He inspected a non-existent spot on his spotless yellow and blue checked shirt. He'd combed his hair and slicked it down. Dockers puddling over his shoes provided the only off note.

"Anything new on that front?" I asked, and then, "Never mind," when I saw Walter's frown at the use of the idiomatic phrase. Most likely he wouldn't know anyway. Once again he inspected his shirt.

"Your shirt's fine, Walter. In fact, you look absolutely spiffy. Let me shorten those pants for you the next time I do mending."

He beamed. "Thank you, Bella. I'm not good at sewing." Interesting that he didn't stutter today.

I looked around at the deserted yard. Was anyone in charge? "Where's Jeremy?"

He jerked a curved thumb toward the house set on a rise beyond the overflow area and creek. "Fixing up his place. Want to see it?"

"Uh no, that's okay." Jeremy—and his house—were the last things I wanted to encounter today. Would having a murder on the property hinder the ranch's ability to get a contractor's loan? It certainly wouldn't help, but that was not my problem.

"Walter," I said, trying to be clear and choosing my words carefully, "Did you by any chance find a notebook after everyone left last night?"

"Sure," he said. "I was going to give it to you, but I thought you'd lose it."

Wow. Could it really be this easy? "Tell me you didn't go into the tent after it."

"I didn't go into the tent after it," he repeated, and smiled, letting me in on the joke. "I found it on that bench by the women's bunkhouse."

I didn't know the bench, not that it mattered. "And you hid it?"

"Sure, in a secret place. Want to see my room?"

I looked around. Still no sign of another human. "You bet."

I followed Walter into the men's quarters, past rows of di-sheveled bunk beds, possessions left behind and other signs of *inhabitus interruptus.* "Where are all the guests?"

"The sheriffs said everyone out, don't come back 'til they say to."

"That's awful. Where would they go?"

Walter shook his head like it was too much to think about. He led me out of the common sleeping room into other, smaller quarters, an apartment with two bedrooms, one door of which was closed. The bedrooms were connected by a bath. A hall led to the small living room we stood in now, and I could see a dining and kitchen area to the left. Cozy. He pointed with pride to the bedroom with the open door. "That's mine."

I stepped across the threshold into a narrow room with a single bed, its brown corded spread stretched across the mattress with military precision. Posters of opera greats such as Pavarotti, Beverly Sills, even contralto Marian Anderson singing at the Lin-coln Memorial in 1939, almost hid the walls. "Very nice, Walter. How did you get into opera?"

He grinned his pleasure at the compliment. "My mom. She's dead."

"I'm sorry."

He inspected the trousers spilling over shoes that looked too big for his small body. Talking about his mom must be hard. "Marcus sleeps in the other room, the one with the door closed. He keeps it locked."

"Why is that?"

"To keep people out." Obviously uncomfortable at saying more, he pointed toward the living area. "Sometimes when

Marcus has a headache, we eat in there and watch cops shows afterward. That's special."

"I'm sure it is. Marcus had a headache New Year's Eve. What gives him headaches?"

He shook his head. "Dunno. They're worse lately."

"That's too bad. Do you know why?"

"Nooo," he said, drawing the word out in a way that made me think he might.

"I'll bet Jeremy is a big help when Marcus isn't feeling well," I prompted. "Where does he sleep?"

He shrugged. "Here and there, more in the old house now. Sometimes he's not around."

Of course. Despite all his protests to me about finding a soul mate, Jeremy probably had a girlfriend. I glanced at the clock on Walter's bureau, alarmed at the time. Mike and Chris were due home around three and it was past that now. "Walter, I have to go. Can you give me the notebook, please?"

He reached under his mattress and drew out Ben's familiar dog-eared tablet, which looked pretty good for what it had been through. The sight of it sent a shiver up my spine, but I held out my hand, "Give it to me please."

"Sure, Bella."

I resisted the urge to ruffle the sandy hair that someone, probably Marcus, had cut into a perfect bowl shape.

As I turned to go, Walter asked, "Can I have a ride to Saint Pat's? The early bird bingo game starts at five and I need to set up tables." He grinned. "Father Burton gives me an extra card for that."

Nice of him. "Happy to have the company," I said.

He reached into the top drawer of his bureau, pulled out a twenty and slid it into a soft cowhide wallet. "Christmas gift. From Jeremy," he said, caressing the wallet before stuffing it into his back pocket.

Expensive gifts aside, I wondered about his relationship with Jeremy. Jeremy claimed he brought Walter with him thirty years ago. A long time. I wondered if that was the straight story and what might have been edited out. The subject of another conversation with Walter. Or maybe Marcus, if he'd speak to me.

"Walter, before we go, I need to use the bathroom. That okay?"

"Sure," he said, pointing to the bath between the bedrooms. I headed that way, taking both my purse and the notebook.

I stood at the sink, washing my hands. I looked at myself in the medicine cabinet mirror. An old woman stared back at me, one who'd had too much stress and too little sleep.

The cabinet door stood partially ajar. Like many people, I can't resist the urge to see what people keep in their cabinets. I opened the door and checked the well-stocked shelves. All the usual stuff, toothpaste, hairdressing and the like. The top shelf held two prescription bottles, both for Marcus Daniels. One was for 800 mg of Ibuprofen, presumably for his headaches. The other was for Valium, with several refills. My heart knocked against my ribs. They'd found Valium in Loreli's body. But that was five years ago. Should I take the bottle? Better not. If Marcus missed it, Walter would remember I'd used the bathroom.

I grabbed the notebook, my purse and opened the door. "Let's go, Walter." I took a step and stopped, my hand still on the knob, at a loss for words. Jeremy stood before me; Walter had disappeared. "Hey, how are you?"

"More to the point, Bella, how are you?" He eyed the notebook. "Walter tells me he gave it to you and that it belongs to your dead reporter friend."

Not good. "Where's Walter?"

"Outside, waiting for you." He held out his hand. "I think since he found it on our property, you should give it to us so we can turn it over to the sheriff's office."

I dropped the notebook into my purse. "Sorry Jeremy, I'm here on assignment for the *Chronicle*. Since Ben worked for them, the notebook's ours." I didn't know if that was true or not, but it sounded good.

Jeremy stood for a long moment staring at me. Then he turned and strode toward the door.

* * * * *

Soon we were rocketing west along Los Lobos Road toward home. The conversation with Jeremy had shifted my priorities. I had the notebook, it was safe and Amy would have to wait. I needed to get Walter to the church and to see with my own eyes that Mike and Chris were okay.

Walter fiddled with the radio dial, reminding me of Chris. "Who'll drive you home after bingo?" I asked.

"No worries, I always get a ride," he said. "I can take care of my self."

"I hope so," I said. "I want to take you out for coffee soon," I said.

"I'd rather have pizza."

"Okay, pizza it is. Next week sometime?"

"Sure. It's a date, Bella." He smiled.

Walter had tuned to the public radio station and the sound of some aria I didn't recognize filled the car. He crossed one leg over the other and his pant leg caught in the top of his socks, exposing his shoes. Sneakers.

Big sneakers.

Big, black, high-top, sneakers with Day-Glo laces!

The Subaru swerved as though on its own, and he grabbed the dash. "Watch it, Bella."

"Sorry," I said, "I need to ask you something."

He turned, worried at my tone.

"Was..." I heaved a deep breath, "...that you in front of my bathroom stall last night?"

The engine knocked, the tires thumped and the soprano screeched while I waited for an answer. I reached over and snapped the radio off. *"Was it?"*

Walter sat busily arranging his pant legs over the sneakers. "I..I just wanted to p...protect you. That's all." His stutter had returned.

"Protect me?" My hand hit the steering wheel. Walter jumped as though he'd been slapped. "You scared the heart out of me. Why didn't you say something?"

"I d...d...don't know," he whimpered, close to tears.

I needed to back off, but I couldn't. "Why did you turn off the lights and leave me in the dark?"

"To hide you from the b...bad people, just like I hid the notebook."

I pulled over to the curb, my knees knocking like pins whacked by a bowling ball. "What bad people?"

Silence, then, "I...I don't know."

"Walter, I think you do."

A plane droned overhead while I waited for an answer. "May... maybe." He pulled at the front of his shirt. "Please don't ask. Please, I just *can't*."

Okay, Bella, deep breath. This isn't working. We'd talk again in a day or two. He was either afraid, or protecting someone, or both. But if he knew something, he could be in danger.

I decided to change tack. "It's okay not to tell me *why* you protected me, but please tell me *how*."

"I was very smart," he said.

"I'm sure you were."

We sat there by the side of the road in the thin winter sunlight and Walter relayed an improbable, but sadly true, series of events: how he'd driven Marcus home early New Year's Eve because the older man had a headache. How he'd doubled back to the Community Center later because he'd seen our two vehicles, knew I'd be driving home alone and followed me. How he decided to tail me to the Small Wilderness preserve after I'd stopped at the church that Friday a week later. "Okay, I understand, I guess, but why did you leave the ski mask on my bike seat?"

"So you'd know it was me and wouldn't be scared."

"Except I didn't know you owned a ski mask."

"I...I didn't think of that."

"There's a lot you didn't think of, Walter. You can't just run around protecting people who may not need, or want, it." I started the car. "It's going to take me a while to get over this. Actions have consequences."

"Consequences—like you're not taking me out for pizza, and you're not going to fix my pants?" he said, his eyes brimming over.

"You've heard that word before, haven't you?"

He nodded, wiping his eyes with the backs of his hands. "From Marcus."

I couldn't help smiling. "Okay, how about next Tuesday for pizza? Bring your pants with you."

"Sure, Bella. I always wear pants."

"I mean the ones for me to shorten."

"I know that, Bella."

My cell chirped. Mike. Where were our pain meds, Chris needed something stronger, and when was I getting home?

"Ten minutes," I said, glancing at the young man next to me. "I'm dropping Walter at Saint Pat's."

After seeing him safely to the church, I drove alone with my thoughts the half mile west toward home. I glanced at the notebook, now on the seat next to me. It sang a siren's song of "Look inside me, take just a peek." And I would have, if I'd had gloves to protect any fingerprints. A deep sigh didn't relieve my frustration. The truth was, I had to turn it over to the sheriff's department. The notebook was evidence, and if I gave it to Amy, we'd be in deep doo-doo.

Could things get worse?

31

Things could indeed get worse, and did. The three of us stood in the kitchen, like politicians trying to find common ground. Mike's duffel sat at his feet. Chris had arrived barehanded, having lost his backpack as well as his cell phone, skateboard and money to the punks who assaulted him.

I studied the men in my life, trying to decide who looked worse: Chris, with filthy clothes, greasy hair and three days worth of chin whiskers, holding himself with infinite care to protect his taped ribs. Or Mike, way too pale, and obviously sleep-deprived. A dog could gnaw on the tension between them. I was hoping they'd have the guy version of a heart-to-heart on the ride home, so Mike would understand why Chris had run away.

That didn't happen, so where did we go from here?

Only Sam seemed unaffected, pressing as close to Chris's legs as he could possibly get. My nephew rewarded him with absent minded pats.

When the silence got too thick, Chris ambled over to the refrigerator and began to rummage through it while I busied myself with the tea kettle. Extra strength Earl Grey with three sugars was called for.

"Is feeding your face all you can do?" Mike asked.

Chris paused, a chicken leg halfway to his mouth. "Like, what should I do?"

"Give us some answers for one. Like where'd you get the money for your little misadventure? Dealing drugs?"

Chris backed up, stumbling over Mike's duffel. He gave it a savage kick and tossed the chicken leg on the floor. Sam pounced, unable to believe his good luck. Two red spots blossomed on Chris's cheeks. "Is that what you think? That I'm into drugs?"

Enough already. "Wait a minute, you two. We need to discuss this like rational adults."

Mike ignored me. "What else am I supposed to think? When I was a cop, kids plus money equaled drugs."

Chris's eyes shot hot sparks. "You are, like, so lame."

Mike said nothing. He walked over to the message center, and picked up the phone. He glanced at the small picture of Ethan, his dead son. Was he thinking that Ethan would have been less trouble than my nephew? I'd seen him do that before in our sometimes-rocky relationship with Chris. I'm sure the action wasn't lost on my nephew.

I started to interfere again, then thought: No, let them play this out.

Mike thrust the cordless phone at Chris, who had grabbed another chicken leg from the refrigerator. "Here, call your folks."

Chris took a bite and chewed slowly. "Later."

Mike grabbed the second leg, tossed it to Sam and shoved the phone into Chris's hand. "Now."

"Okay, okay. I get it."

I sucked in my breath as Mike raised a hand toward Chris, then lowered it. Chris retreated to the hall, punching numbers into the phone.

The teakettle shrieked. I turned off the burner and poured water over the leaves, releasing the fragrant aroma of Earl Grey. So distraught was I that I jumped when Chris thrust the phone at me. "They want to talk to you."

Swell. I held the phone between thumb and forefinger. "Hello?"

"What have you heathens done to our baby?" Janet screamed into my ear.

Baby? I held the phone away and stared at it. Better choose my words carefully. "Look, Janet, as they say in the media, mistakes were made. Chris has some growing up to do, but I'm sure he's learned a lot from this experience."

"And what have you learned, eh Bella?" Ed, my former brother-in-law, chimed in on an extension.

"Pipe down both of you, and listen."

Janet, never one to allow facts to get in the way of a good rant, bellowed, "We're going to sue."

I thought about Marcus's threatened suit against the paper, and perhaps against me. They'd have to stand in line. "What for?"

"Defamation of character, for starters."

Defamation of character? Janet was on shaky ground with her comprehension of legal terms. Last I heard that referred to statements that harmed someone's reputation.

"...alienation of affects..."

Affects?

...and, and, contributing to the delinquency of a minor," she finished with a flourish.

"Chris is eighteen, not a minor," I pointed out.

"We'll think of something," she countered.

"Look, there's nothing to be gained by shouting at each other over the phone. Why don't you two take a few days off and fly out here? You can see for yourselves that our home provides a stable environment and get out of the snow and ice for a while."

"Bella, what do you not get about this? We're through with Chris. Done. Finished. *Kaput.* Besides, we can't take time off. We have to move the two orphans back to the foster home."

"The kids you just took in and set up in Chris's room?"

"We put them in the basement. I set up my sewing in Chris's old room."

"Nice." Would she catch the irony? *Silly me.*

"You wouldn't believe what we've gone through. The music blares up through the heating vents all night long, they eat me out of house and home, and...and, their mouths are worse than Chris's. That's saying a lot."

"Goodbye, Janet." I pressed end.

"Told you," Chris said over his shoulder as he made for the back door. Sam, not to be left behind, followed.

"I need sleep," Mike said and headed for our bedroom. So much for the long-delayed conversation about my secret life of the last three days. *Thank God.*

32

Mike was out two minutes after his head hit the pillow. I pulled a blanket over him and followed Chris to his hidey-hole in the barn. I entered the area Mike had walled off for him thinking about Janet's two orphans in their basement, now forced back into foster care. Had we done right by Chris allowing him to sleep out here? Maybe he'd feel more like part of the family if he slept inside.

"Knock, knock," I said, and then louder, "Knock, knock."

Chris removed his ear buds, sat up and leaned on his elbows. "Hey, how you doin'?" The hard sounds of rock blasted through the tiny devices. No opera for him, and why should there be? He was his own person, as was Walter. His eyes looked red and swollen. The exchange with Mike had hurt him.

"I've been better," I admitted.

"Bummer. Anything I can do?"

I started to give the standard "No, thanks," and stopped. "There is one thing that would make me feel better."

"What?"

"Tell me where you got the money."

He had the grace to smile. "I, like, walked into that one."

"Well?..."

He stared up at the Jimmy Hendrix poster, one of his retro favorites, on the wall beside the futon. "It's complicated."

"Isn't everything? I've got all day."

"Well, you know my mom..."

"I met her once or twice."

He brushed aside my feeble attempt at humor. "You know what I mean. She opened a college fund when I started kindergarten. Gave me the passbook. Like, it was in both our names." He swallowed hard. "After she...died, I hid the passbook so you-know-who wouldn't get her mitts on it." He stopped and gulped several times.

I touched his arm. "It's okay."

"When I decided to leave Cleveland, I got a copy of mom's death certificate, faked an ID showing I was already eighteen, and closed the account." The song finished and his deep, shuddering sigh took its place. "Now she's gone, and the money is too. She must think I'm a real loser."

I pointed to a spot beside him. Sam had already staked out his place at the end of the bed. "May I?"

Chris scooted his back against the wall. "Sure."

I sat down, reached over and smoothed his hair. He let me. "In the first place, you're too young to be a loser. You can't claim loser status until you're at least my age."

"I've made some mistakes," he said, and his voice caught.

"Some doozies," I admitted. "Not to preach"—though of course that's exactly what I was doing—"but if you learn from them, then they don't count."

He considered that. "Still, she must hate me."

"She doesn't Chris, motherhood doesn't work that way."

"How would you know about motherhood?"

"Touché. But I know Bea and she would never hate you."

"Now everything's gone," he said, and sighed deeply.

"No it isn't, Chris. Money's important, but it isn't everything. You were old enough when she died to remember her. I'll bet you've got some great stories."

He nodded, and made a strangled sound.

I smoothed a wrinkle in the beige corded bedspread. "Tell me one."

His eyes danced in the light of memory. "When I was little she always took me to the park so I could play on the slide. Used to scare the crap out of her. You know she was afraid of heights?"

"Yeah, I remember. That didn't stop her from taunting me to jump off the garage roof with an umbrella. I broke my arm that time. It still aches on rainy days."

"Bummer."

"Well, one time at a new park, she decides the slide is too high for me and she'll, like, go down with me. To protect me, you know?"

"Makes sense."

"Not really. She gets up to the top and just freaks. Can't put even one leg on the slide, much less her butt."

I smiled at the picture. Bea and I were an awkward pair. My dad used to call us "The Graces." "What'd you do?"

"We stood there for, like, maybe five minutes. Finally, we had to back down the steps, one at a time. I had to go first and hold onto her. She moaned the whole way down with at least ten kids lined up behind us." He rolled his eyes. "Ohmigod, it was *so* embarrassing."

"But it's not now?"

He considered. "Now it's funny."

"See, it's become a good memory, and that's better than money."

"I'd rather have the money."

"You won't always feel that way." I looked around the room, at the tangle of clothes on the chair, the posters and thrift-store MP3 player, acquired since he got here. "Do you have a picture of your mom?"

He shook his head. "Naw, Janet got rid of all those."

"Would you like one? I have a bunch."

His eyes brightened. "Awesome."

"There's something else you can do for me."

"What?"

"Tell your story to Uncle Mike."

"About the slide?"

"No, the money."

"Why waste my time?" Chris flopped over and turned his face to the wall. "He's such a dick."

33

Thursday, January 22nd, 5:37 PM

Chris and Mike had both zonked for the night. I gladly left them to their slumbers, and after grabbing a bite to eat, headed for the West Wing. I sat at my desk in the old mill and listened to the wind howling and rain hissing against the sliding door like an angry cat. We needed rain, but why tonight, when so much misery abounded? I shivered, pulled my cardigan around me, and cranked up the dial on the wall heater next to the desk.

Ben's notebook, waiting to divulge its secrets, stared back at me from its resting place beside my computer keyboard.

Feeling the cell vibrate in my sweater pocket, I pulled it out and checked its lighted face: another message, the sixth, from Amy. She'd have to wait, and she would, I hoped, until morning, and not show up at my door. I wanted to gather a few bread crumbs to toss her way before Mike delivered the notebook to the sheriff's department.

Too bad he didn't know that yet. What a conversation awaited us in the morning.

I donned light cotton cosmetic gloves Amy had given me. I'd never found a use for them until now. Feeling curious eyes burning into the back of my neck, I turned to face my old friend and confidant, Emily Divina. "My, my, you're looking fetching tonight." And she was, the lamp's soft glow softening her stern countenance and adding sparkle to her eyes, a kind of reverse "Picture of Dorian Gray" effect.

"Emily, here we are again, eh?" If not breaking the rules then at least bending them around the edges, a habit left from convent life with its many rules begging to be bent.

I grabbed the notebook by the edges in order to preserve any fingerprints not already destroyed by careless handling. A purple rubber band held the old pages together. I pulled the desk lamp closer; Ben had filled almost three quarters of the current page. My heart beat a little faster, and the rain seemed to pound a little harder, as I read.

Halfway through, I set the notebook down, again handling only the edges. Below the date and time, meticulously noted, were ruminations on what we'd already discussed: drinking from wrinkled paper bags by some guests, what appeared to be midnight requisitioning of the fire pit, the rundown condition of the buildings, brief profiles of two anonymous guests I recognized as Honker and Captain.

It seemed like pretty mundane stuff. Why wouldn't he share it with me? I read on, the last paragraph answering my question: an observation that Amy's "spy" continued to dog his every step. My hackles rose.

"Okay Emily, that explains it."

I removed the band and thumbed through the older pages. On each of them Ben had noted the date and time. Meticulous fellow. Too bad he wasn't so picky when it came to scruples. He'd started this notebook in early November when he'd been working on a story detailing the misdeeds of a city council member. He'd cited several websites, and since Amy suspected him of cut-and-paste journalism, I noted the web addresses.

I'd joked about maybe the book containing Ben's grocery list, and in a couple of cases that proved to be true, again with the time and date duly noted.

The page for December 31st at 10:30 AM looked like more of the same at first glance: three phone numbers in a column, and a fourth scribbled within parentheses below the third.

Written below that and circled several times was a single name.

My heart pounded in rhythm to the rain hitting the window. I sat a long time listening to the rain, staring at the numbers, trying to quiet my mind. The first and fourth number had unfamiliar prefixes, cell phones perhaps. I concentrated on the first number, which looked familiar. On a hunch, I grabbed my own cell and checked its directory to confirm my suspicions. The number was Magda's. Thank goodness I hadn't deleted it.

Feeling the familiar sensation of eyes watching me, I turned to Emily. "What made the schmuck think he could get away with this?"

In a cold sweat of realization, I pawed around for the phone book, first on the jumble of my desk, and then in the magazine rack, finally dragging it out from under a jumble of yarns in my knitting basket. The second number was Dominic's at Sereno Cellars, the one I'd made the condolence call to New Year's night. The third number was a shocker: the Blue Stetson ranch.

Once again I turned to Emily. "Looks like Ben was our blackmailer/extortionist." He must have first called Magda, then Dominic, then Marcus at the Blue Stetson. Was Marcus the killer or had Ben also tried to sell him information about Loreli's murder? And who was the fourth number? I began to dial.

"Hey, Bella."

I jumped, clasping a hand to my chest and dropping the phone. Unless Emily had suddenly developed a deep voice, I had a visitor. Mike stood in the doorway, clad in bathrobe and slippers, hair tousled by sleep. "I think you've got some 'esplaining' to do, Lucy."

Oh dear.

"Couldn't sleep, so I turned on the TV. Your friend Ben's murder is all over the tube, and your name came up as well. What the hell is going on?"

I indicated my reading chair beneath Emily's portrait. "Sit down, Mike. It's a long story."

While he rested his elbow on the chair arm, held his chin in his hand and closed his eyes, I explained about the confidential assignment from Amy, her suspicions about Ben, my new job as research assistant, the long night at the Blue Stetson, Ben's murder, the subsequent fallout at the paper, and how I might not now have a new job, or any job, for that matter.

He drew a long sigh and raised his head. "And here I thought it was something serious." A ghost of a grin played around his mouth, then faded. "Why can't you be straight with me, Bella?"

The words stung and I lashed out like rain against the window. "Well, it's not like you've always been straight with me," I said, thinking of events last summer, and even before we met, when he'd left the Chicago PD under a cloud and hadn't told me until years later, and then, only when he had to.

Mike drew another long sigh and rested his elbows on the chair arms. He brought his hands together in a steeple and talked into them. "I understand why you keep sticking your nose in where it doesn't belong—"

"Wait a minute. I just seem to fall into these things."

"No you don't, you go looking for them. Because you couldn't solve your sister's murder, you feel like you have to keep getting involved in these other ones."

His words shocked me into silence. Could that really be true?

"This time you've really done it, Bella," he continued. "Your job at the paper is probably toast, and the fallout from this debacle will affect mine at the sheriff's office as well. I mean, how can I defend you?" He stopped to gather his thoughts for another fusillade and squinted at me. "Why are you wearing those gloves? Oh dear God, tell me you're not..."

"Mike, you need to see this. This is Ben's notebook. Walter hid it after the murder. I'm using gloves to protect any fingerprints. Come here."

He heaved himself out of the chair, crossed the short distance to my desk, and stood peering over my shoulder. "Look at these phone numbers," I said. "I'm pretty sure Ben was the caller who tried to extort money from Magda and Dominic. The third number is the Blue Stetson. He may have tried to get money from Marcus because—"

He finished my sentence. "Marcus killed Loreli."

"There's something else. When I was at the ranch today, I used Marcus's bathroom and found a prescription for Valium in the medicine chest."

Mike's gray eyes narrowed. "Loreli had Valium in her system."

"If he killed Magda too, what was his motive?" I asked.

"Maybe she found out between the time she left the New Year's Eve benefit and the Polar Bear Dip the next morning that Marcus killed Loreli."

"Ben might have called her back that night and she confronted Marcus. When I talked to her earlier, she was certainly angry and upset enough to do so if she'd learned more."

"Exactly. And despite all his talk about the importance of rescue swimmers at the Polar Bear Dip, Marcus wasn't around New Year's day," Mike said.

"That we know of. Maybe he was out there, waiting for her."

"Good point," Mike said. "We figured out from the video that he and Loreli had problems in their relationship before she went to rehab. And now you saw his Valium. The phone number in the notebook and the video are probably enough circumstantial evidence to bring him in for questioning. I have to take the note-book to the sheriff first thing in the morning."

"I know that, Mike. That's why I showed it to you."

"Good girl. What's the fourth number?"

"I don't know, probably another cell. You can check it out tomorrow."

Mike stayed silent for a while I wondered what would come next. He surprised me by rubbing my shoulders in a husbandly fashion. "What am I going to do with you?"

I pulled away. "Don't go there, Mike. That question fell out of favor about the time Eleanor Roosevelt became first lady."

He grinned. "Touché." He turned my face to his and assumed his familiar "I'm in the mood for love," look. "Time for bed."

I jumped out of the chair and turned to face him. "You've got to be kidding. I haven't had any sleep for two nights and neither have you, and I'm not in the mood."

"I could put you there." He wrapped his arms around me, and as he pulled me close, his eyes found my new (to me) sofa. "We haven't christened that yet."

"It's too small, and besides, I told you I'm not in the—" I tried to say this as he all but smothered me with kisses. He'd brushed his teeth and I knew he'd planned this from the beginning.

I looked over his shoulder and saw Emily staring at us. "Wait." I covered her portrait with an afghan.

* * * * *

Later, when we'd moved to the warmth and expansiveness of our bed, I lay awake listening to Mike sleep. I placed my hand on his bare hip, cool to the touch, marveling at the audacity,

the gall, of feeling desire and making love in the midst of chaos. I guess, like food, passion reminds us that we're still alive.
Lucky us.

* * * * *

The next few days settled into a routine, as though such a
thing were possible, much less normal. Chris told his story to
a chagrined, and I suspect, much relieved, Mike. I hope they'll
both work harder at their relationship. Mike moved Ethan's picture from right next to the phone to the shelf above the message
center, still at eye-level but not quite so accessible, again a gesture not lost on Chris.

Somewhere in the midst of last Tuesday's chaos, I had the
presence of mind to call the school and tell them Chris would
be out all week due to an accident. He didn't get off Scott-free,
however. On Thursday, I drove over and picked up his assignments for the week.

* * * * *

Friday, January 23rd, 4:30 PM
"Hi Bella, I've got news for you," Mike's voice came over the
ether.

"What about?" I sat hunched over the desk phone with purse
and keys in hand, ready to leave the office for the day. It had
been another rugged one, but I was still employed. Amy was apo-
plectic over the notebook going to the sheriff, but she understood I had no choice. Marcus had not been questioned yet, but
I understood it was imminent.

"About the fourth number in Ben's notebook," Mike said. "And this is confidential. It's a throw-away cell."

"Can you trace it?"

"Not easily, but not impossible either. It's a brand sold by Radio Hut."

"Was it bought online?"

"Doubtful. If the phone was purchased for nefarious purposes, the buyer would likely pay cash."

"Or use a stolen credit card online."

"True. But we'll start with the brick and mortar locations and maybe we'll get lucky. Scully wants me to spend the next few days visiting franchises in the area, checking sales records. Maybe a clerk will remember the buyer. If we can pinpoint the location, that narrows the field considerably. Worth a shot."

"Sounds tedious."

"It is, but so's a lot of police work. That's why they pay me, so Scully and the other high-priced dicks can concentrate on the big picture."

"Ryan would take issue with the terms 'high price' and 'dicks.'"

He chuckled. "That's part of the fun. Gotta go, see if Little Mike can handle the shop Monday morning."

"Better have him cover the afternoon as well. Chris's hearing is at two."

"I may not be able to make it."

"Don't even think that, Mike. We're both going."

"Yes, Ma'am."

34

Tuesday, January 27, 7:55 AM

While the kettle chugged its way to a boil, I scurried around the kitchen in my furry slippers adding Irish Breakfast to the already-warmed pot and retrieving my favorite cup from its place in the corner of the cupboard.

On mornings like this, the old furnace didn't quite do its job, but even its wheezings of sporadic warmth provided comfort and solace. I took a moment to be grateful for it, and for one huge obstacle behind us.

Yesterday afternoon the judge let Chris off with stern warning to keep a lid on his temper, write a letter of apology to Miranda and her parents, and sentenced him to a hefty dose of community service, which included working with the homeless.

We could use the help. February, Saint Pat's month, was fast approaching. Besides homeless women, with and without children, local churches like ours also kept intact families. We were seeing more and more of those as families lost their homes in the real estate crunch.

We'd been socked with a double whammy. Besides sheltering more homeless, many parishioners who normally volunteer for a one-night stint had been laid low by a nasty flu bug slinking around the Central Coast. As program coordinator, I had plenty to do, and wouldn't normally be one of the two people who stayed the night with people transported from the county shelter after they had dinner and showers there. My job entailed finding fifty-six willing and physically able volunteers, two a night for the month of February. The quota was difficult to fill under normal circumstances, impossible with parishioners hacking and coughing. Thank God Chris was eighteen and could pinch-hit as a junior member of a two-person team.

I sliced a juicy Cuyamaca orange, grabbed a pumpernickel bagel-half from the toaster and slathered it with butter. Not even waiting to sit down, I sank my teeth sank into the crunchy dough. I let the first salty, buttery morsel slide over my tongue. *Heaven.*

The phone rang. I swallowed, grousing, "Good morning," like it was anything but.

"Good morning, Bella. Did I awaken you?" asked Father Burton.

"No, Father. I've been awake for hours." A small exaggeration. "What's up?"

"We have a small problem."

Oh dear. Father Burton's "small problems" were usually disasters-in-the-making.

"Apparently the toilet in the gym bathroom at Saint Alban's overflowed and the plumber can't get there today because of all the broken pipes in the area."

"I hoped they turned the water off," I said, wondering what this had to do with me. Then it hit me; Saint Alban's had the homeless duty this month. Suddenly the bagel felt like lead in my stomach. "Let me guess, they want us to start our stint a week early."

"It's only for tonight, and I told them you'd have to give the okay. We don't have to do this, Bella."

"Yes, we do. Where else would the homeless stay?" My hackles rose. "It's not like they have a lot of choice in the matter."

"That's for the county to worry about."

"We can manage," I said, wondering, even as I said the words, how we would manage on such short notice. I grabbed my homeless schedule from the bottom of the pile on the kitchen desk. "Let's see, I'll call the main shelter and coordinate with them to bus the clients here instead of Saint Alban's." They wouldn't be happy about using the extra gas but I couldn't help that. Running my finger down the page, I stopped at the names of two of our most enthusiastic and reliable volunteers. "Then I'll call the Jenks. They'll be glad to pinch hit for one night."

"Another small problem," Father said.

I fortified myself with a gulp of Irish Breakfast. "And that would be?"

"I spoke with Don Jenks after mass yesterday. Mary Alyce has the flu."

Crap. At that point, I heard a scratching at the door, familiar, but more intense than usual. Sam had only been out a few minutes, but even that was too much for the old dog.

"There are some rules for tonight I want to go over with you. First of all—"

"Father, someone's at the door. I'll get us some volunteers and check with you later about the rules. Assume we're on for tonight."

I let Sam in, polished off my breakfast and called Anne Swenson at the main shelter to tell her that their staff would have to bus tonight's clients the twelve extra miles to Saint Patrick's and move their cots from Saint Alban's to our parish hall, news she received with unflappable aplomb.

My next calls did not go as well. After working my way down the list, I'd failed to recruit a single volunteer for tonight, much less two.

Unless a pair of angels dropped from the sky, Chris and I would have to take the duty. Knowing he was still on the school bus, I pulled up his number on my cell and relayed the bad news.

"Auntie Bella, this really suc—"

"How many times have I told you—watch the language?"

"Sorry. But it's like, I have to study tonight."

"Chris what just happened yesterday?"

"I got sentenced to 150 hours of community service."

"Exactly. This is chance to reduce that by twelve or thirteen hours."

"Thirteen *hours*? You're sh—kidding me!"

"This is an emergency. We have to be there at seven tonight when the van brings the clients and stay until they're picked up in the morning. Then I'll drive you to school. What time's your exam?"

"Second period."

"Good. You can study on the early shift from ten 'til one AM, then you can sleep until six."

Complete silence then, "That's only five hours. How can I take a chemistry exam on five hours sleep? Can't I just stay in bed until it's time to leave for school?"

"No, we have to make coffee, get everyone up, and put out cereal and fruit for breakfast."

More silence. "You still there?"

"Yeah. Can Edam come over tonight? She's my study partner."

"Edam? I thought that was a cheese," I said without thinking.

"It's a family name," he replied, as though that explained why parents would saddle a kid with that kind of first name. "Can I?"

"The rule is no guests, and that includes Edam. Too much responsibility for the church."

"Geez..." More silence. "What's for dinner?"

Did I just win that one? "How about sub sandwiches?"

"Cool. I'll have meatball. Double provolone, please."

"You got it."

35

Tuesday, January 27th, 8:20 AM

"What's going on?" Mike stood behind me, cell phone in hand. How did we ever function without these things? Instead of his usual gray work uniform, he'd chosen what I think of as a "politician shirt," a blue windowpane-checked number. Also Dockers and his new brogues. He smelled of a tad too much Brut. My new overnight bag swung jauntily from one shoulder.

Unsure of whether to whistle or gape, I opted for the latter. "You got a hot date?"

He grinned. "I wish." He patted the bag. "Okay if I use this? Mine's a wreck."

"I guess. What's going on?"

He waved the phone at me. "I was just talking to Scully. We're leaving for the conference a day early."

"What about the cell phone investigation?"

He waved away my question, saying instead. "We're going to stop on the way up and meet the Salinas detectives over that body discovered there a few weeks ago, the one I told you about?" I nodded and he continued: "The case was a low priority for a while, but suddenly it's hot. They matched his dental records with a dentist here in Tolosa."

"Okay." Quickly I filled him in on Saint Alban's crisis of plumbing. I could tell he was only half listening, but as I explained how Chris and I were taking the duty, a frown crossed his face. "I don't like the idea of you two being alone out there all night, especially so soon after Ben's murder."

My stomach gave a little flutter. He was right. I'd been too frantic with everything else for the thought to even cross my mind. "Mike, it's perfectly safe."

Was it? "After all the clients get there, we don't let anyone else in unless the shelter calls ahead of time. And they leave us a cell phone. We can speed-dial 911 or the shelter if there's an emergency."

"Take Sam with you."

I eyed Sam, obviously more interested in his breakfast than becoming a watchdog. "No canines allowed."

"Well, just be careful." He peered into the fridge. "What's for breakfast?"

"Bacon, eggs, toast. Whatever you want to fix. I have to get dressed for work."

After taking a quick shower, I stood shivering in bra and panties trying to find something suitable to wear to work and comfortable—and warm enough—for tonight. Mike walked in and whistled. "*Hoo-wee.* Scully's outside. Shall I tell him to wait twenty minutes?"

He lunged for me and I gave him a gentle but firm little nudge backward. "You're expected in Salinas at 10:30, remember?"

"You're right." He grinned. "Never hurts to try." We stepped apart, realizing that we wouldn't see each other for several days.

"Didn't we just do this?" I asked, thinking of Mike's trip to San Jose last week, when he brought Chris back. Today was different somehow, we'd left something unsaid, something unfinished, but I wasn't sure what.

"Gotta go." He stepped forward for our hug.

"Wait," I said, remembering the unfinished business. "You didn't answer my question. How can you leave without wrapping up the cell phone investigation?"

He gave me a sheepish grin. "Forgot to tell you. That part of it is finished. Found a guy at the Santa Maria mall late yesterday after Chris's hearing who sold the phone to a guy for cash. The salesman remembered him because when he handed over the money, he saw a scar on his forearm."

Kathy's guy in the bathroom had a similar scar.

At that moment, Ryan honked from the driveway and the bedroom phone rang, a distracting cacophony of sounds. I grabbed the phone: Anne Swenson calling from the shelter with more questions. When we finished our conversation a few minutes later, the detective and Mike were gone.

I thought later that if I hadn't been interrupted by the phone call, I'd have told Mike about Kathy also seeing a scar and things might have been different.

36

Tuesday, January 27ʰ, 6:25 PM

After another exhausting day at *Crisis de Jour*, the staff's name for the *Chronicle*, I stood at the kitchen counter unpacking the bag of subs. It had taken the kid at the deli forever to build them and he'd forgotten Chris's double provolone.

I checked the wall clock. Thirty-five minutes to eat and get to Saint Pat's. I dumped the subs on paper plates and flew around gathering things we'd need for tonight: a sleeping bag, pillow, tooth brushes, tea and a couple of mysteries for me, Chris's book bag so he could study.

The phone rang. "*Hell-o,*" I barked.

"Bella?" The man at the other end sounded distressed. "Are you all right? This is Dominic."

"Dominic, good to hear from you," I said, abashed at my rudeness. "Sorry, but Chris and I have to take homeless duty at seven. Can I call you back later?"

"This will take only a second," he said. "Something's happened that makes it imperative that you look at "Two Years before the Mast.""

Huh? I stared at the phone, feeling both abashed and guilty. "I haven't had a chance, but I'll take it with me tonight. I'll have some free time after our clients go to bed."

"Excellent," he said, "let's talk after you do." He rang off, and I stood gaping at the receiver, wondering what that was all about.

At that moment, Chris came in from the barn, where he'd been changing clothes. Like me, he'd opted for warm and comfortable, a black T-shirt, gray around edges from repeated washings, a frayed flannel shirt, Levis and boots. I pointed to the jumble on the floor and asked him to pack the car. He eyed the sub. "Can't I eat first?"

"Yeah, but make it snappy. We only have about thirty minutes." He wolfed down the sandwich, reminding me of Sam, and didn't seem to notice the dearth of cheese.

While he ate, I fed Sam and put him in the barn for the night. Sorry, boy," I said to him in response to his hangdog look at the prospect of an evening all by his lonesome.

Back in the kitchen, I pointed to Chris's backpack. "Do you have everything you need to study tonight, and a change of clothes for tomorrow?"

Chris looked at me, eyes wide, cheeks pouched out like a chipmunk. He swallowed hard. "Crap. Edam has the study guides. You'll have to drive me over to pick them up in Mariposa Bay."

I fought the urge to throw something at the wall. "Chris, how could you? There's no time for that. Could she bring them to the church?"

"She's not allowed to drive on weekday nights."

"Swell. What's the solution to this problem?"

He thought for all of a nanosecond. "I could drive Uncle Mike's truck over to pick up the study guides and come to the church later."

I eyed the keys hanging on a hook by the back door. Did I have a choice?

* * * * *

Tuesday, January 27ʰ, 6:57 PM

I pulled into the parking lot on the far side of the church, surprised to find it empty. Even though I'd arrived a few minutes early, I expected the shelter van to be there ahead of me.

I turned off the engine and waited for the Subaru to calm itself down. Twelve hours until I sat in this seat again, exhausted, but needing to rush home, shower, feed Sam and let him out and arrive at the paper by 9:30 AM.

Stop it Bella, at least you have a home to go to.

I was already exhausted, and if the plumbing at Saint Alban's wasn't fixed by tomorrow night, this would be just a warm-up. Too bad Mike wasn't around, he could be pressed into service. Maybe Chris would take one more night. I wouldn't be up to another one after working all day. In a pinch, Father could take the duty himself.

Right.

Best not to over-think it. Right now I just had to put one foot in front of the other for the next twelve hours. I opened the hatchback, retrieved the box with our sleeping gear and followed the path that led past the church to the parish hall, a separate building behind the church proper. The box was large, and while not heavy, its clumsiness forced me stop to draw deep breaths of frigid air into my lungs. Not a good night to sleep under a bridge.

I approached the hall, relieved to see the beams of the outside spot reaching beyond the entrance to the tall trees and bushes beyond. Father Burton waited behind the glass door. He opened it just enough for me to wedge my body and the box through.

"Here," I said, hefting the box toward him, "bedding for my nephew and me." His bushy white eyebrows shot up in surprise, but he took the box.

"Ready for tonight?" he asked, shifting the box to get a better grip.

"Ready as I'll ever be. How about you?"

A smallish smile, one that I took as a good sign. We'd need Father's cooperation for tonight to go well.

I followed him into familiar territory, down the short hall that led to the meeting room, past a small kitchen on the left and the bathrooms on the right. Despite the chill outside, the inside temperature felt about right. Like similar facilities everywhere, the room carried a faint institutional smell of damp cardboard and floor wax.

Father flicked on the overhead lights and I was relieved to see the shelter had delivered the thirty cots we'd need for tonight. They were stacked in piles of five in one corner of the room. I'd been counting on Chris to set them up. Where was that kid? A small knot of worry formed in my gut.

The priest handed the box back to me and gestured toward the small storeroom adjacent to the bathrooms. "There's a cot in there you can put your sleeping bag on."

I'd spent plenty of time in that room, a wasteland of parish relics, hunting for Connie's records of the homeless program after her murder. At least the room had a door for privacy. "Fine." I inclined my chin toward the box. "Let me drop this off."

Another small smile. "We can go over the rules for tonight when you get back."

37

Tuesday, January 27th, 7:10 PM

"All right, the rules," Father said, when I'd joined him in the small, well-equipped kitchen. He leaned against a long counter in front of an open area where volunteers passed food through to the larger room, pencil at the ready to tick items off his list. "First, I understand some of these people have cars. They are to park on the street, no exceptions."

"But—" I protested.

"No exceptions," he repeated. "I don't want oil stains on the driveway."

"What about the shelter van? With thirty people, it will have to make several trips and it's a long walk from the street on a cold night like this."

"No exceptions." *Tick.*

"Fine." I muttered through tight lips.

"Next rule."

"Wait." I held up a finger and glanced at the time. The first van-load was ten minutes late. I grabbed my cell, called the driver and relayed the new instructions about parking on the street.

"Second rule," Father said, "No eating in the cot area." He indicated a table and chairs set up in front of the serving counter.

Tick.

"That's reasonable," I said. The parish hall had an ongoing ant problem.

"Third rule. No smoking, even outside."

Blood rushed to my face. "A lot of our guests smoke. I'm not sure we can enforce that."

"Just do it." *Tick.*

I clamped my hands on my hips, took a deep breath and glanced around, trying to tamp down my irritation. Something was missing from the counter, the large coffee pot, the brew from which fuels many a parish meeting. "Father, where's the coffee maker?"

"I put it away." He pointed to a microwave the size of a boot box. "They can drink instant."

My temper, already on simmer, hit full boil. "Coffee, especially in the morning, is such a comfort. I'm not sending them out on the street for a whole day without at least one cup of strong java. Now get me the pot."

"As you wish." He ducked down to retrieve the pot from a cupboard under the counter.

One tick for my side.

I became aware of a general commotion at the entrance and the first load of guests spilled through the door. Father took one look, enough apparently. "I'll just leave by the back entrance. Be sure to lock it after me."

Cindy, the driver, a heavyset woman with big, brassy hair and a persona to match, took in the surroundings, her eyes coming to rest on the jumble of cots in the corner. "Why haven't those been set up?"

"Look," I said, "it's one of those things that fell through the cracks. We didn't know we were taking the duty until this morning, all my volunteers have the flu, I got off work late, my nephew was in school all day—"

She touched my arm, green eyes soft with understanding. "Don't worry, it's not your fault. I was just venting." She handed me a clipboard with the chore list, emergency numbers and a basket. "For car keys. Collect 'em when the client first arrives. If they need to go back to their car, one of you must accompany them." She cast her eyes around the hall. "You do have a partner?"

"My nephew. He's not here yet." A combination of irritation and fear shot through my body.

She pulled her keys from the pocket of a brown bomber jacket that looked like a veteran of several wars. "One other thing. If someone leaves, either on foot or by car, they can't come back in. And no one comes in after lights out unless the shelter calls first. You okay here?"

I nodded, wondering if I really was.

"Great. I'll get the next load of clients."

The door shushed behind her, and seven guests stood in a huddle, staring at me. Obviously I was leading this parade. What to do first? My name would be good. I grabbed a piece of chalk and wrote "Bella Kowalski" on the board used for menus. Too complicated. "You can call me 'Mrs. K.'" Several people nodded, but no one moved. "Could I have some volunteers to set up the cots, please?"

A young man with short, dark hair and dime-sized bling in each ear approached, a baby clinging to one shoulder. He stuck out his free hand. "I can do that, Mrs. K. I'm Jose, and this here's my son Michael."

I grabbed his hand. "Thanks, Jose."

Jose put two fingers to his lips and whistled. "Yo, Ernesto." He pointed to a man accompanied by a teen, hopefully his daughter. "Give us a hand."

The teen, a wisp of a girl with smoky, doe eyes, gave his arm a gentle "go" shove. "Sure, man," he said, and moved toward us.

Jose then called out to a woman with a shaved head and copper earrings the size of small plates. "Zora, put out the snack food."

"Who was your slave last year?" she said, but started toward a box of small plates, chips, cookies, crackers and fruit under a foldout table next to the wall. Another box beside it held breakfast items: peanut butter and jam, plastic bowls and spoons, canisters of coffee, creamer and sugar. We'd worry about those later.

"First time?" Jose asked, and I nodded.

"Don't worry, you'll be fine. Who's your *obrero?*"

"*Obrero?*"

He smiled, looking much like his son. "Your worker."

"My nephew. He's not here yet." Obviously.

He held the baby out to me. "While you're waiting how 'bout you let Michael drool on you?"

"Thanks, I thought you'd never ask. How old is he?"

"Five months, yesterday."

I took the infant, who cooed as he settled into softer landscape. I buried my nose in the soft down of his hair, almost swooning from the fresh, new-person smell. Where was Mom? I wondered.

The two men and Zora fell to work. Others joined them and soon the hall filled with the metal screech of cots being opened, the clatter of foodstuff and utensils set out, and the *snap, snap* of blankets and sheets unfolding.

Minutes later, what the shelter terms an "intact family" arrived: Maria, Tony and Sky, their four-year-old. Tony handed me his keys as his wife and daughter headed for the snack table.

"Did you park on the street?" I asked.

He shrugged. "Had to. Someone put cones across the lot entrance."

Father Burton, God's *obrero*.

Maria approached, holding Sky's hand. "Tony and me worked late tonight," she said, and I nodded. I'd seen on the roster that they were employed by a cleaning company. Who watched Sky while they worked? Hopefully she didn't stay alone in the car. The homeless live in peril, often one step from disaster.

"We missed dinner at the shelter," Maria continued. "Can we, uh, have our cereal now? We have to leave before breakfast." She pushed an errant strand of mahogany hair off her face. Sky, her mirror image, repeated the self-conscious movement.

"Come with me." I stepped around the corner into the kitchen, opened the fridge and retrieved the milk, checked the date, and set it on the counter. A package of shredded cheese sat on the lower shelf at Sky's eye level. Her hand reached out, fingers wiggling.

Maria pulled her hand back. "That doesn't belong to us."

The girl whimpered and stuck her thumb in her mouth.

I pulled the Cheddar out and handed it to Maria, surveying the contents of the refrigerator. "I wish we had more to go with it."

"This is plenty, thank you."

Memo to Bella: Replace cheese tomorrow.

Maria filled a small Styrofoam bowl with the orange strings and give it to Sky. She grabbed two more bowls, and while she poured cornflakes for herself and Tony, the girl licked pinches of her favorite food from her fingers. With each tiny nibble, her eyes smiled at me. Cheerios and cheese, not much of a family dinner. But the little girl's smile reminded me why I did this work.

The next half hour went by in a buzz and a blur as our guests finished setting up and I handed Michael back to his dad. Cindy delivered the rest of our clients, wrote up a chore list and gave me the clipboard with emergency numbers. We had one empty cot, in case someone arrived late.

After she left with a wave and a "see ya," I glanced once more at the wall clock. Chris was now more than hour late.

38

Tuesday, January 27th, 8:20 PM

Just as I shifted into high-worry gear, with Chris dead by the side of the road, he breezed in, swinging a fast food bag.

"Where have you been?"

He gave me a "whaat?" look. "The truck needed gas, and"—he waved the bag—"I got another sub since the first one didn't have double cheese." So he'd noticed. He set the sack on the table and grabbed a paper plate. "Guess the time kinda got away from me."

"Doesn't matter," I said, and it didn't.

Several people were missing. They couldn't all be in the bathroom. "Did you see anyone smoking outside?"

"Sure, what's the big deal?"

"Father said no smoking."

"He would."

"Attitude, Chris."

Memo to Bella: Have Chris pick up butts before Father finds them.

Jose wandered over with Michael riding shotgun in the crook of his arm. "How 'bout I set up for breakfast, Mrs. K?"

I surveyed the second box under the table. "That can wait for morning."

Jose frowned. "Not much time before the van comes." He was right. We were supposed to wake everyone at six, and the van arrived to transport them to the main shelter around seven. One puny hour to use the bathroom, fold their bedding, complete assigned chores, drink coffee and eat a cold breakfast.

"You're right, of course." I held out my arms. "I'll take Michael again." Then my eye landed on Chris. "On second thought, give him to my nephew."

"*Auntie Bella!*"

Jose grinned. "Here man. Good practice."

From the way Chris held Michael, you'd have thought the kid was an unexploded bomb. Michael didn't care; he gurgled, eyed Chris's sandwich, and promptly spit up on Eddie Van Halen's image.

"Gross!" Chris held his favorite retro rock T-shirt away from his body with one hand and clutched the baby around the middle with his other arm.

I handed him a damp paper towel. "Here, just wipe it off. A little spit-up isn't fatal."

Jose just grinned. My nephew caught the grin and scanned the room for help. "Where's your wife, man? She needs to do this."

The grin vanished. "Jail."

"Jail?" Chris's eyes widened. *Bounce, bounce* went Michael on his knee. "What for?"

"Chris, that's not—"

It's okay, Mrs. K," Jose said. "Drugs. I thought having Michael would help, but it didn't make no difference." He stared at the paint spatters on his boots.

Chris's knee stopped mid-bounce. "You raising him by *yourself?*"

"Yeah, makes it hard to find the work, you know. I do yard and outside paint jobs so's he can stay with me." He paused and indicated a battered stroller snugged into a corner. "We're gonna walk over and see her tomorrow."

"County jail's at least five miles from the day shelter," I interjected.

Jose shrugged.

Chris eyed his sandwich. "I'm not hungry. Want it?"

Jose shook his head. "Thanks man, had plenty at the shelter." He inclined his head toward Maria and Tony, who sat cross-legged on their cots passing sections of the *Chronicle* back and forth. Sky hunkered down at the dining table, happily finger-painting with four other kids and an art-student volunteer from the local JC. "They can probably use it."

"Cool." Chris walked over and offered the sub to the couple who accepted it with touching eagerness. I remembered Father's rule about not eating in the cot area.

Memo to Bella: Spray for ants in the morning.

The clock said 9:30, half an hour after our guests' assigned bedtime, when we finally got things together for morning: the large urn filled with water and coffee, trash removed, everyone finished in the bathroom. I flicked the overhead lights a few times.

Chris approached with Sky, his new best buddy, attached to his shirt tail. Their faces were so streaked with red, yellow and green paint they resembled fake Indians. "What's with the lights?"

"Bedtime in five minutes."

"You're, like, kidding, right?" Alarmed by the tone of Chris's voice, Sky scampered back to her parents. Thumb in mouth, she watched him. Chris smiled to let her know things were okay, then turned back to me. "It's friggin' noon."

"Not quite, Chris. Look around you, these people are tired." Some were already sleeping, covers hiding their heads. "They've had a long day and they're up at six." I grabbed a folding chair, and started for the kitchen, indicating that he should do the same.

We placed the chairs facing each other, one for the butt, the other for feet, next to an island used to store kitchen utensils. "We're supposed to sit on these all night, Auntie Bella?"

"I'm not happy either, but do you see any soft chairs around?"

He shrugged like it was no big deal. "No, but you're not expecting me to go to bed in five minutes, right?"

Teens. "We talked about that. You study for your test 'til one, then wake me for my shift."

"Are you serious? I'm not gonna study that long."

"Your choice. The test's tomorrow." My patience was in a freefall. "Do whatever you like. I'm going to bed." Torn between the need for sleep and curiosity as to why Dominic wanted me to read "Two Years before the Mast," I pulled the book from my bag. With luck I could get a chapter or two in before dropping off.

* * * * *

I awoke to a darkened room alive with night silence. Where was I? Then I remembered: Saint Pat's storeroom. Like ghost ships, the dark hulks of stacked boxes stared back at me. The cot I lay on had slept plenty of other bodies and I was glad I'd brought the sleeping bag. I'd done pretty well sleep-wise; not even the Dana book had kept me awake past the second page. I didn't remember turning off the light. Maybe Chris did.

Chris. I threw back the sleeping bag and checked my watch. 1:20 AM. Why didn't he wake me?

That became obvious in the kitchen. He sat on one chair, stockinged feet up on the other, ears sprouting speaker buds, head thrown back, mouth agape, eyes closed, chemistry book askew on the floor. The volunteer on duty wasn't supposed to sleep, but realistically, it had probably happened before.

"Chris, wake up!"

"Whaat?" His head shot up, eyes unfocused, as though he'd just emerged from a dark tunnel.

"Go to bed. It's almost 1:30."

"Okay." He got up and lurched toward the storeroom.

He took a few steps, stopped and turned. "Forgot to tell you. Marcus Daniels dropped Walter off."

"Where is he?" I looked around, stomach clenching. This wasn't supposed to happen.

"Sleeping with the others. On the one empty cot."

"We're not supposed to admit anyone unless the main shelter calls."

"Great. How was I supposed to know that?"

Good question. I'd forgotten to tell him. "What did Marcus say?"

"Asked if Walter could stay here overnight."

"Did he say why? Was there another emergency at the ranch?"

"Dunno. Didn't think it was any of my business."

"Look, I'll deal with it. You did the right thing. Go to bed." The kid had his test in the morning. After he stumbled off, I picked up the phone to call the shelter and explain the situation, then stopped mid-dial. What if they sent Walter packing?

Memo to Bella: Easier to ask forgiveness than permission.

Okay, deep breath, decisive action called for. I checked the phone book and dialed the Blue Stetson. After hearing "We can't take your call right now, I said, "Hello, Marcus or Jeremy. This is Bella Kowalski." I rattled off my cell number. "One of you need to come over to Saint Pat's and pick up Walter. We're not allowed unauthorized guests. Please call me, or better yet, come and pick him up as soon as possible."

I stuck the phone in my sweatshirt pocket and tip-toed out of the kitchen and into the darkened sleeping area. Sure enough, Walter lay on the once-empty cot close to the far wall, face relaxed in peaceful slumber. I retreated, aware of the musty air, and snores and snuffles from thirty sleeping people. I could hardly wait to get home to my own bed. Maybe I'd call in sick tomorrow.

39

Wednesday, January 28th, 3:23 AM

While waiting for Marcus, I made myself extra-strong tea and turned to the first chapter of "Two Years before the Mast." Concentration proved impossible. Every creak of the building took me out of the story, every rustle in the bushes set off internal alarms. I sighed with frustration and, as I set the book in my lap, my eye wandered to the tooled leather cover. I speculated, not for the first time, on the book's value. Why was he so interested in me reading, and then discussing, it?

I rubbed my hand over the cover, mesmerized by the smoothness of it, and opened it to the title page, which I'd skipped before. Might this be a signed first edition? If so, it would be worth a fortune. The page was without signature, but below the title someone had scrawled in pencil: "See back."

Intrigued, I turned to the back page which contained a pocket identical to the one used in books before computerized record keeping. Instead of a card with stamped dates, the pocket contained a folded paper. Not unusual, people often leave things in books. Kathy Tanner once found a hundred dollar bill in a shelved book.

I pulled the paper from the pocket and, with infinite care, unfolded the single yellowed page. I stared at it slowly comprehending that I held a certificate from Oakland's Highland Hospital attesting to the live birth of Jeremiah, a baby boy, April 30th, 1966, mother Angelina Sereno, student, and father Todd Burton, also a student. I did the math; the child would now be forty-three.

Understanding came slowly, but it came, followed by waves of shock that shot through me like electronic darts. A clammy sweat seemed to be melting me from the inside out and I bit my lips to keep my teeth from chattering. Feeling lightheaded, I dropped the paper in my lap and gripped the seat of the chair until the feeling passed.

When it did, I again picked up the paper, fully realizing that I held in my shaking hand the mother lode, the missing link, the treasure map. Jeremy was the couple's child, born before Father Burton entered the priesthood.

Jeremy claimed to have been born in the Bay Area and, according to Magda's obituary, Angelina spent time in San Francisco. Even though she later married a Mr. Minetti, now deceased. Father (thinking of him as "Todd" boggled the mind) and Angelina had remained an item. I wondered how they compartmentalized their minds to carry on an illicit relationship and still think of themselves as serious Catholics. Not my concern, but if Angelina was Jeremy's mother, he'd be heir to the Sereno fortune and the winery, squarely on the money trail that Mike claimed was the source of most murders.

Was it an accident I found the paper or did Dominic, sick as he was, slip it inside the book? Did he urge me to read it, knowing my curiosity would lead me to the birth certificate? If Jeremy had murdered Dominic's sisters, the old man would have grown suspicious after Magda's death. This might be his quirky way of making sure someone else knew the family connection. Why me? And why not turn it over to law enforcement? But the latter would lead to an ugly family scandal and certainly a rift with his aunt if his suspicions were unfounded. Also, he might be afraid of Angelina and Jeremy, and with good reason.

The more I thought, the more it made sense. Despite the hour, I pulled my cell from my pocket to call Mike. This couldn't wait.

40

Wednesday, January 28th, 4:07 AM
Staring at the lighted face of the cell, I heard a rap on the glass door. What now? Another rap, and then another, louder and more insistent. I ran to the door. Expecting Marcus, I jumped when I saw Jeremy's face, framed by cupped hands, peering through the glass. He looked different, unkempt and harried, sinister somehow. In his present state, I wasn't about to let him near our homeless guests, so I opened the door just enough to slip through and stood with him outside under the spotlight, trying not to shiver in the cold night air.

The dark eyes narrowed. "What the hell? Let's go inside."

"Sorry, I can't let you in. No unauthorized persons."

"Your nephew didn't have a problem letting Marcus in."

"He didn't know. Stay here. I'll get Walter."

My cell buzzed. I wrested it from my sweatshirt pocket and stared at the number. Mike. My heart knocked against my ribs. How could I relay my suspicions with Jeremy here?

Be still, tweaky heart. I held up my index finger for Jeremy to wait, ignoring his scowl. "Hi Mike."

"This is important. You alone?" I glanced at Jeremy, whose eyes seemed to darken until they became part of the night.

"Bella, you okay?"

"Uh, I'm fine. What's up? How's the conference?"

"Not there yet, we're still in Salinas working on the case of the remains found in the Pinnacles."

I turned my back on Jeremy. "Really?"

"Turns out the guy's name is Dave Farris. Remember I told you he had dental work done in Tolosa County?"

"Yeah, that's why you went up there."

"Turns out Farris's last known address was ClearChoice rehab."

ClearChoice. The name on the letterhead of the notepad in Loreli's Secrets Box.

"It gets better. Our friend Jeremy was the registered owner of the rehab."

"How interesting." I deliberately made my tone noncommittal.

"And better. Jeremy has a military background. We played hell getting this info, but he served as a Navy Seal before becoming a fireman, and re-upped with a private military corporation five years ago when everyone thought he'd moved to Tucson."

"I'll certainly...um, make note of that," I said.

"Bella, I don't like what I'm hearing. Is someone there?"

How to say this? "That's a possibility."

"I take it that means yes. I'll send the sheriff to Saint Alban's."

"Good idea." I looked back over my shoulder. Jeremy didn't appear to be listening, but the tightness of his back and shoulders said otherwise. "Talk later." I slipped the phone back in my pocket and suddenly realized Mike had said 'Saint Alban's' rather than Saint Patrick's."

I grabbed the phone and as I pressed the send button to auto-call Mike, Jeremy said, "Put it back in your pocket, Bella."

I did as he said, every nerve in my body screaming for me to cut and run. But I couldn't abandon thirty people inside. And I certainly couldn't let him anywhere near them. In need of a plan, I forced a smile. "I'm afraid you do have to leave. I'll bring Walter by the ranch on my way to work." *Liar, liar, pants on fire.*

Jeremy and I stood toe to toe under the glare of the spotlight and a single word streaked across my mind. *Killer.* Jeremy killed Magda to keep her from discovering the truth about Loreli's death, and Ben because he was blackmailing him. He must have listened to the message I left at the Blue Stetson about Walter being here.

"Mike just reminded me the shelter doesn't allow—"

"Didn't sound like you were discussing the shelter."

Gulping, I forged ahead. "If someone finds I let you and Walter in without authorization, the whole program could be in trouble."

"No, Bella." Keeping his eyes on me, Jeremy reached into his pocket and palmed something slim and dark. I heard a snick and saw a gleam under the light. "You're the one who's in trouble."

Mesmerized by the switchblade, I didn't react. He lunged out, grabbed the front of my sweatshirt, spun me around and

held me by the waist. As his arm rose to put the knife to my ca-
rotid artery, I saw the bite scar on his arm.

*The dog in Loreli's kayak, Kathy, New Year's Eve, the man in the bath-
room, the Radio Hut sales person, all pointing in a straight line to Jeremy.*

"Come on. We're getting out of here." The blade pressed
against the side of my neck.

"Where are you taking me?"

"Your favorite place. The pier." Tethered as I was around the
middle, I couldn't see his face, but his voice dripped malice.

My insides plunged. "The Cayumaca pier? Why?"

"A payback Bella, for the hell you've given me, nosing around
where you don't belong, refusing my job offer. I'm going to start
a drug and alcohol rehab at the ranch, not a juvenile facility. Did
you know that?"

"Uh, no. Why did you say it was a juvenile facility?"

"Figured you'd heard about ClearChoice."

I played dumb. "I don't know what you're talking about."

"Sure you do. Your husband just told you."

The tip of the blade nicked my neck. I should stand my
ground, refuse to budge, but fear had frozen my muscles and destroyed my will. He'd frog-marched me several steps on the walk-
way that led around the church to the parking lot when I heard,
"Jeremy." A pause, and I heard a rustle in the bushes behind us.
"Hasn't there been enough killing?"

Father Burton stood to the left of Jeremy. His face was ashen
and tears streamed from his eyes. Gone was the tough old lion, in
its place someone merely old. He held up three arthritic fingers.
"The Sereno sisters and that reporter."

"Just for the record, I didn't kill the reporter. But none of
that is your business." Jeremy paused as though he'd just thought

of something. "Go inside, old man, and grab her handbag. And if you pull any funny stuff, Bella here won't be the only one dead."

My heart sank when Father nodded and slipped inside, returning a few seconds later with my handbag which I'd left in plain sight. He handed it to Jeremy and whispered, "What you do *is* my business. After you leave, I'm going back to the rectory and call the sheriff. I should have done it long ago."

Jeremy tightened his grip on my midsection. "Old man, you're not gonna call anyone. That clear?"

Father's shoulders slumped. He opened his mouth to say something, then turned and headed toward the rectory.

"Father!" I called. He didn't hear me, or chose not to.

The wail of a distant siren filled the night air. "Mike called the sheriff," I said. "You'd better let me go."

His body tensed as though weighing my words. The siren wailed again, closer now. Jeremy gave me a vicious shove. "Get going, sister. You're my insurance policy. One wrong move and I'll slit your throat." He half-pushed, half-dragged me toward the parking lot on the other side of the church. I didn't fight him because the sheriff was on his way. But the siren grew weaker, then died, the call for somewhere else. I felt like a shipwrecked person watching the rescue plane disappear into the clouds.

Rounding the corner of the church, I expected to see the Blue Stetson van in the parking lot. Instead, there sat a black Lexus, a blonde behind the wheel. Angelina got out and opened the driver-side rear door, then stood behind it as a chauffer might.

"Fetch that rope from the trunk, Mother," Jeremy barked, and then "After you, Bella." I planted my feet in front of the open door. If Jeremy wanted me in the back seat he'd have to knock me out. And that's exactly what happened.

41

"Slow down, Mother. A speeding ticket would be inconvenient."
Mother? Speeding ticket? The words delivered in a familiar voice forced my eyes open. Fighting both pain and nausea, I finally figured out I was in the back seat of a car. Angelina's Lexus. More pain as my brain conjured up images of Walter asleep at Saint Pat's, Father Burton walking away, Mike's phone call.

"Don't be such a wuss, Jeremy." Angelina shook her head and her blonde pageboy unleashed a storm of dandruff. Funny what you notice when your ass is on the line. There seemed to be no reason not to use one of Mike's colorful phrases.

Jeremy leaned over and pushed his face into mine. A fetid odor radiated from his mouth—perhaps from too much death. "Did that little blow to the head affect your memory, Bella? We're taking a little stroll on the pier, and then you're going for a swim. Like a big girl." He leaned closer. "Who's your uncle now?"

I stared into blank space, outwardly stoic, brain screaming, *"Not that. Anything but that."* I'd confided in Jeremy about Uncle Jimmy throwing me off the dock when I was a kid. Now he was using my own fear to torture me. A chill passed over me and my face numbed as though shot with Novocain. Moments passed with only the sound of Brubeck's "Take Five" filling the ether.

Lights from a vehicle appeared in the rearview mirror. Deputies? My heart surged with hope and then fell with a sickening thud as the car passed, two dots of red fading into the night. But with despair came rage, followed by rational thought. Mike would call law enforcement again and send them to Saint Pat's this time, or Father would do the right thing and call. All I had to do was delay and outthink a psychopath and his murderous mother.

Good luck, Bella. "A nighttime swim," I said, working scorn into my voice. "You can't get away with that. No one will believe I went off and left thirty homeless people alone. And my husband knows I'm not suicidal."

"Yours is a simple abduction, robbery and murder, my dear." Aunt Angelina drove with one hand, holding up my handbag with the other to prove her point. "Happens every day and the beauty is, blame will fall on one of the homeless people you're so fond of." She tossed the handbag over the front seat. It landed by Jeremy's feet and he kicked it aside.

"What about you, Jeremy? Is your concern for the homeless and addicted all a sham?" I said through clenched teeth.

He stared straight ahead, giving no indication he'd heard, except for the working of a muscle in his jaw.

"Why are you doing this?" I asked, although I knew. I'd seen the scar on Jeremy's wrist, a legacy of the bite Loreli's dog had delivered at the murder scene. I now knew Angelina was his mother, making him an heir to the Sereno fortune after Dominic died, and giving him a motive for Magda's murder. Also, he must wonder how much the reporter/blackmailer Ben had told me and how much I'd discovered on my own.

"I didn't kill Ben Adams, but when I saw you with the bastard's notebook at the Blue Stetson, I knew you'd go through the damned thing and find something incriminating. After the cops left the night before, I tore the place apart looking for that damned notebook, and Walter had it all the time. Mother and I decided you had to die, and it was just a matter of finding the right situation. You provided that when you called the ranch tonight. Isn't that true, Mother?"

Angelina stared at the windshield, saying nothing.

Like Ben's idea to confront Jeremy at the Blue Stetson, theirs seemed a risky plan born of desperation. Mike and law enforcement knew he owned ClearChoice and had been trained in military assassination techniques. Jeremy and his mother might not realize it yet, but their goose was, if not cooked, at least oven-ready. My only hope of saving myself lay in saying or doing something to buy time. The Brubeck ended and the guitar of Wes Montgomery began with no bright ideas on my part.

By now the deputies must have arrived at Saint Pat's. Maybe someone there heard or saw something. Maybe Father Burton would tell what he knew. Maybe a person of faith would pray now.

Thoughts of family filled my mind. Would I ever see Mike again? What about Chris? And my mom? Strained as our relationship was over Bea's death, I hoped someday for reconciliation. How awful it would be for her to have another daughter murdered. Would I see Bea on the other side?

I stared out the window, desperate to think of a delaying tactic that would save my life. But seeing familiar landmarks like the smoke stacks of Mariposa Bay and a few minutes later, the phosphorescent surf pounding against the shore, I knew we'd soon be at the pier.

I closed my eyes. Time to pray.

* * * * *

The engine geared down and my eyes flew open. Angelina slowed the Lexus and pulled into handicapped parking next to the pier. I looked around hoping for divine intervention in the form of an early morning fisherman. The empty parking spaces, the deserted bathrooms, the pier stretching to infinity, dashed that hope.

Angelina fished a blue and white handicapped sign from the glove compartment and hung it behind the mirror, from which she now looked back at us. "Don't be long," she said.

"Don't worry, Mother. This won't take long, will it, Bella?" He offered me a Jack Nicholson grin, his eyes radiating sick pleasure. How could I have ever considered him attractive?

"For God's sake, Jeremy untie her hands. That's a sure sign of murder."

"This is my show, Mother."

"My God," Angelina sighed, "what have I given birth to?"

"Time to go, Bella." Jeremy opened the door, slid out and dragged me out by the rope that bound my hands, producing excruciating pain.

"Hurry up." He jerked harder and I almost passed out from the agony.

"Don't screw up," Angelina called to Jeremy. "If the cops show up, I'm leaving."

Mother of the year had spoken.

In darkness broken only by wisps of early morning fog, he frog-marched me toward the end of the pier. Halfway there, all shame vanished. "Please, please, Jeremy. I won't say a word.

Please don't kill me. Mike and I will leave the country. Please, please."

He gave me a whack between the shoulder blades that reverberated all the way to my toes. "Shut up."

As we moved along, I became all too aware of the inky water lapping just under our feet. How cold would it be? Probably as cold as New Year's Day. Would mine be a quick death, or long and drawn out? Would it hurt? Would my heavy sweatshirt weigh me down? At least I had on flats instead of athletic shoes. Could I kick them off as I fell? I looked up and saw a shadow at the end of the pier. "Help! Help!" I screamed.

Another pounding on my back ricocheted through my body. "Shut up, Bella." He clamped his hand over my mouth as the shadow disappeared into nothingness. Soon my body would be nothing.

The mind is a wondrous thing and mine completely blanked until we stood by the rail at the end of the pier. I stared down at the waves hitting the pilings, taking my last breaths, savoring them while I could.

Footsteps behind us and the snick of a knife opening. I whirled around. Angelina stood there with Jeremy's switchblade. "You left this behind."

Was this good or bad? Was she going to kill me, or maybe Jeremy?

She gave her son a one-armed shove and commanded me, "You, turn around."

Oh my God. It was me. I did as I was told only because I couldn't bear to see the knife coming at me. Shoulders tensed for a stab in my already-aching back. I jumped when the blade nicked my wrists. She'd cut the rope. *She'd cut the rope.* My heart surged with hope as I watched it fall between the planks and slither into the sea.

She pocketed the knife. "Okay," she said, dusting her hands together, "now they can't trace the rope to me. I'm going to walk away. Wait two minutes, and do what you need to do. And don't screw up."

She took two steps and turned as though she'd forgotten something. "Did you remove the wallet and credit cards and leave her handbag on the pier?"

Silence except for the lapping of waves against the pilings. "I thought you were going to do it."

"You knucklehead." While they wrangled over who was supposed to do what, I decided if I couldn't be brave at least I'd be lighter. I quietly slipped out of my sweatshirt and shoes and tossed them over the railing.

Declaring she'd take care of the handbag, Angelina disappeared into the darkness, leaving a hollowed out spot in my gut. With her gone, Jeremy took immediate charge, shoving me to the railing. He didn't notice my missing clothes. "You're in luck," he said. "The ocean's quiet tonight. See for yourself."

I bent over the railing and my last thought as he shoved me over the edge was, "You didn't wait two minutes."

* * * * *

Water. Cold, so cold. Lungs freeze. Pray for quick death. Wave knocks me into piling, try to grab, barnacles rip skin, burning pain, please, please, let me die. Undertow pulls me out, then in. Panic. Bob to surface, snatch lungful of air and water, sink. Despair. Pray. Another wave, hit piling, more burning pain, more despair, wave pulls me out, then in, bob to surface. Breathe, Sink. Pray. Anger. Repeat. Again. More anger. God, please let me die.

Next bob, see something. Each time, gulp more air, less water. Plan B, God? Get bearings. Light from pier. Good. Bob to surface, look up. See rope between pilings. Better. Try to grab, miss. Catch incoming wave, hit piling, pulled out and in, bob to surface, breathe. Reach! Miss again. And again. Arms on fire. Can't do this. Yes, you can. Time incoming wave, ride with it, reach, grab rope. Got it! Hang on. Raise head, breathe. Pray.

What now? Rope loosens. Might break. Can't hang on. Yes, you can. Try to scream. Can't. Try again. Still can't. Can't hang on, either. Yes, you can. More light on water. Try to scream again. Still can't. Voices. More light. More voices. Sound of motor.

Sound of scream. Me.

Strong arms lift me into boat, wrap me in blankets. "You're safe, Ma'am."

* * * * *

Wednesday, January 28th, early morning.

The Search and Rescue boat rocketed toward shore and the foot of a pier ablaze with the strobes of squad cars. "Looks like they caught your friends," remarked my rescuing angel whose badge said "Al."

I drew the blanket tight around me. "They're no friends of mine." Al smiled and I thought, "I will love this man until the day I die." As we approached shore, he killed the engine and two young men—was it? Oh my God it was!—Chris and Walter, dashed into the surf to pull the boat onto the sand.

I leapt from the boat and ran through the waves to envelop them in a two-armed hug. "What took you so long?" I asked, alternately laughing and crying.

Before either could answer, deputies surrounded us and news crews appeared with cameras and microphones. A paramedic grabbed my arm. "You need to go to the hospital, Ma'am."

"Bella, you're a mess," Walter said, and Chris punched his shoulder.

I couldn't disagree with Walter's assessment: hair plastered to my head, sopping clothes ripped by barnacles, cuts on hands and limbs streaming blood. Once again I became aware of burning pain from the salt water.

"I can walk to the ambulance."

"No way, Ma'am." A gurney was produced, deputies cleared space ahead of us and I was ferried like Cleopatra to the waiting ambulance. I raised up on my elbows (earning a sharp rebuke from the paramedic) to look for Detective Scully, then remembered he was in Salinas with Mike.

Mike. Must call him.

Walter and Chris walked on either side of me, each holding a hand. The warmth of their hands seeped through my skin and radiated through my body. Never had I felt so protected, so loved. "Okay, you two. What happened?" I asked.

Before Walter could open his mouth, Chris said, "Walter woke up when he heard Jeremy's voice outside, listened through an open window and heard Jeremy say he was taking you to the pier. After you left, he went to Father Burton, who was busy calling 911. Father stayed with the homeless people while we came after you."

I squeezed Walter's hand. "That was very brave, and exactly the right thing to do."

He smiled, but there was a sadness in his eyes that might never leave. Jeremy, his hero, had not only killed several people, he'd betrayed both him and Marcus.

"Jeremy's n...not a good person, is he?"

"No Walter, he's not. Though he's been good to you, hasn't he?"

Walter nodded and his eyes filled. "Should I have given him that reporter's notebook?"

"No Walter, again you did the right thing."

We approached the ambulance. Jeremy and Angelina sat in the back seat of a nearby squad car. As we passed, Walter gave Jeremy a little wave, which Jeremy ignored. I longed to fly through the window and choke him. He'd left behind a trail of broken lives.

A van neared the pier and screeched to a stop. Marcus ran to us and put his arm around Walter. "Thank God you're all right. I took you to Saint Pat's so you'd be safe from...," his voice broke and he looked at the squad car with Jeremy and Angelina, "from Jeremy." He put his arm around Walter who leaned into him. "I just want you to know son, that no matter what happens now, I'll take care of you. Do you understand?"

Walter nodded and enveloped himself in Marcus's sturdy frame.

Still hanging on to Walter, Marcus turned to me. "Tonight I decided to drive up the coast to think about Jeremy and what I needed to do. I've been suspicious since New Year's Day when I missed the dip because of my damn headache. Maybe if I'd been there Magda wouldn't have died."

"It's okay, Marcus," I said. "You had no way of knowing."

"But I did. My suspicions have been building ever since Magda died and tonight I decided to get Walter away from Jeremy at least for the night, and decide what to do tomorrow. I planned to have Todd…er, Father Burton, keep him, but he said Walter would be better off with you in the shelter."

I nodded and he continued: "I knew when Jeremy and Walter came to me years ago, Jeremy had problems, but I thought I could make a difference in his life, and it seemed for a while I had. The swim team in high school and college, the military, becoming a fireman, even his ill-fated rehab center. But nothing worked. Jeremy's a monster, isn't he?"

"Marcus, everyone knows you did your best." Before I could say more, Chris's cell rang. He fished it out of his sweatshirt pocket, peered at the face and handed it to me. "Uncle Mike."

"Bella, you okay? I've been out of my mind."

"I'm scratched up and wet, but glad to be alive. I tried to call you back about Saint Alban's. Jeremy stopped me."

"You must have pressed send without realizing it. The call went through."

"The call went through? You actually *heard* what happened tonight?" My heart played hopscotch in my chest.

"A lot of it. We've got plenty to build a case against him and Angelina," Mike said. "You're a hero."

Why didn't I feel like one? "Thanks. I kept expecting law enforcement to show up, and they didn't."

"I sent them to Saint Alban's by accident. Guess I get the Darwin Award for stupidity on that one, huh?"

"Mr. Darwin, when will you be home? I can't wait to see you."

42

Saturday, January 31ˢᵗ, noon

"Hey Ryan," Mike called as we entered Nosh 'n Nibble, a popular eatery snugged into the corner of a strip mall at the north end of Mariposa Bay. The detective stood at the counter contemplating a pizza menu on the wall. He looked good since he and Mike had started to play racquetball.

"Good to see ye." He offered Mike a wide Irish grin with lots of teeth, but his wide-set blue eyes, one of which wandered a bit, flicked with uncertainty when he turned to me. "Bella."

Mike gave me a one-armed hug. "Hope you don't mind me bringing Bella along for an update. She's been nagging me to death."

The detective nodded. "You certainly deserve one after all you did to build the case against those two. As long as what we say doesn't go beyond this room. Ye know what I'm talkin' about, Bella?"

Meaning I worked for a newspaper. "Scout's honor, Detective Scully."

"Ryan." He smiled and indicated the menu. "How do ye like yer pizza?"

"With anything but anchovies," I said, and Mike added, "Or pineapple."

While they quibbled about beer and salad choices and who'd pay, I fetched forks and napkins and chose a corner booth away from prying eyes and inquisitive ears.

"Why don't you tell us what's happened since the arrest," Mike said after the two had set before us Caesar salads, glasses and a frosted pitcher of Guinness.

Ryan filled our glasses, took a long sip and held up his glass to admire the dark brew. "Aye, our lad's been singing like a canary on cocaine hoping to cut a deal and avoid the death penalty."

Mike: "Like that's gonna happen. Hasn't his lawyer told him to shut his pie hole?"

Ryan, looking puzzled: "Ah, ye mean mouth. He's not listening. Like many of his ilk, Jeremy wants us to know how clever he's been. On the other hand, he's also trying to claim he was merely Angelina's pawn."

Me: "Can't have it both ways. I've been wondering for days how Jeremy got to this state of affairs."

Ryan: Well, in the spring of 2003, our lad Jeremy decides to open a rehab facility. The money's good, he's had drug and alcohol counselor training in the military, and, being something of a loner, he's tired of fire department politics. He borrows money from Angelina—"

Me: "His mother." It seemed so weird I had to keep reminding myself.

Ryan: "—and sets up his rehab in an old motel out by the airport. He gets a license easily because of his background and a few patients trickle in. But startup costs are high and Angelina claims she can't spare more capital."

Mike: "Why didn't he tap Marcus?"

Ryan: "He knew his benefactor didn't have it. He limps along a few months, thinking things will get better as word gets out about the place."

Me: "And Loreli arrives in October."

Mike: "Then in November both Dave Farris and Ben Adams arrive at ClearChoice and the plot thickens."

I counted back on my fingers. Ben was barely eighteen, just a kid.

Ryan, leaning across the table and lowering his voice: "By the end of 2003, Jeremy's broke. Then he finds out his new client, Dave Farris, is a fifty-year-old trust fund baby with no living relatives. Jeremy's antennae light up. He invites Dave to empty a few bank accounts and buy into ClearChoice for a half million."

Mike: "Except Jeremy's plan doesn't include the hapless, and soon to be very dead, Dave."

Ryan: "Don't forget he was trained to kill in the military."

Me: "Don't they weed out people who like killing too much?"

Mike: "Normally yes, but don't forget Jeremy's had training in psychology and manages to fudge the test."

Scully: "We digress. Jeremy drags Dave off to a remote area of the Pinnacles and throws him into a canyon where he's not found for five years."

Mike: "Thanks to an anonymous tip to Salinas's law enforcement."

Me: "No doubt from Ben trying to up the pressure on Jeremy to pony up."

Ryan: "That's exactly right, but we're getting ahead of ourselves." He took a fortifying sip of Guinness. "In January 2004, Jeremy offs Dave, and Loreli finds his disappearance suspicious. Then he spies her going through his bank statements. He also overhears her discussing her suspicions with Ben and decides she has to die."

Me: "Seems like he should've killed Ben too."

Ryan: "Too risky. He can explain Dave's absence by saying he left voluntarily and died later, but what if two more clients die? Jeremy figures he'll pay Ben to keep quiet."

Mike: "But Ben freaks and gets the hell out of Dodge on his own. Five years pass and he realizes he has salable information. When he sees the newly-returned Jeremy in town, he phones the Blue Stetson and gets Walter, who innocently gives him Jeremy's cell number, and Ben places the anonymous blackmail call New Year's Eve."

Me: "Let's go back to 2004. How did Jeremy get the drug into Loreli? Dominic claimed she treated rehab seriously."

Ryan: "She did. Marcus takes Valium and Jeremy helps himself and laces some vitamin capsules with the drug. He uses one on Dave to lure him to the Pinnacles and, a few weeks later, places another by Loreli's morning juice glass. Then he drives to Angelina's, sprints the short distance to Bush Lupine Point and suits up. When Loreli appears, he follows her across the bay, sneaks up behind her and breaks her neck as he's been taught."

Mike: "A perfect plan, except her dog bites the hell out of him."

Ryan: "Despite that, he swims back to Bush Lupine Point, hides his gear in the bushes and makes his way back to Angelina's home."

Me: "Gutsy."

Ryan: "True, but the fact that the dog died as well made the department suspicious and we withheld that information. But nothing came of it and, because Loreli had drugs in her system, hers was declared a death by misadventure."

Mike: "Jeremy treated the wound himself, and had plastic surgery later."

Me: "Which left that small scar Kathy saw. Like he'd slit his wrist at some point."

Mike: "If he had, several people would still be alive."

Ryan: "True enough. He claims Angelina harassed him into leaving town."

Me: "Seems like his leaving would be suspicious in itself."

Ryan: "Our lad was clever, took his time and planned carefully. Told Walter and Marcus he was going to Tucson and arranged for a service to handle his mail from there."

Just then I smelled sausage, cheese and garlic behind me. Our pizza had arrived.

"Shall we take a break?" Ryan asked.

43

Ryan gathered three small plates close to him, lovingly loosened each piece with a fork, placed it on the plate, and handed one to each of us. "Do yer think we can finish that?" Ryan asked, eyeing the half-empty pitcher of ale.

"Don't know," Mike said, "but we can try."

Much as it pained me, I pushed my glass aside. "In that case, I'm the designated driver."

Mike and I sprinkled hot pepper flakes and grated Parmesan on our slices while Ryan placed his black olives in a tidy mound on the side of his plate.

"Aren't you going to eat those?" Mike asked, reaching across with his fork.

We munched in contented silence for several minutes, then Ryan reached for a second slice, saying: "Shall we get back to business?"

Mike: "Okay, fast forward five years. Dominic gets sick and Angelina realizes if Magda dies too, she'll inherit."

Me: "Why would a sixty-something woman, with no experience, want a winery?"

Ryan, draining his glass and standing: "I'll let you answer that Mike, while I make a wee visit to the loo."

Mike made a "go" motion and turned to me. "Angelina planned to liquidate the winery, sell the land to developers—"

"Developers? Real estate's in the tank."

He popped a stray olive into his mouth. "True, but it won't always be, and she planned ahead. Decided the best way to bring Jeremy back into the family fold was to make sure he eventually inherited Sereno Cellars. When he came back to town, she decided they should off Magda."

"So Jeremy killed Loreli to keep her quiet, and Magda for profit."

"Exactly. Two different motives, which threw us off initially. Jeremy got Ben's anonymous call, and then ran smack into Magda on New Year's Eve. Not knowing what she knew, he moved the timetable to the next morning."

"So all the while he danced with me, he was planning murder."

Mike gave me a one-sided grin. "That'll teach you to dance with strange men."

"Marcus had a migraine at the party, so he didn't show up at the Polar Bear Dip, which made Jeremy's task easier."

"True. He got lucky there."

Ryan, resumed his seat and poured another glass of Guinness.

Me: "Jeremy was there on the beach after Martin brought Magda ashore. Why place himself at the scene?"

Mike: "It would look weird if neither he nor Marcus were present, and he was unwilling to throw the blame on Marcus, though he might have if things got sticky."

Ryan: "Our lad's not done yet. He plants the knife in Martin's unlocked car, then calls Vader who trots into Sheriff Whitley's office and the next thing you know, Martin's a person of interest. Fast forward a few weeks after Magda's murder. Jeremy hasn't responded to Ben's blackmail threat. Our journalist is getting desperate, as well as—how do you Yanks say—'scared shitless.' In desperation he enlists a land developer he knows to pressure Amy into the undercover story."

Mike: "Earning his own Darwin Award for stupidity."

Me: "Ben wanted to confront Jeremy in a safe environment, thinking he wouldn't off him there."

Mike: "So much for that good idea."

Ryan: "Alas that is true."

Me: "After I fall asleep, he sees his chance and seeks out Jeremy, when what he really needs to do is just leave."

Ryan: "Once again Jeremy's forced to react rather then act. But here's the strange thing. Jeremy claims he didn't kill Ben."

Me: "That's what he told me, too. And Father Burton as well."

Ryan: "Trust me, Bella, he killed Ben. He certainly had motive, and who else did?"

Me: "Maybe Ben's so-called informant, the heavyset man talking to Ben thinking he was Jeremy." A thought noodled around the edges of my brain, but my cell chose that moment to buzz and the idea vanished as I took a call from Chris. "What's up?"

"Can you come home right now?" he asked.

"I'm in a meeting, but we're almost through. Is there blood, or have you called 911?"

"No, I'm applying to the Culinary Institute and I need your help."

"Great, I'll see you in a few minutes."

"Teenage angst," I said in response to Mike's questioning look. "Where were we?"

Mike: "What happens to Father Burton?"

Ryan: "He's out of the priesthood, but the diocese will lawyer him up if it looks like he's complicit in any of the murders."

Me: "Don't forget, he called 911. But that doesn't absolve him. He had choices."

"True." Ryan rose, shrugging into his windbreaker. "Put the thought of the heavyset man out of your mind. Mike and I have been in the business long enough to recognize guilt when we see it, haven't we Mike?" My husband gave him the smug smile of someone who'd made up his mind. "By the way," Ryan said, "Jeremy and Angelina will be arraigned at three on Monday. I can get you in, Bella."

I shook my head. "No thanks. I never want to see those people again."

44

Thursday, February 7th, 2PM

A Sereno Cellars groundskeeper showed me to Dominic's office in the tasting room and then quietly withdrew. Dominic sat in a wheelchair, legs and lap bundled in a creamy cashmere afghan despite the warmth of the room. The temperature enhanced the pleasantly tart aroma of fermenting grapes that pervaded the building. Still, it did nothing to allay my sadness and trepidation at this meeting.

Dominic faced me in front of an immense bay window that overlooked an informal garden ablaze with early Iceland poppies. I'd come in response to his call asking me to return the birth certificate. I was also here on another mission, but Dominic didn't know it yet.

His smile was wan, but his soft dark eyes danced with life. "Bella, thank you for coming on such short notice. Better late than never for our book discussion, eh?"

I returned his smile despite the gravity of recent events and took his proffered hand in both of mine. "How are you doing?" I asked.

He put his head back and let out a guffaw that held no trace of offense or self pity. "How am I doing? Well, my dear, as well as could be expected considering that my aunt and my nephew are in the pokey for the murders of my sisters and I've got terminal cancer."

I put a hand to my mouth. "Oh Dominic, I'm so sorry. I didn't think—"

He raised a hand as though the gaffe were of no consequence and indicated an armchair opposite. "Sit here close to me so I can inhale that divine perfume you're wearing."

"It's Jergen's Lotion," I admitted, sinking into the plush leather chair.

"My mother wore that." He turned the wheelchair slightly. "As you can see, I'm watching my garden grow, as I won't be here next year."

I opened my mouth to offer a platitude and then shut it, choosing instead sympathetic silence.

When I had produced the birth certificate, he looked it over and said, "Just put it on the desk. I don't think Jeremy and Angelina can get their hands on it from where they are."

I did so, again with no comment. Dominic rang the house for tea, then turned back to me. "I'm glad we could spend some, how do they say, quality time together." His smile faded. "I'm sure you have questions."

"Oh, I do," I said. *You don't know the half of it.* I studied the vintner who looked even thinner than at Magda's funeral three weeks ago. "Are you sure you're up to questions, that it's not too painful?"

"I'm as good as I'm going to get," he said with a long sigh. "Fire away. I've already given my statement to sheriff's detectives."

I brushed a spot of lint from my dark skirt to gain time. I had to ease into this gradually. "Let's start with the birth certificate.

With Loreli and Magda both gone, I understand why you wanted someone else to know that Jeremy was Angelina's son, but why me? We'd only met a couple of times."

He grinned. "Simple. You have innate good sense and I knew you'd provide me with sound advice about my options, that is, to say nothing or go to law enforcement with my suspicions and risk alienating my aunt and nephew if they were unfounded."

"Thank you." What else was there to say?

An affirmative nod. "After Magda's death, I began to suspect Jeremy."

"Why was that?" I asked in a whisper.

"This sounds bizarre, but there was just too much death around the man and I couldn't put our family's future in his hands." His eyes filled and his voice broke. "Better no future at all than one in the hands of that bastard. As for my beloved aunt..." He left the sentence unfinished.

"When did you suspect the two of them of being in cahoots?"

"Well, early in December I saw them together at a farmers' market, then lost sight of them in the crowd."

"It doesn't seem unusual that mother and son would be out together."

"Not normally, but I didn't know Jeremy was back on the Central Coast. Neither he nor Angelina had bothered to call." He shifted the chair close to me and lowered his voice. "They reunited about ten years ago, but often these birth mother and child relationships don't coalesce and that seemed the case here."

I nodded. "Too much water over the dam, and all that, to form a bond based on trust."

"Except in this case the bond was based on greed," Dominic said.

"Sad. How long have you known Jeremy was Angelina's son?"

"From the beginning. I was quite young when Angelina became pregnant. As you can imagine, my parents were upset, and Mama especially, railed on and on about how she and Papa couldn't hold their head up in polite society with his sister pregnant out of wedlock." He took a deep shuddering breath. "I do think Angelina would have kept the baby if they hadn't carried on the way they did, and things would have been different."

"Maybe." I knew he'd like to think so. I wasn't so sure. Some people are just born bad, and I suspected Jeremy might be one. "Did Magda and Loreli know he was Angelina's son?"

"Actually, no."

"*Really*?" I couldn't have been more surprised. "Ever since I found the birth certificate, I've assumed that Jeremy introduced Marcus and Magda."

At that point, we heard bustling in the corridor and the housekeeper arrived with the tea on a tray. Dominic's face lit up. "Maria, thank you so much. This is Bella Kowalski, a friend of both Loreli and Magda."

"*Bueno,*" she said, nodding and smiling as she placed the tea on a small table between us.

"*Hola,*" I responded and put out a hand which she grasped warmly. While Dominic beamed, we exchanged pleasantries in her native language, with her doing most of the talking because of my *poco* Spanish.

When she'd taken her leave, and we'd done the traditional tea ceremony of pouring, choices of one lump or two and milk or lemon, with the addition of *biscotti* to lend an Italian flavor to the proceedings, Dominic asked, "Where were we?"

"How Loreli and Marcus met."

He took a sip from a bone china cup. "Ah, she volunteered at the ranch, and the rest, as they say, is history." His facial muscles sagged as though he'd suddenly remembered how sad that history was.

"But the video in the Secrets Box showed Jeremy taking pictures at that party in 2003. I assumed from that you socialized frequently."

"Not at all. That was my fiftieth birthday party. Happier times."

"Of course. So Jeremy was at the party as Marcus's foster son, not because of any familial association?"

He nodded. "Because of Todd's, that is Father Burton's, status as a priest, we had to be extra careful as you may well imagine, and it was damned awkward at times."

"Angelina and Father Burton were anything but careful." *Ouch, Bella, why don't you say what you really think?*

Dominic bit into a *biscotti* and chewed, considering. "True, but I've lived long enough to know that some things are just unexplainable."

I looked at him, dying to ask the question, *"What else was unexplainable, Dominic?"* But I couldn't force it out. Damning myself for a coward, I said instead, "I agree," and sipped from my cup, taking solace from the tea's smoky flavor. "At what point did you became suspicious of Angelina and Jeremy's newfound closeness?"

Dominic set the cup on the tray and laced his work-worn hands over the afghan in his lap. "After I saw them at the market, I called and waited for Angelina to tell me Jeremy was back. She didn't and I wondered why not."

"I can imagine."

"After that I drove by her house several times—"

"You drove all the way from Dos Pasos?"

He held up a hand for him to let me finish. "Almost every time, the white van with the Blue Stetson license plate was parked in the driveway."

"It could have been Marcus or Walter."

"Unlikely. Angelina hates Marcus and she terrifies Walter."

"With good reason," I said, and received a small smile in return. "Go on, please."

"A week or so before Christmas, she called requesting Jeremy's birth certificate, which I kept with other family papers in the safe." He gestured toward a safe that dominated one wall of the paneled room.

"It's legally hers."

"True, but some instinct told me to stall, say I couldn't find it or perhaps it was in the bank's safety deposit box. She kept nagging and I don't handle conflict well in my condition."

"Of course not."

"Then Magda died New Year's Day and I realized Angelina would inherit when I'm gone, and Jeremy after her. She had asked for the birth certificate *before* Magda died to prove lineage after I was gone. That seemed highly suspicious. With a closed adoption, a copy would be difficult or impossible to get."

"They'd have to rely on DNA testing, and that could be awkward considering the circumstances."

"Exactly."

"You could have changed your will."

He gave me a wicked smile. "Oh, I did, but she doesn't know it yet."

Good for him. I stared up at the shelves of books that covered one wall. "Another thing I wonder. Why didn't you just mail the birth certificate to me?"

"I wanted it out of my safe the day of Magda's funeral and giving it to you in the book was the quickest way. My memory's failing and I have to write down passwords and combinations. Angelina insisted upon staying here for a few days after the service and I knew she'd snoop around until she found the combination to the safe."

At that point, Maria arrived to gather the tea things, and with more smiling and pleasantries, just as quickly departed. "What are your plans now?" I asked.

He smiled. "What you mean is, am I going to check myself into a care center?" He looked around at the room, with its leather furniture, velvety wood paneling and floor-to-ceiling bookcases. "Some problems really can be solved by throwing money at them, and my care is one of them. As you can see from Maria, I have a dedicated staff. And with hospice when the time comes, I should be fine, God willing."

"You will be, Dominic. I've never known anyone with more courage."

His eyes misted over and he looked so exhausted I decided to take my leave without posing the question I'd come to ask. I leaned over and put my arms around him, feeling his frail body shudder beneath the afghan. "Dominic—?"

He pulled away and stared up at me, pleading not just with his eyes, but his whole being, "Please don't say anything."

I looked down at this man of integrity, who'd always tried to do the right thing, and realized I couldn't make his life a living hell for the few months left to him. "I won't. I have to go now." We left it at that, with the unspoken understanding that it would be too painful for us to meet again.

I walked for the last time through the tasting room, shoes tapping on the wood floors, and out into healing sunshine, knowing I would go to my grave believing, but unable to prove, that a Dominic desperate for justice had arranged for Vito, his former lover, to kill Jeremy.

But instead of Jeremy, Vito had mistakenly killed Ben, who with his newly dyed hair, resembled Dominic's nephew. I realized where I'd seen the heavyset man before that night at the Blue Stetson. Vito, rumored to have an unsavory Mafia past, had appeared in the video taken at Dominic's birthday party back in 2003. Pretty slim evidence for the justice system, but my heart recognized the truth my eyes saw, and my ears heard. You see, the phrase Vito uttered that night, the one I was too shell-shocked to dredge up for Amy, was "For Dominic."

45

Seven months later:

Jeremy pleaded guilty to killing Ben in exchange for life imprisonment rather than the death penalty, a sort of cock-eyed justice in Bella's opinion. Rumor is Angelina's gained at least forty pounds from the hearty prison food.

The Chicago suits fired Amy, who stayed in bed for three days, greasy haired, and eating cold Chinese food with her fingers. She then moved to San Francisco and went to work as a media consultant for an insane sum of money.

Chris lives in Napa, attending the Culinary Institute and living with an eclectic assortment of fellow students. Amy promised to keep an eye on him, but it's unclear to Bella who needs to watch whom.

Mike still accepts cold case investigative work on a piecework basis, but feels the limitations of not being a sworn officer. Walter continues to live with Marcus and work at Saint Pat's under Father Rodriguez, back from the Philippines. Walter and Bella go out for pizza regularly.

Bella still ponders the moral ambiguity of protecting Dominic in his last days and hopes a merciful God will understand. She works full time as obituary writer and researcher and has a good rapport with the *Chronicle's* new managing editor who hails from Detroit.

Marcus Daniels plans to open the rehab facility the first of the year. While the ranch's other buildings continue their steady decline, he and his homeless guests are looking forward to receiving the first of several loads of FEMA trailers purchased from a cash-strapped federal government with money left to him in Dominic's will.

The End

Made in the USA
Charleston, SC
05 May 2016